A finely honed su...
C.J. to proceed with extreme caution.

The squirming baby in Dana's arms giggled, somehow snatched the wet rag out of her hand and threw it with unerring accuracy smack into Dana's face.

"Babysitting?" C.J. asked.

"Funny you should say that." Hot little flames sparked in her eyes. "My cousin Trish breezed back into town today."

C.J. felt the blood drain from his face.

"Oh?"

"Yeah. She brought me a present. Now, it's a very nice present, to be sure, but heaven knows I wasn't expecting anything like this."

"I'm sorry," C.J. said, "but am I missing something?"

She marched over to C.J. and smacked a triple-folded sheet of paper into his palm.

It was a birth certificate and the first word out of C.J.'s mouth was particularly choice when he read who the daddy was.

"Cameron James Turner," the paper said.

Dear Reader,

I love, love, love the holidays—the decorations, the music, the food (okay, maybe I love the food a little *too* much). I also love all the moments during the season when I realize just how blessed I am to have friends and family there to "get my back" whenever I face the unknown, or waffle about taking that risk I know I'd regret forever if I didn't take it. Talk about a priceless gift. And here's another one—the peace that comes from knowing I'm loved for who I am.

So as you join Dana and C.J. while they inch their way toward the realization that the best relationship is the one in which each partner cherishes each other's uniqueness, why not take a moment to thank that special person who's got *your* back, who loves you *because* you're you? I can't think of a better or more appreciated gift.

And you don't even have to wrap it.

Karen

BABY STEPS

KAREN TEMPLETON

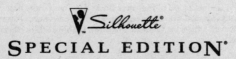

SPECIAL EDITION®

Published by Silhouette Books

America's Publisher of Contemporary Romance

 **SILHOUETTE BOOKS**

ISBN-13: 978-0-373-24798-1
ISBN-10:   0-373-24798-2

BABY STEPS

Copyright © 2006 by Karen Templeton-Berger

This edition published by arrangement with Harlequin Books S.A.

® and TM are trademarks of Harlequin Books S.A., used under license.
Trademarks indicated with ® are registered in the United States Patent
and Trademark Office, the Canadian Trade Marks Office and in other
countries.

Visit Silhouette Books at www.eHarlequin.com

Printed in U.S.A.

Books by Karen Templeton

Silhouette Special Edition

††*Marriage, Interrupted* #1721
††*Baby Steps* #1798

Silhouette Intimate Moments

Anything for His Children #978
Anything for Her Marriage #1006
Everything But a Husband #1050
Runaway Bridesmaid #1066
†*Plain-Jane Princess* #1096
†*Honky-Tonk Cinderella* #1120
What a Man's Gotta Do #1195
Saving Dr. Ryan #1207
Fathers and Other Strangers #1244
Staking His Claim #1267
***Everybody's Hero* #1328
**Swept Away #1357
***A Husband's Watch* #1407

Silhouette Yours Truly

*Wedding Daze
*Wedding Belle
*Wedding? Impossible!

††Babies, Inc.
 †How To Marry a Monarch
 *Weddings, Inc.
**The Men of Mayes County

KAREN TEMPLETON,

a Waldenbooks bestselling author and RITA® Award nominee, is the mother of five sons and living proof that romance and dirty diapers are not mutually exclusive terms. An Easterner transplanted to Albuquerque, New Mexico, she spends far too much time trying to coax her garden to yield roses and produce something resembling a lawn, all the while fantasizing about a weekend alone with her husband. Or at least an uninterrupted conversation.

She loves to hear from readers, who may reach her by writing c/o Silhouette Books, 233 Broadway, Suite 1001, New York, NY 10279, or online at www.karentempleton.com.

To Gail
for giving this couple another chance
to finally get together
(and for unfailingly knowing when I most
need a word of encouragement)
and to Charles
for loving this book
and wanting it to be the best it could be.
How blessed can a girl get?

Chapter One

"You get back here, Cass Carter!"

Dana Malone zipped across the sales floor after her rapidly retreating partner, nearly landing on her butt when a crawling baby shot out in front of her from behind a St. Bernard-sized Elmo. Half a wobble and a shuffle later, she was back on track. "What do you mean, *I* have to do it—*ouch!*"

"Watch out for the new high chair," the long-legged, denim-skirted blonde tossed back, cradling the tiny head jutting out from a Snugli strapped to her chest.

"Thanks," Dana grumbled, rubbing her hip as she snaked her way through cribs and playpens, Little Tikes' playhouses and far too many racks of gently used baby clothes. Her two partners—and their skinny little fannies—could navigate the jumbled sales floor with ease. For Dana, the space was a minefield. As was Cass's request. "Have you lost your *mind?*

I can't pick the store's new location by myself, Cass! What on earth do I know about real estate?"

"This is Albuquerque, for heaven's sake," Cass said as she slipped into the store's pea-sized office. "Not Manhattan." She shimmied past her desk, heaped with paperwork and piles of newly consigned clothes, then swiped a trio of original Cabbage Patch Kids dolls in mint condition from the rocker wedged into one corner. "How difficult can it be to choose one strip mall store-front over another? Here, take Jason for a moment, would you?"

The weight of the month-old infant—and the ache—barely had a chance to register before Cass, now settled into the rocker, reached again for the softly fussing infant. Dana allowed herself an extra second of stolen new-baby scent before relinquishing her charge, watching Cass attach baby to breast with a neutral expression. The baby now contentedly slurping away, her partner lifted amused blue green eyes to her. "C.J.'s already got several potential locations lined up. All you have to do is weed out the ones that won't work."

A trickle of perspiration made a run for it down Dana's sternum, seeking haven in her cleavage. "I'd just assumed we'd all do this together."

"I know, sweetie. But I'm pooped. And Blake's on my case as it is about coming back to work so soon. Besides, between our lease being up next month and the store about to burst at the seams—"

"What about Mercy? Why can't she do it?"

"Why can't I do what?"

The third side of the Great Expectations triangle stood in the office doorway, sports car-red fingernails sparkling against a frilly little skirt Dana wouldn't have been able to wear when she was twelve.

"Go property scouting," Dana said. "You'd be much better at it than me."

Meredes Zamora swiped a dark curl out of her face as she squeezed into the office. "I'm also much better at juggling five customers at a time. You get rattled with two."

"I do not!"

Both ladies laughed.

"Okay, so maybe I do get a little flustered."

"Honey," Mercy said, not unkindly, "you start *stuttering*."

"And dropping things," Cass added.

"And—"

"Okay, okay! I get your point!"

It was true. Even after nearly five years, even though wallpaper books and Excel spreadsheets held no terror for her, Dana still tended to lose her composure under duress. Especially about making business decisions on her own—

"He's expecting your call," Cass said.

Dana suddenly felt like a bird being eyed by a pair of hungry cats. "Who is?"

"C.J."

She sighed in tandem with the soft jangle of the bell over the front door. In a flounce of curls and a swish of that miniskirted fanny that had, Dana was sure, never felt the pinch of a girdle, Mercy pivoted back out to the sales floor, leaving Dana with the Duchess of Determination. She decided to ignore the feeling of dread curdling in her stomach as a slow, sly grin stretched across Cass's naturally glossed mouth. "You've never seen C.J., have you?"

Curdled dread never lied. Especially when it came to Cass, who, now that her own love life was copacetic, had made fixing Dana's woeful lack in that department her personal crusade.

Wiping her palms on the front of her skirt, Dana pivoted toward the door. "Mercy probably needs me out front—"

"No, she doesn't. Sit." Cass nodded toward the pile of clothes on her desk. "Those things need to be tagged anyway."

Scowling, Dana plopped behind the desk, snatching a tiny pink jumper off the pile. "Twelve bucks?"

"Fifteen. Macy's has them new for forty." Cass shifted in her chair, making Jason's hand fly about for a moment until his tiny fingers grasped her bunched up blouse. Envy pricked at Dana's heart as Cass continued, more to the baby than to Dana, "C.J. is…mmm, how shall I put this…?" *Zing* went those eyes. "Magnificent."

So she'd heard. Dana *phh'd* at her.

"As if it would kill you to spend the afternoon with the man with the bedroom, blue eyes." Cass tugged her skirt back over her knee. "Butt's not bad, either."

Just what Dana needed in her life. Lethal eyes and taut buns. She scribbled the price on the tag, then jabbed the point of the ticket gun into the jumper, entertaining vaguely voodoo-esque thoughts. "I think that's called sexual objectification."

"Yeah. So?"

She grabbed the next item off the pile, a fuchsia jumpsuit with enormous purple flowers. "Twenty?"

"Sure. Sweetie, I nearly drooled over the guy myself when he helped me sell the house a few months ago. And don't you dare tell Blake."

Dana's head snapped up. "Excuse me? You were seven months pregnant, recently widowed—"

Never mind that Cass's second husband had been a dirtwad of the first order, but a friend has a duty to point out these things.

"—your ex-husband was hot to get back together, and you were salivating all over your Realtor?"

"Yeah, well, it was like having a close encounter with a chocolate marble cheesecake after a ten-year diet. Fortunately, since I'm not all that crazy about chocolate marble cheese-cake, the temptation passed."

*Un*fortunately, Dana had a real thing for chocolate marble cheesecake. Which Cass knew full well. As did Dana's hips.

"This wouldn't be you trying to fix me up, by any chance?"

"Perish the thought."

Dana sighed, wrote out another price tag. "You forget. I had inside information." She plopped the last garment on the "done" pile, then folded her hands in front of her on the desk. "C. J. Turner's idea of intimacy is cozying up to his cell phone on his way to one appointment, making follow-up calls from another. The man is married to his business. Period."

A moment of skeptical silence followed. "You got this from Trish, I take it?"

"Not that I know any details," Dana said with a shrug. Her much younger cousin and she had never been close, despite Trish's having lived with Dana's parents for several years. She'd worked for C. J. Turner for six months before vanishing from the face of the earth, more than a year ago. Before the alien abduction, however, she had talked quite a bit about the apparently calendar-worthy Realtor. Professionally, she'd sung his praises, which was why Dana had recommended him to Cass when she'd needed an agent's services. Personally, however, was something else again. "But I gathered the man hasn't exactly listed himself on the Marriage Exchange."

Cass gave her a pointed look from underneath feathery bangs. "So maybe he hasn't met the right woman yet."

"Boy, you are sleep-deprived."

"Well, you never know. It could happen."

"Yeah, and someday I might lose this extra thirty pounds I've been lugging around since junior high, but I'm not holdin' my breath on that one, either."

"You know, sweetie, just because Gil—"

"And you can stop right there," Dana said softly before her partner could dredge up past history. She rose, grabbing the pile of newly marked clothes to cart out front. "I've already got one mother, Cass."

"Sorry," Cass said over the baby's noisy suckling at her breast. "It's just—"

"I *am* happy," Dana said, cutting her off. "Most of the time, anyway. I've got a good life, great friends and I actually look forward to coming to work every day, which is a lot more than most people can say. But trust me, the minute I start buyin' into all the 'maybes' and 'it could happens,' I'm screwed."

Silence hovered between them for a few seconds, until, on a sigh that said far more than Dana wanted to know, Cass said, "C.J.'s card's in my Rolodex."

"Great," Dana said, thinking, *Why me, God? Why?*

"You keep staring out the door like that, your eyeballs are gonna fall right outta your head."

C.J. smiled, relishing the blast from the lobby's overzealous air conditioner through his dress shirt, fresh out of the cleaner's plastic this morning. "Haven't you got phones to answer or something, Val?"

"You hear any ringing? I don't hear any ringing, so I guess there aren't any phones to answer." The trim, fiftysomething platinum blonde waltzed from behind the granite reception desk to peer through silver-framed glasses out the double glass door at the gathering clouds. "You giving that cloud the evil eye so it'll go away, or so it'll come here?"

One hand stashed in his pants pocket, C.J. allowed a grin for both the storm outside and the Texas tempest beside him. Out over the West Mesa, lightning periodically forked in the ominous sky; in the past ten minutes, the thunder had gone from hesitant rumbling to something with a real kick to it. If it weren't for this appointment, he'd be outside, arms raised to the sky, like some crazed prehistoric man communing with the gods. Ozone had an almost sexual effect on him, truth be told. Not that he was about to let Val in on that fact.

"Ah, c'mon, Val—can't you feel the energy humming in the air?"

"Oh, Lord. Next thing I know, you're gonna tell me you're seeing auras around people's heads—"

The phone rang, piercing the almost eerie hush cloaking the small office. Already cavelike with its thick, stone-colored carpeting and matching walls, the serene gray décor was relieved only by a series of vivid seriographs, the work of a local artist whose career C.J. had been following for years. Normally the place was hopping, especially when the three other agents he'd brought on board were around. But not only were they all out, even C.J.'s cell phone had been uncharacteristically silent for the past hour or so.

Unnerving, to say the least.

"I hear you, I hear you," Val muttered, sweeping back around the desk, assuming her sweetness-and-light voice the instant she picked up the receiver. A wave of thunder tumbled across the city, accompanied by a lightning flash bright enough to make C.J. blink. Behind him, he heard a little shriek and the clatter of plastic as Val dropped the receiver into the cradle. Some twenty-odd years ago, an uncle or somebody had apparently been struck by lightning through the phone; nobody in her family had touched a telephone during an electrical storm since. Still, the quirk was a small enough price to pay for unflagging loyalty, mind-boggling efficiency and the occasional, well-deserved kick in the butt.

She was standing beside him again, her arms crossed over a sleeveless white blouse mercilessly tucked into navy pants, warily eyeing the blackening sky.

"Looks like you're about to get your wish…oh, *Lordy!*" Another crack of thunder nearly sent her into the potted cactus by the door, just as a white VW Jetta with a few years on it pulled into the nearly empty lot. His three o'clock, no doubt, he thought with a tight grin.

Not that Cass Carter hadn't given it the old college try, with her enthusiastic recital of Dana Malone's virtues. Nor could he deny a certain idle curiosity about the person belonging to the warm Southern drawl on the other end of the line, when Dana herself had called to make an appointment. Still, if it hadn't been for all the business Cass and Blake Carter had brought to the agency over the past few months, he would have gladly handed off this particular transaction to one of the other agents. He rarely handled rental deals these days, for one thing. And for another, God save him from well-intentioned women trying to fix him up.

His last…whatever…had been well over a year ago, a one-night stand that should have never happened. And he shouldered the blame for the whole fiasco, for a momentary, but monumental, lapse of good judgment that—thank God!—hadn't turned out any worse than it had. *By the skin of his teeth* didn't even begin to cover it. But the affair had brought into startlingly sharp focus exactly how pointless his standard operating procedure with women had become.

It would be disingenuous to pretend that female companionship had ever been a problem, even if C.J. hadn't taken advantage of every opportunity that presented itself. At twenty, he'd considered it a gift; by thirty, somewhat of an embarrassment, albeit one he could definitely live with. Long-term relationships, however, had never been on the table. Not a problem with the career-focused women who were no more interested in marriage and family than he was, liaisons that inevitably self-destructed. But it was the gals for whom becoming a trophy wife was a career goal—the ones who saw his determination to remain single as a challenge, yes, but hardly an insurmount-able one—that were beginning to get to him.

What he had here was a mondo case of bachelor burnout, a startling revelation if ever there was one. But far easier to avoid the mess to begin with than suffer through cleaning it up later—

The phone rang again; Val didn't move. "What do you suppose is taking her so long to get out of her car?" she said, her voice knifing through his thoughts.

Twenty feet away, the car door finally opened, and out swung a pair of beautifully arched feet in a pair of strappy high-heeled sandals. C.J. watched with almost academic interest as the woman attached to the feet pulled herself out of the car, the wind catching her soft, billowing white skirt, teasing the hem up to mid-thigh. Her little shriek of alarm carried clear across the parking lot.

In spite of himself, C.J. smiled: he now knew she wore garterless stockings with white lace tops.

"Val? Would you mind checking to be sure all those property printouts for Great Expectations are on my desk?"

"Since I put them there, there's no need to check. Cute little thing, isn't she?"

She was that.

Assorted debris and crispy, yellowing cottonwood leaves whirlwinded through the parking lot, whipping at long, tea-colored hair swept up into a topknot, at long bangs softly framing a round face. He could see her grimace as she tried to yank the hair out of her eyes and mouth, hang on to her shoulder bag and hold down the recalcitrant skirt all at once. Huddled against the onslaught, she made a dash for the front door, the weightless fabric of her two-piece dress outlining a pleasant assortment of curves. She hit the sidewalk the precise moment the first fat raindrops splatted to earth; C.J. pushed open the door, only to have a gust of wind shove an armful of fragrant, soft female against his chest. His arms wrapped around her. So they wouldn't fall over.

"*Oh!*"

Wide gray-green eyes met his, her skin flushed underneath that unruly mass of shiny hair, now adorned with several leaves and a Doublemint gum wrapper. Inexplicably, he thought of freshly laundered linens and gardens and cool evening breezes at the end of a hot, sultry day.

And, because some habits are simply harder to break than others, he also thought of the pleasant things one could do on freshly laundered linens with a woman who smelled like sunshine and fresh breezes and exotic flowers—

She shot backward as if stung, a full lower lip hanging slightly slack, glistening with some natural-colored lip goo that suited her fair skin to a tee.

C.J. smiled. "Dana Malone, I presume?"

"Oh!" she said a second time, then started madly plucking things out of her hair. Her hands full, she looked frantically around, as if trying to find someplace to stash the evidence before anyone noticed. Always the gracious hostess, Val brought her a small wastebasket. Dana gave a nervous little smile, wiggling her fingers for a second until the disintegrating leaves drifted into their plastic grave. "The wind…" she began as she dusted off her hands, tugged at the hem of her tunic. "A storm's comin'…you were closer than I expected…oh."

Her blush heightened, as did her Southern drawl. Mississippi, he guessed. Maybe Alabama. Someplace that brought to mind verandas and Spanish moss and ladies who still wore white gloves to church during the summer. She wiped her hand on her hip, those glistening lips twitching around a nervous smile. "I don't usually make such spectacular entrances."

"And it's not every day lovely women throw themselves into my arms."

"Oh, *brother,*" Val muttered behind him as a slightly indignant, "I did not *throw* myself anywhere, I was *blown,*" popped out of Dana's mouth.

Val cackled. C.J. turned his gaze on his office manager.

"Don't you have someplace to be, Val?"

"Probably," the blonde said, her reply swallowed by a flash of lightning and a window-rattling clap of thunder, as the sky let loose with torrents of rain and marble-sized hail that bounced a foot off the ground.

Dana whipped around to face outside, her palms skimming her upper arms. "Oh, my goodness," she breathed, radiating what C.J. could only describe as pure delight. "I sometimes forget how much I miss the rain!"

Don't stare at the client, don't stare at the— "So you're not from New Mexico, either?"

She shook her head, her attention fixed on the horizon. "Alabama. But I've lived here since I was fourteen." Now her eyes cut to his. "Did you say 'either'?"

"South Carolina, here. Charleston."

"Oh, I love Charleston! I haven't been back in a while, but I remember it being such a pretty city—"

Val cleared her throat. They both turned to her.

"Those printouts are right where I said they were," she said. "On your desk. For your appointment." She paused, looking from one to the other. "Today."

"Oh! Yes! I, um…" Dana lifted a hand to her hair, her face reddening again. "Do y'all have someplace I can pull myself back together?"

"Ladies' is right around the corner," Val supplied.

C.J. watched Dana glide away, her fanny twitching ever so slightly. Then he glanced over to catch Val squinting at him. "What?"

"Nothing," she said, her backless shoes slapping against

her heels as she finally returned to her station. But when he passed her on the way back to his office to get the printouts, he thought he heard her mumble something about there being hope for him yet, and he almost laughed.

But not because he found her comment amusing in the slightest.

Dana squelched a yelp when she flipped on the light in the mushroom-colored restroom and caught a load of her reflection. Not that her heart rate could possibly go any higher than it already was after catching her first glance of C.J.

Those eyes…

That *mouth*…

Wow.

"Cass Carter," Dana muttered, sinking onto a stool in front of the mirror, "you are *so* dead." She shook her head, which sent the last few hairpins pinging off the marble countertop, her tangled hair *whooshing* to her shoulders. Then, with a small, pitiful moan, she dropped her head into her hands.

The man went *way* beyond chocolate marble cheesecake. Heck, he went way beyond any dessert yet known to man. Or woman. He was…was…

In a class all to himself, is what. Who knew people could actually look that good without airbrushing?

Well, this musing was fun and all, but it wasn't getting her fixed up. She plucked out another leaf and a crumpled straw wrapper, then dug her brush out of her purse to beat it all back into submission again. Dana stood and bent over at the waist, brushing the dust and grit out of her hair. Maybe the blood would rush back to her head, reestablish some semblance of intelligent thought processes. Grabbing the slippery mass with both hands, she twisted it into a rope, then coiled it on top of her head, standing back up so quickly she got dizzy.

So she sat down again, clamping the coiled hair on top of her head while she rummaged through her bag for the loose hairpins she was forever finding and dropping into the leather abyss.

Wow.

So much for the blood to the head theory.

After the kind of sigh she hadn't let out since Davey Luken's clumsy kiss in the seventh grade, she jammed a half-dozen pins into the base of the topknot, finger-fluffed her bangs. Yeah, well, Dana hadn't dated as much she had, as long as she had, not to gain an insight or two along the way. Because for all C. J. Turner's Southern charm and suaveness and brain-fritzing masculinity, he also positively buzzed with I-am-so-not-into-commitment vibes. Must've driven Trish right around the bend.

Only then did Dana burst out laughing as she realized what she'd felt, on her hip, a split second before she pulled out of C.J.'s arms. Heeheehee…she'd bet her entire collection of Victoria's Secret knickers the man had not been amused by *that* little reflex reaction.

Although, come to think about it, it hadn't been all that little.

Still chuckling, Dana stood again, tugging and hitching and flicking leaf pyuck off her bazooms, only to take a long, hard, honest gander at herself in the mirror. Generally speaking, she was okay with her body. For the most part, things curved in and out where they should, even if a few of the outs were a little farther "out" than average. But she'd long since learned to work with what she had, to spend a few extra bucks to have highlights put in her hair, to use makeup to emphasize her large gray green eyes, to wear clothes that made her feel feminine and good about herself. Dowdy, she didn't do.

However, that didn't mean she wasn't a realist, or that while she knew any number of full-figured women—her mother included—in very happy relationships, neither did her father look anything like C. J. Turner. Nor had any of her former boyfriends. The odds of C.J. being interested in her in that way, even as a passing fancy, were slim.

Well, that certainly takes the pressure off, doesn't it? she thought, giving those bodacious bazooms a quick, appreciative pat. If nothing else, they'd always have Paris. Or something.

She flicked off the light to the ladies' room and walked out into the hall, chin up, chest out, feeling pretty and confident and...

"Ready to go?" C.J. said from the lobby, his model-bright smile lighting up those baby blues.

...seriously out of her depth.

"Sure am," she said, smiling back, praying for all she was worth that she didn't snag her heel on the Berber carpet and land flat on her equally bodacious fanny.

"Yes, that'll be fine, I'll see you then," C.J. said into his cell phone, clapping it shut and slipping it back into his pants pocket. Not a single call between lunch and Dana's appointment; since then, the damn thing had rung every five minutes. "Sorry about that," he said. From the other side of the vacant storefront, she waved away his concern.

"At least this way," she said, making a face at the bathroom, "I don't feel guilty about takin' up so much of your time."

"It goes with the territory," he said. "Take all the time you need."

Her back to him, she lifted both hands in the air and waggled them as she click-clacked over the cement floor toward the stockroom.

Chuckling softly, C.J. decided he wasn't quite sure what to make of Dana Malone. She exuded all the charm and femininity befitting her Southern upbringing, but none of the coyness. No eyelash fluttering, no feigned helplessness. On the contrary, her incessant fiddling with the printouts, the way she worried her bottom lip as they inspected each property, told him she was genuinely nervous about the position her partners had put her in. And becoming increasingly embarrassed—and ticked off—about being unable to make a decision.

The storm had lasted barely ten minutes, but leftover clouds prowled the sky, leaving the air muggy, the temperature still uncomfortably high. And, after a half-dozen properties, Dana was grumpy and irritable. Now, at number seven, C.J. stayed near the front, his arms folded across his chest as he leaned against a support pillar, watching her. Trying to parse the odd, undefined feeling that kicked up in his gut every time she looked at him.

"It's okay, I suppose," she finally said, her words literally and figuratively ringing hollow in the vast, unfurnished room. "It's certainly big enough. And the double doors in back are great for deliveries...."

She looked to him, almost as if afraid to say it.

"But?" he patiently supplied.

Her shoulders rose with the force of her sigh. "But...there's not much parking. And you can't really see the front of the store from the street. I mean..." Annoyance streaked across her features as she fanned herself with the sheaf of printouts. "I suppose we really don't need more than five or six spaces in front." She crossed to the front window, her skirt swishing softly against her legs. "And this big window is not only perfect for display, it lets in lots of outside light for the play area Mercy wants to put in. Right now, the toddlers have the run of the shop, and we're so afraid one of them is going to get hurt...."

He thought he heard her voice catch, that she turned a little too quickly toward the window. "And maybe that Mexican restaurant next door would pull in enough traffic to compensate for being on a side street…." Fingers tipped in a delicate shade of rose lifted to her temple, began a circular massage.

"So we'll keep looking," C.J. said mildly as he straightened up. "Next?"

A couple of the papers fell from her hand as she tried to shuffle them; he went to retrieve them for her, but she snatched them up before he had a chance, pointlessly pushing back a strand of hair that kept falling into her eyes. "Oh, um, this one near the Foothills might not be bad. Great square footage for the price, lots of families in the area…" Then her brow creased. "But I don't know, maybe we should stick with something more centrally located…oh, *shoot!*"

"At the end of our rope, are we?"

"There's an understatement…oh! What are you doing?" she asked as C.J. took her by the elbow, ushering her through the glass door.

"Break time. For both of us."

"I don't—"

"You're making yourself nuts. Hell, you're making *me* nuts. This is only a preliminary look-see, Dana. No one expects you to sign a contract today."

"Good thing," she said, her hand shooting up to shield her eyes from the glaring late afternoon sun as they walked back to his Mercedes, "since it's all a blur." He opened the car door for her; she didn't protest. Once he'd slid in behind the wheel, she plonked her head back on the headrest and closed her eyes. "But what a weenie-brain," she said on a sigh. "I can't even eliminate the dogs."

C.J. felt a smile tug at his mouth as he pulled out into traffic. "I can assure you I've met a fair number of people who'd qualify for that title, Dana. You're definitely not one of them."

She seemed to consider this for a moment, while her

perfume sambaed around the car's interior. Something high-end and familiar. But, on her, unique. "Thank you," she said at last, her eyes still closed. "But I sure do feel like one." Her eyes blinked open. "Why are we pulling in here?"

"Because it's at least five-hundred degrees out, you're obviously fried, and this joint makes the best ice-cream sodas in town. My treat."

A pickup festooned with yapping mutts rumbled up the street behind them as a whole bunch of questions swarmed in Dana's hazy gray-green eyes.

"You hate ice-cream sodas?" he asked.

A startled laugh burst from her throat. "No! I'm just…" She shook her head, dainty, dangly earrings bobbing on tiny earlobes that had gone a decided shade of pink. "But I think I'll stick with Diet Coke."

A four-by-four roared past, spraying soggy gravel in its wake.

"It's that woman thing, isn't it?"

Her eyebrows lowered. "Excuse me?"

"Where you won't eat in front of a guy. If at all."

Her mouth twisted, her gaze slid away. "I think it's kinda obvious I'm no anorexic."

"Good to know. Because I'm here to tell you that not-eating business annoys the hell out of me. But hey—" he popped open his car door, then loosened his tie, having already given his jacket the heave-ho three properties ago "—if you really want a Diet Coke, knock yourself out."

"Actually…" She hugged her purse to her middle, as if trying to shrink. "I can't stand the stuff."

"Then it's settled." He shoved open his door, then went around to open hers. "Maybe if you just chill for a bit, you'll be able to think more clearly. Damn," he muttered as his phone rang again. He grimaced at the number—a deal he'd been trying to close for nearly a month—then at her.

"Hey—" she said, as they both got out of the car "—you've got ice-cream sodas to pay for, far be it from me to hinder your earning capacity." She glanced up at the sky. "Wonder if it's going to rain again? It sure feels steamy, doesn't it?"

It did. But somehow, he mused as he answered the phone, he doubted the humidity had anything to do with it.

Chapter Two

Dana would lay odds the diner probably hadn't changed much in twenty years. At least. Formica soda fountain and booths, nondescript beige vinyl upholstery. It was clean, though, and light, and hummed with conversation, laughter, canned mariachi music. Despite the dearth of patrons this late in the afternoon, C.J. swore the tiny restaurant would be packed by six. Dana believed it. Although Albuquerque had more than its share of tony eateries, this was one of those unassuming little holes-in-the-wall the well-off liked to think they'd "discovered," where the menu selections were few but the serving sizes generous, the food simple but excellent and the staff treated everyone like a lifelong friend.

And, if she'd been here with Mercy or Cass, she'd definitely be more relaxed. But sitting across from C.J., she was about as relaxed as Sallymae Perkins's hair on prom night.

Plus—to make matters worse—she also had to admit that none of the places they'd looked at was going to work.

"Sorry," she said, her mouth screwed up as she poked at a lump of ice cream in the bottom of her collarbone-high glass, dolefully considering the wisdom of broiled chicken breasts and salad with lemon juice for the next three nights.

"Don't apologize." C.J. certainly seemed unfazed, slouched in the booth, the top two buttons undone on an Egyptian cotton shirt only a shade lighter than his eyes. Light brown hair sprinkled with gray shuddered in the breeze from a trio of lazily *fwomping* overhead fans, as his mouth tilted up in a half smile. A gentle smile. A tired smile, she thought, although she doubted he'd admit it. Especially since she was, in all likelihood, as least partly to blame. "That's why we're here."

"But I took up half your afternoon—"

"Would you stop it?" he said gently. "That's what the first rounds are for, to get a feel for what the client really wants."

Lazy raindrops began to slash at the window by their booth, while, in the distance, thunder rumbled halfheartedly. What she really wanted, Dana thought with a stab, had nothing to do with anything C. J. Turner had to offer. Unfortunately. She speared the chunk of ice cream, popped it into her mouth.

"So why not just ask?" she asked over the whir of the milkshake mixer behind the counter, the high-pitched chatter of a bevy of kids three booths over.

"I did. And Cass gave me the basics." One arm now snaked out along the top of the booth seat; he offered her another smile. "The rest she left to you…damn."

A salesman's smile, she told herself as he answered his phone with yet another apologetic glance across the table. Impersonal. No different from those he'd bestowed on everyone they'd met that afternoon, on everyone who'd called.

Then, out of the corner of her eye, she caught the sudden

appearance of tiny, dimpled fingers hooking the edge of their table. Seconds later a mass of fudge-colored curls bobbed into view, over a set of matching, devilish eyes. Just as quickly, eyes and curls and pudgy fingers vanished, supplanted by a howl.

Dana was out of the booth and on her knees at once, hauling the sobbing baby onto her lap. About two years old, she guessed, smelling of chocolate sauce and baby shampoo.

"Oh, now, now," she soothed as she struggled to her feet, bouncing the child on her hip, "you're not hurt, are you?" Laughing, she glanced over at C.J., whose stony expression knocked the laughter right out of her.

"Enrique, you little devil!" A pretty young woman dashed back to their booth, taking the child from Dana's arms. His wails immediately softened to lurching sniffles as he wound his plump little arms around his mother's neck.

Dana crossed her own arms over the void left in the child's wake, wondering why, after all this time, she'd yet to move past this point. In any case, the emptiness, in combination with the look on C.J.'s face, knocked her off an emotional ledge she hadn't even known she was on. "He's not hurt," she assured the baby's mother, struggling to banish from-out-of-nowhere tears.

The brunette rolled her eyes, then laughed. "He never is. But I've really got to get a leash for him! I turn my back for five seconds to wipe his brother's nose, and he's gone." She jostled the child, more to comfort herself than the baby, Dana decided. "Scared me half to death. Yes, you did, you little terror! Oh, no!" She plucked a tiny hand from around her neck and inspected chocolate-coated fingers, then groaned. "I'm so sorry! He got chocolate on your pretty white dress! I'll be happy to pay for the dry cleaning!"

Dana glanced down at the smudge over her left breast, then shrugged, figuring the young woman had better things

to spend her money on than a dry-cleaning bill. Once assured
a squirt of Shout would make it good as new, the woman
whisked her son away, and Dana slid back into her seat
across from C.J., only to realize, to her mortification, that
she was still teetering on that emotional edge. Yeah, well,
being surrounded by far too many reminders of all those
things that were, or seemed to be, out of her reach, would
do that to a person.

"Are you okay?" came the soft, genuinely concerned—for
himself as well as her, Dana thought—voice across the table.

Looking at him was the last thing she wanted to do. But
what choice did she have? She cleared her throat as discreetly
as possible, then met his gaze. "Just tired, is all," she said, but
the cant of his eyebrows told her he didn't buy it for a minute.

"That stain, though…"

She tried a smile, anything to remove the sudden wariness
in his features. "Hey, you hear a kid cry, you don't even think
about getting dirty, you just want to make it all better."

He watched her for a long, hard moment, during which she
could practically see the gears shifting in his thought. "You
follow your instincts, in other words."

"Well, yes, I suppose—"

"So why do you think your partners elected you to do
the footwork?"

Nothing like a conversational right turn to obliterate self-
pity. Dana blinked, then said, "I have no idea, actually. In fact,
I tried to get out of it."

"Because?"

She sighed, wadding her napkin into a ball. "Let's just say
decision making's not my strong suit. Which I'm sure comes
as no surprise."

"And yet…" C.J. leaned forward, shoving his empty glass
to one side so he could clasp his hands together, his eyes

holding her fast. "Cass tells me you're not only a financial whiz, but have a real flair for decorating kids' rooms, as well."

Another blush stole up her neck. "Well, yes, I suppose, but—"

"She also said if anyone could find Great Expectations' next home, it would be you, because you wouldn't make a decision until you were absolutely positive it was the *right* decision."

He reached across the table, briefly touching her wrist. His fingers were cool, a little rough. And suddenly squarely back in front of him, leaving a mild, buzzing sensation in their place.

"Trust your instincts, Miss Malone. The same way you trust your instincts about how to handle children. It's a gift. Be...be grateful for it. So..."

His posture shifted with his train of thought, giving her a chance to anticipate the next right turn. "Now I have a better idea of what to show you next time." He shrugged. "No big deal."

No big deal, her fanny. Never in all her born days had she met a man who could put her so much at ease and keep her so off-kilter at the same time.

"So," C.J. said, "what day looks good for you to take another stab at this?"

Dana sucked on her empty spoon for a moment, squinting slightly at those lovely, keep-your-distance eyes. The spoon clanged against the inside of the glass when she dropped it in. She looked up, pasted on a smile.

"How's Friday look?"

Grateful for an excuse to look away from that far too trenchant gaze, C.J. scrolled through his Palm Pilot, then nodded. "First thing in the morning looks good. Say...nine?"

"Perfect," she said, then stood. "Is there a restroom here? I hope."

"In back. Not ritzy, but it works."

"That's all I ask," she said, then headed toward the back of the diner. No less than a half-dozen male heads turned to watch her progress.

"Hey, C.J.! How's it goin'?"

With a smile for Felix, the diner's owner, C.J. picked up the check the bulky man had dropped in front of him. "Oh, fine. This heat's a killer, though."

A chuckle rumbled from underneath Felix's heavy, salt-and-pepper mustache. "I'm surprised you haven't already *melted,* my friend. Maria's already smacked me twice for staring!" He leaned close enough for C.J. to smell twenty years' worth of *sopapillas* on his white apron. "These women who think we want them skinny, they got it all wrong, no? Give me a woman I'm not afraid is going to break, anytime."

C.J. swallowed a smile. Felix's wife certainly fit the bill there. He handed a ten to the grinning proprietor, told him to keep the change, then stood as Dana emerged from the restroom…and a vaguely familiar female voice said, "C.J.? What on earth are you doing here?" right behind him.

He turned to find himself face-to-face with an artfully streaked blonde in one of those short, shapeless dresses and a tennis visor, flanked on either side by miniature versions of herself, twin girls who could have been anywhere between three and seven.

He thought back. Five, he decided, had to be the cut-off.

"I thought that was you when I came in," the woman said, perfect teeth flashing, the ends of her straight, gleaming hair skimming her shoulders. "We don't live far, the girls love the milkshakes here." The grin widened. "My goodness, it's been way too long. How *are* you? You look terrific!"

"Um, you, too." Out of the corner of his eye, he caught Dana's approach, her raised eyebrows. "Well, well," C.J. said, glancing at the little girls. "You've certainly been busy, haven't you…?"

"Oh. Hello." The blonde offered Dana a cool smile, and C.J. thought, *I'm dead.*

"Dana Malone, this is…"

"Cybill Sparks," she mercifully supplied, assessing Dana as only a female who feels her territory threatened can. Never mind that he hadn't even seen the woman—with whom he'd had a brief (and not particularly sweet, as he recalled) affair— in years. Or that she'd clearly moved on.

A weird blend of protectiveness and irritation spiked through C.J., even as Dana, her smile as gracious as Cybill's was frozen, said, "C.J.'s my Realtor. We were just scouting out properties for my store."

Which was apparently sufficient to silence Cybill's Incoming Threat alarm. "Oh? What do you sell?" she asked, her smile more natural again. "Not women's clothing, I presume?"

A moment passed. "No, a children's store. Maybe you've heard of it?" Dana grinned for the twins, who had ducked behind their mother's legs and were both smiling up at her with wide blue eyes. "Great Expectations?"

"Ohmigod, yes! I *love* that store! We're in there all the time! With four sets of grandparents, the girls get far more clothes than they could ever wear. It's so great having someplace to unload them. Especially since I can make a few bucks on the deal." She laughed. "Although don't tell any of the grands!"

"Wouldn't dream of it," Dana muttered, but Cybill's attention had already slithered back to C.J. Her hand landed on his arm, her expression downright rapacious. "I've been meaning to call you for, gosh, ages."

"To let me know you were married?" C.J. said lightly.

"No, silly, to let you know I'm divorced! My number's the same, so give me a call sometime." Another tooth flash. "With all those grandparents, it's no trouble at all finding a sitter on short notice! Nice to meet you," she tossed dismissively in Dana's direction, then steered the children toward the counter.

Dana waited until they'd gotten outside to laugh.

"What's so damned funny?" C.J. grumbled.

"You had no idea who she was, did you?"

"Of course I knew who she was," he said, giving his lungs a second to adjust to the breath-sucking heat. "It was just her name that temporarily escaped me."

"That is seriously pathetic."

"Not nearly as pathetic as the way she threw herself at me," he muttered.

"True. For a moment there I thought she was going to unhinge her jaws and swallow you whole. I take it she's an old girlfriend?" she asked over his grunt.

"She'd like to think so. But I swear, the kids aren't mine."

She chuckled again, a sound he realized he enjoyed. Very much. He stole a glance at her profile as they walked to the car, thinking what a bundle of contradictions she was—self-deprecating one minute, completely comfortable with teasing him the next. About another woman's putting the moves on him, no less.

He literally shook his head to clear it.

"So what happened?" Dana said as they got to the car and C.J. beeped it unlocked.

"Nothing, in the long run. Much to her chagrin."

Once in the car, they clicked their seat belts in place almost simultaneously. "So tell me…" Dana briefly checked her makeup in the visor mirror, then turned to him, amusement glittering in her eyes. "Do women launch themselves at you on a regular basis?"

C.J. wasn't sure which startled him more—the question itself or the ingenuousness underpinning it. He met Dana's curious, open gaze and thought, *There's something different about this one,* even as he said, "You do realize there's no way I can answer that and keep either my dignity or your respect intact?"

"My...respect?"

He twisted the key in the ignition, backed out of the lot. "A Realtor who doesn't have his clients' respect isn't going to get very far."

"I see." She faced front again, severing what he realized had been a gossamer-thin thread of connection, leaving him feeling both annoyed and relieved, which made no sense whatsoever. "Thanks," she said, her voice definitely a shade darker than moments before. "For the soda, I mean. I needed that. And I promise not to be such a worrywart on Friday."

"Don't make promises you can't keep," he said lightly, wondering why her soft laugh in response sent a chill marching up his spine.

In combat boots.

Sometime later, Dana let herself into her parents' Northeast Heights home, breathing in the pomander of swamp-cooled air, that night's fried chicken and a brief whiff of fresh roses, at once comforting and disquieting in its immutability. Her pull here tonight was equally comforting, equally disquieting. Tonight, she needed home, even though, paradoxically, this was the one place guaranteed to remind her of those areas of her life currently running on empty.

She found her father first, molded to a leather recliner in the family room, a can of diet soda clutched in one thick-fingered hand, the baseball game on the movie-theater-sized TV screen reflected in his glasses.

"Hey, Daddy. Whatcha up to?"

Gene Malone jerked up his head and grinned, his thinning hair fanned out behind his head like a limp peacock's tail.

"Hey, there, baby!" he said over the announcer's mellow drone. "What brings you around?"

Her father, a Sandia Labs retiree, was rounder, and balder, than he used to be, but the humor simmering behind his pea-soup-colored eyes was the same as always. Dana bent over to kiss his forehead, then crackled onto the plastic-armored sofa beside the chair, staring at the TV. "Nothing much. Just hadn't seen y'all in a bit." Trying to keep from frowning, she studied his face. "How're you feeling?"

"Never better." A heart "episode" the year before had scared the willies out of them; unfortunately, she strongly suspected he wasn't following his diet and exercise regimen as scrupulously as he should. Especially when he said, "You know, this eating more chicken and fish routine really seems to be helping. I haven't felt this good in ages."

Uh-huh. Somehow, she didn't think *fried* chicken was what the doctor had in mind. "Glad to hear it, Daddy. Where's Mama?"

"In the den, sewing. Leastways, that's what she said she was gonna do." The leather squeaked when he shifted. "You know Trish called?"

This was news. "No. When?"

"Day or so ago, I don't remember."

"She say where she was?"

"Have no idea. You'll have to ask your mother."

Wondering, and not for the first time, how two people could live together for so long and talk to each other so little, she left her father to cheer on whoever and headed toward the smallest bedroom—the one that had been Trish's for nearly eight years—which they generously referred to as a den. In a sleeveless blouse and cotton pants, Faye Malone sat with her back to the door, as comfortably padded as the futon beside her. As usual, she was keeping up a running conversation with the sewing machine while she worked, pins stuck in her mouth, tufts of touched-up-every-three weeks auburn hair sticking out at odd angles where she'd tugged at it while trying to figure something out.

Heaven knew, having Faye for a mother had never been exactly easy, and not only because of the woman's habit of walking out on anyone who didn't agree with her. Or her nearly obsessive protectiveness when it came to family. All her life, Dana had variously loved and feared the woman whose scowl had been known to set people to rethinking opinions held dear from the cradle. Tonight, however, Dana envied her mother her single-mindedness.

And her strength.

"What's that you're making, Mama?" she asked, once Faye had removed the pins from her mouth.

Her mother jumped and pivoted simultaneously. "Lord, honey, you gave me a start," she said, laughing, dropping the pins into an old saucer by the machine. "This? Oh, um…just a little something for Louise at church." She cleared her throat. "Her daughter's havin' her first baby next month."

Dana sat on the end of the futon that had replaced the old iron daybed, fingering the edge of the tiny royal blue and scarlet quilt. The vent over the door blasted too-cool air at the back of her neck, making her shudder. "Pretty," she managed, trying to keep her voice light, to ignore the tension vibrating between them. Not to mention the unmistakable wistfulness in her mother's voice, that she'd never get to watch *her* daughter grow big with a grandbaby.

"So…" Eager to change the subject, Dana clasped her hands, banging them against her knee. "Daddy said Trish called?"

"Oh, yes!" Her mother pulled off her glasses, tucking them into her shirt pocket. "I would've mentioned it, except there didn't seem to be much point."

"So she didn't tell you where she was, I take it?"

"Not a word."

"She say she was coming back?"

Her mother shook her head. "Although she had that funny little hitch in her voice, like when she'd done something wrong and was afraid we'd get mad at her? To this day, I don't know what my sister was thinking, marrying that…creep. Man wasn't worth the price of the marriage license. *And* cost Marla her own daughter."

An observation made many times over the past dozen years. Dana's aunt's second marriage, to a man the family fondly referred to as The Cockroach, had had a disastrous effect on her already troubled daughter. After Trish's third attempt at running away, and since Dana had been more or less on her own by then, Dana's parents had offered to let the teen come live with them in Albuquerque. And on the surface, especially after Aunt Marla's death a few years back, Trish had certainly seemed to be getting her life on track. She'd settled down enough to finish high school, gotten through community college, and had finally landed that job at Turner Realty. She'd even talked about becoming an agent herself, one day.

But threaded through Trish's marginal successes ran not only a string of rotten relationships with men, but a chronic resistance to letting either Dana or her parents get close enough to help her. Other than the occasional call during the past year to let them know she was still alive, she'd cut herself off from the only family she had.

Sad, but, since her cousin had consistently rebuffed Dana's attempts at being chummy, none of her concern. If Trish was out there somewhere, miserable and alone, she had no one to blame but herself.

"She asked about you," she heard her mother say.

Dana started. "Me? Why?"

"Beats me." Mama threaded a needle and moved to the futon, where she preferred to do her hand sewing. "I thought it was odd, too." She fell into the cushion with an *oof.* "Although she did ask how you were getting on since…"

Her mother caught herself, her lips puckered in concentration as she stared at her sewing.

At the beginning, Mama had meant well enough, Dana supposed, doing her level best to take Dana's mind off her situation. Tonight, though, Dana realized she'd lost patience with pretending. And with herself for allowing the silence to go on as long at it had.

"Go on, finish your sentence. Since I had my operation."

Faye smoothed the quilt with trembling hands. "I'm sorry, honey. It just sort of slipped out."

Dana sighed. "It's been more than a year, Mama. Way past time for us to still be sidestepping the subject, don't you think?"

"I…I just don't want to make you feel bad, baby."

Stomach wobbling, Dana snuggled up against her mother, inhaling her mingled scent of soap and sunscreen and cooking.

"I know that," she said softly, fingering the tiny quilt. "But ignoring things doesn't change them. Not that I'm not okay, most of the time, but…but there are definitely days when I feel cheated, when I get so angry I want to break something. And if I can't unload to my own mother about it, who *can* I tell?"

"Oh, honey." Faye dropped her handiwork; Dana let herself be drawn into her mother's arms, suddenly exhausted from the strain of putting on a brave face, day after day after day. Whether it had been holding Cass's baby, or the toddler in the diner, or even the strange mixture of kindness and wariness in C.J.'s eyes that had brought on the sudden and profound melancholy, she had no idea. But today, this minute, all she could see were the holes in her life. And with that thought came a great, unstoppable torrent of long held-back tears.

Why did the ordinary rites of passage that so many women took for granted—boyfriends, marriage, motherhood—seem to slip from her grasp like fine sand? In her teens and twenties, there had always been "later." But watching relationship after relationship crash and burn—if they ever got off the ground to begin with—had a way of eroding a girl's self-confidence. Not to mention her hopes.

Was it so wrong to want a family of her own, to ache for a pair of loving, strong arms around her in bed at night, to be the reason for someone's smile? Was it foolish to want a little someone to stay up late wrapping Christmas presents for, to wonder if they'd ever get potty trained or be okay on their first day of school, to embarrass the heck out of by kissing them in public, to tuck in at night and read to?

Or was she just being selfish?

And her mother listened and rocked her and told her, no, she wasn't being selfish at all, that someday she'd have her own family, a husband who'd cherish her, children to love. That she had so much to offer, she just had to be patient. Things happen for a reason, Mama said, even if we might not understand the particulars when we're in the middle of it.

So what, exactly, Dana wondered over her mother's murmurings, was the reason for C. J. Turner's appearance in her life? To torment her with eyes she had no reason to believe would ever sparkle just for her, a pair of arms she'd never feel wrapped around her shoulders, a chest she'd never be able to lay her head against?

She sucked in a breath: What on earth was she going on about? She didn't even know the man! Were nice guys so rare these days that simply being around one was enough to send her over the edge? Because even in the midst of her pityfest, she knew the meltdown had nothing to do with C.J. Not really. No, it was everything he represented.

All those things that, for whatever reason, always seemed to elude her.

But even the best crying jags eventually come to an end. Dana sat up, grabbed a tissue from the tole-painted box on the end table, and honked into it, after which her mother pulled her off the futon and led her to the kitchen. Yeah, yeah, the road to Jenny Craig was paved with comfort food, but there you are. And as she ate—fried chicken, coleslaw, potato salad—and as Amy Grant held forth from the clock radio on the counter, punctuated by the occasional war whoop from the family room, the conversation soon came back around to her cousin.

"So…" Dana wiped her fingers on a paper napkin, perking up considerably when her mother hauled a bowl of shimmering cherry Jell-O out of the fridge. "What was Trish asking about me? And is there whipped cream?"

The can of Reddi-wip plonked onto the table. "Just if you still lived alone, still worked at the store." Mama scooped out two huge, quivering blobs into custard dishes. "I gave her your number, I hope that's okay?"

"Sure. Not that she'd ever call me." The first bite of Jell-O melted soothingly against her tongue, reminding her of the last dessert she'd eaten. As well as the lazy, sexy, South Carolina accent of the man who had bought it for her.

Her mother was giving her a pained look. So Dana smiled and said, "Speaking of the store, I started looking at possible sites for the new location today."

"Well, it's about time! A body can't hardly breathe in that itty-bitty place y'all are in now. Find anything?"

Yeah. Trouble. "Not yet."

"That's okay, you will, honey. You just have to keep looking."

A twinge of either aggravation or acid reflux spurted through Dana as she stared hard at her spoon. And how long, exactly, was she supposed to *keep looking?* She thought back to how she'd spent weeks searching for the perfect prom dress, finally finding one she absolutely loved in some little shop in the mall. Except…the neckline was too low. And it was red. With a full skirt. And all those sparklies…

So she'd kept looking. And looking. Until, by the time she finally realized that was the only dress she really wanted, it was gone. So she'd had to settle for something she hadn't liked nearly as much because she'd dithered so long.

Because she'd believed herself unworthy of something so perfect.

She nearly choked on her Jell-O.

She was still doing it, wasn't she? Refusing to even try something on because of some preconceived notion that it wouldn't work. And maybe it wouldn't, once she got it on (she stifled a snort at the double entrendre). God knew she'd left plenty of clothes hanging in dressing rooms over the years. But at least she owed it to herself to *try*, for crying out loud—

"Dana, honey? Why are you frowning so hard?"

Dana blinked herself back from la-la land and smiled for her mother, even as fried chicken and potato salad tumble-dried in her stomach.

"Yes, I'm fine," she said, thinking, *Damn straight I have a lot to offer.*

And absolutely nothing to lose.

Chapter Three

C.J. clattered his keys and cell phone onto the Mexican-tiled kitchen countertop flanking a professional-grade cooktop he never used, gratefully yielding to the house's deep, benign silence. His briefcase thumped onto the stone floor as he glanced at the message machine: nada. Good. However, since his cleaning lady, Guadalupe, only came twice a week, his cereal bowl greeted him where he'd left it more than twelve hours earlier, bits of dried corn flakes plastered to the sides, a half cup of cold, murky coffee keeping it company. He tossed the dregs into the stainless steel sink, splattering his shirt in the process, aggravating the vague irritability clinging to him like seaweed.

C.J. yanked open the dishwasher and rammed the dishes inside, then grabbed a beer from the Sub-Zero fridge. Moments later, he stood on his flagstone patio, his gaze skating over the infinity pool, its mirrored surface reflecting the cloudless, almost iridescent early evening sky, then across the pristinely kept golf course dotted with fuzzy young pines and delicate ash trees beyond. And backdropping it all, the rough-cut Sandia Mountains, bloodred in the sunset's last hurrah. A light, dry breeze shivered the water's surface, soothing C.J. through his shirt. He took a pull of his beer and thought, glowering, *What more could I possibly want?*

Other than dinner magically waiting for him, maybe.

And not having to make a certain phone call this evening.

Back inside, a couple of touches to assorted wall panels instantaneously produced both cool air and even cooler jazz. Damn house was smarter than he was, C.J. thought grumpily, continuing on to the master suite at the back of the house.

From the middle of the king-size bed, a yard-long slash of gray surveyed him—upside down—through heavy-lidded yellow eyes. The cat pushed out a half-assed meow that ended in a yawn huge enough to turn the thing inside out.

"Don't let me disturb your rest," C.J. said as he tossed the day's dress duds into the leather club chair in the corner, adding to the mountain of clothes already there, waiting to be hauled to the cleaners. He'd barely tugged on a soft T-shirt, a pair of worn jeans, when he felt a grapefruit-sized head butt his shin.

"Nice try, fuzzbutt, but you've still got food in your dish, I looked. Which is more than I can say for myself. Unless you want to make this phone call for me?"

The cat flicked his tail in disgust and trotted away, and C.J. mused about how he wouldn't mind having a tail to flick in disgust himself, right about now.

He rolled his shoulders as he returned to the kitchen, his aching muscles a testament to the fact that too many years of twelve- and fourteen-hour days were beginning to take their toll. Still, work was what he did. Who he was. Besides, what was the alternative? Watching reality TV for hours on end?

He glanced at the microwave clock. Eight-thirty-two. Two hours later in Charleston. If he put this off long enough, he'd miss his father's birthday altogether. A tempting, if unrealistic, thought. "Forgetting" the occasion would only add fuel to the implacable fire of bitterness and resentment lodged between them.

The cat writhed around his ankles, startling him. The house was beginning to cool off. C.J., however, was not.

Eight-thirty-six. Frosted air teased his shoulders as he opened the freezer, yanked out a microwaveable dinner. He peeled back the corner and stuck it in the zapper. Fifteen minutes. More than enough time.

He snatched his cell off the counter, hesitated another moment, then dialed. His father answered on the first ring, his voice bombastic, irritable, condemning the caller for having interrupted whatever he'd been doing. "Turner here!"

"Dad. Happy birthday."

A moment of silence followed. Then: "That you, Cameron?"

"Who else would it be? Unless I have a half brother you forgot to mention."

Again, brittle silence stretched between them. Ah, yes— one did not joke with Cameron James Turner, Sr.

"Wondered if you were going to remember."

"Of course I remembered." Although he hadn't sent a card. Hadn't in years, since Hallmark didn't make one that said *Thanks for never being there for me.*

"Well," his father said. "It got so late."

"I just walked in the door. Long day."

That merited a grunt, but nothing more. Then, "Business good?"

"Fine."

"Growing?"

"Steadily."

"Glad to hear it," his father said, but perfunctorily, without any glow of pride. Not surprising, considering how small potatoes his father obviously considered a four-person real estate agency. In Albuquerque. C.J. glanced at the microwave and mentally groaned. How could two measly minutes seem like an eternity? "So. You do anything for your birthday?"

"Like what?"

"I don't know—go out with friends?"

"Why would I do that?"

Why, indeed? "Well. I just wanted to say…happy sixty-fifth. 'Night—"

"Not so fast, hold on a minute. You planning on coming out anytime soon?"

Shock sluiced through C.J. He and his father hadn't seen each other in more than a dozen years. "What did you say?"

Why?

"Simple enough question, Cameron. I'm getting my affairs in order, need your signature on some papers."

C.J.'s fingers strangled the phone. He should have known. "I can't get away right now. You'll have to courier the papers to me."

"But they have to be witnessed—"

"So I'll have them witnessed!"

The dial tone snarled in his ear; his father had hung up on him, shutting C.J. off, and out, as he always had. Always would.

C.J. slapped the phone shut. From two thousand miles away, he felt the burning look of disapproval etched into his father's overlarge features, the disappointment shadowing blue eyes like C.J.'s own. He'd never understood why, nor had he ever felt compelled to dig around for answers he wasn't sure he wanted, anyway. The basics were simple enough: his father had denied him nothing, except himself.

And while C.J. would never intentionally treat another human being as dismissively as his father had him, his well didn't exactly run deep, either, judging from his lack of any real connection with the women he'd dated over the years. Clearly, he'd inherited his father's factory-defective heart.

But Dana's different, came the thought, as unexpected and unwelcome as a bee sting.

Followed immediately by *Don't go there, Turner.*

Not a problem, he thought with a rueful grin. Not after all he'd gone through to reach a place where he was finally as much in control of his life as was humanly possible. And blissfully, gloriously free—free from the pressure to be someone he wasn't, free from either his own or anyone else's expectations.

At his feet, the cat meowed, a tiny interrogative *eeerk.*

Almost nobody, anyway.

The microwave beeped. In a daze, C.J. popped open the door, grabbing his dinner with his bare hand. He cursed, dropping the hot tray with a great clatter.

Free, he mused, to make a fool of himself without witnesses.

He let the cat out back, then followed, his meal and drink in tow, to sink into one of the pricey, thickly padded patio chairs the decorator had picked out. The sky had gone a deep, soothing blue; C.J. took another pull of his beer, then let his head loll back against the cushion. Overhead, the first stars had begun to twinkle. And if he wanted to sit here for the next two hours watching them, he could. If he wanted to turn the volume up all the way on the sound system, he could. If he wanted to leave the toilet seat up, or his towels on the floor, or two weeks' worth of clothes piled on his chair, he could.

It was as close to heaven as any man could wish for, he thought, forking in a bite of tasteless…something.

"Such a shame you have to go out in this heat to look at more properties today," Mercy said from her perch on the counter beside the cash register, dunking a donut into her coffee.

Squatting in front of a display of infant toys, Dana lifted her eyes, caught the smirk. "Uh, yeah. You look *real* broken up about it."

"Oh, come on," Mercy mumbled around the last bite of donut, then dusted off her hands. A geranium-pink tank top emblazoned with a rhinestone heart set off her ebony curls, today caught up in a series of clips studded with even more rhinestones. *Subtle* was not one of Mercy's strong suits. "I can think of a lot worse things than tootling around the city with a good-looking guy."

"Whom you haven't even met, so how do you know how good-looking he is?" Dana stood, moving over to a rack of toddler dresses to yank out a 3T that had gotten wedged in with the 2s. "And you have powdered sugar on your chin."

The brunette rubbed at the spot. "Did I get it?" Dana glanced at her, nodded. "And I trust Cass's taste in men. So…" Mercy slithered off the counter, tugging at the hem of her short white skirt, then knotted her hands around the top of the chrome rack, chin propped on knuckles. "How hot are we talking, exactly?"

Her just-try-it-on initiative about C.J. notwithstanding, Dana wasn't about to give her partners any ammunition toward the cause. This was one uphill battle she intended to tackle on her own, thank you. So she shrugged and said, "He's okay, I suppose. If you like that type."

"*Type* as in *gorgeous?*"

"No. Type as in 'I-don't-*do*-serious'."

"Oh, that." Mercy batted the air. "Not a problem."

Dana couldn't help the laugh. "And you're saying this because…?"

"Yeah, yeah—I know what you're getting at. But *I'm* still single not because I don't think there's a man alive who doesn't, deep down, want to come home to the same woman

every night, but because I'm…particular." She flounced over
to the door, peered out at the still-empty parking lot. In this
heat, it was unlikely they'd get many customers. "A girl's gotta
have standards, you know."

Dana eyed the leftover donuts still on the counter, forced
herself to look away. "And one of mine is that the sight of
children and wedding rings doesn't make the guy puke."

Mercy *pff'ed* her disdain through glossed red lips, then
tented her hand over her eyes. "Speaking of standards…bad-
ass vehicle at three o'clock. Yowsa."

Dana glanced over to see the familiar silver sedan glide into
a parking space. "Oh, no! I was supposed to meet *him,* at the
agency," she said over a pounding heart, suddenly not at all
sure she was ready to put her new resolve to the test. Especially before her second cup of coffee. "What on earth…?"

Both women stood, transfixed, as C.J. got out of the car,
slipped on his suit coat. Poor guy, dressed for a board meeting
in this weather. Still, that first glimpse of tall, handsome man
in a charcoal suit was enough to make anyone's heart stutter.
Including Mercy's, apparently.

"He's *okay?*" she said, eyes wide. "Hey, you don't want
him, toss him this way. I got no problem with leftovers."

"What happened to your standards?"

"Trust me, *chica.* He meets them."

The door swung open, and he was in. And smiling.
"Morning, ladies," he said, his voice still holding a hint of just-
out-of-bed roughness that made Dana swallow. Hard.

Then she smiled, thinking, *Okay, toots. You can do this.*

Damn.

The Dana Malone smiling broadly for C.J. from across the
store was not the same Dana Malone he'd left three days ago.
Where was the nervousness, the shyness, the insecurity, that

had—C.J. was pained to admit—made it much easier to blow her off as any kind of a threat to his hard-won autonomy?

You are man, he reminded himself. Strong. Above temptation. Impervious to…smiles.

While he stood there, thinking about how strong and above temptation he was, the curly-haired dynamo standing beside Dana jutted out a slender, long-nailed hand. "Hi! I'm Mercedes Zamora. Partner Number Three."

"Oh! I'm sorry!" Dana said. "Mercy, this is C. J. Turner—"

"I know who the man is, honey," Mercy said with a warm—*very* warm—smile. Out of the corner of his eye, C.J. caught Dana's glare. The phone rang. Nobody moved.

"Merce?" Dana tugged one of the woman's long curls. "The phone's ringing."

"What?" she said, still grinning at C.J. like an overeager retriever. Dana tugged again, harder. "Ow!"

"The *phone?*"

"Well, why didn't you just say so?" Mercy said, rubbing her head. But as she turned away, she glanced over her shoulder at C.J., then gave Dana a look he decided was best left untranslated.

Dana rolled her eyes, shrugged in a we-love-her-anyway gesture, then said, "I'm sorry…wasn't I supposed to meet you at your office?"

"You were. Except it occurred to me I might get a better feel for what you all needed if I saw the shop first."

She laughed. "There's a thought," she said, then ducked behind the counter and held up the coffeepot, grinning. "Can I tempt you?"

Uh, boy.

It wasn't fair, the way that nearly weightless dress, barely darker than her skin, caressed her curves, skimmed her breasts, her thighs, fell in a graceful sweep to her ankles.

It wasn't fair, the way her thick hair, corralled into a braid, exposed her delicate jaw and neck, the way that same wisp drifting around her temple still eluded capture. As she swept it back, he noticed she wore simple pearls in her earlobes.

It wasn't fair, her having earlobes.

"No. Thank you."

"Your loss," she said, pouring herself a cup.

"So," C.J. said, turning to face the sales floor. And frowning. "Hmm. Now I understand why you need a bigger space."

"You don't miss a trick, do you?" he heard behind him, and he smiled. But it was true. He'd never in his life seen so much stuff crammed into one store. Not an inch of wall space had been left exposed, and you took your life in your hands navigating the floor, as well. There were even mobiles and stuffed animals and wall hangings suspended from the ceiling. Something…indefinable spread through him, gentle and warm and oddly…scary.

He grinned anyway, taking in the racks of tiny clothes, the miniature furniture, the shelves of whimsical lamps and tea sets and fancy dress dolls. The combined scent of rich coffee and her perfume as she came to stand beside him. "This reminds me of what I'd always imagined the Old Woman's shoe to look like on the inside. No wonder you nixed all the places I showed you. Which means…damn. You're probably going to hate everything I picked to show you today, too."

"Now, now…guess we won't know until we try, right?"

Tempted to peek behind the counter for the telltale pod, C.J. instead crossed to a display of christening gowns, fingering one whisper-soft garment frothed in ivory lace.

"The workmanship's incredible, isn't it?" she said. "That one's nearly seventy years old."

C.J. let the fabric fall from his fingers, stuffed his hand in his pocket. "You'd think the family would want to hang on to something like that, pass it down."

"If there's someone to pass it down *to*." Before he could decide if he'd only imagined the slight edge to her voice, she said, "Let me grab my purse and we can get going, I've got an appointment with a decorating client at twelve-thirty."

She disappeared into the forest of racks and displays, leaving her perfume in his nostrils and a decided sense of foreboding in his brain.

On the surface, Dana mused upon her return to the shop two hours later, one probably couldn't call the outing successful. Because C.J. had been right—all the new places sucked, too.

"Well?" Mercy said the instant the door *shooshed* shut behind her.

"Nothing."

"Oh. Well, did you find a place, at least?"

Dana gave her a dirty look. One that belied what she was really thinking, which was that on a personal level, things couldn't have been more successful. As in, there was a lot to be said for having spent a whole two hours in the man's company without angsting about how she looked or what she said or even what he thought about her. Not more than once or twice, anyway. "Where's Cass?"

"The baby kept her up all night with colic, so she's taking the day off. Says she'll switch one day next week with you, if that's okay."

"Yeah, sure," Dana said distractedly, leaning on the counter and leafing through the mail. "Although we really need to think about hiring another body or two. So we could, you know, have lives?" The phone rang. Without looking, she reached for the receiver.

"Great Expectations—"

"Dana?"

"Speaking. May I help you?"

"Dane…it's me. Trish."

She jerked upright, the mail forgotten. "Trish? Where are you? Mama's worried sick about you."

"I'm okay. Which I told her last week when I talked to her. Listen…I need to see you."

It took a second. "You're here? In Albuquerque?"

"Yeah, just for a couple days, though."

"Where? Give me a number where we can reach you—"

"You coming into the shop tomorrow?"

"What's tomorrow? Saturday? Yes, I'll be here all day—"

"When do you get in?"

"Around nine, I suppose. But wouldn't it be better to get together at my place? Or Mama's house—?"

Click.

Dana stared at the phone for a second, then slammed it down.

"What was that all about?" Mercy asked.

"*That* was my airhead cousin."

"The one who disappeared?"

"The very same." Dana huffed a sigh. "Says she's in town, but won't tell me where she is. Said she's coming to the shop tomorrow, although God knows why."

Swishing a lime-green feather duster over a display of ornate frames, Mercy shrugged. "She probably wants money."

"Yeah, well, she's in for a rude surprise, then, since between the medical bills from last year and our expansion, this is one dry well. If she needs help, she can jolly well haul her butt back home and go to work like the rest of us poor slobs."

Mercy laughed.

"What's so funny?"

"Anyone who didn't know you would think you were this wussy Southern belle, all sweet and helpless. But let me tell you, if I had to pick someone to be on my team against the bad guys? I'd pick you in a heartbeat."

Dana tilted her head at her friend. "Yeah?"

"Yeah."

The phone rang again the very moment a mother with four stair-step children tumbled into the shop.

"Great Expecta—"

"Hey, I'm on my way to another appointment," C.J. said, and Dana's face warmed with pleasure. Dumb. "But I just thought of a place I bet would be great for the shop. Don't know why I didn't think of it sooner. Must be the heat. In any case, I'm tied up until five, but wondered if you wanted to see it then? It only came on the market this morning, and I don't know how long it's going to last. And the great thing is the owner's willing to sell, so you could apply the rent toward the purchase price if you all want to buy eventually—"

"Slow down, slow down," she said, laughing. "Yes, five would be fine. But let me meet you there."

She wrote down the address on a scrap of paper, then hung up, deciding she was feeling all fluttery and trembly inside because of the prospect of finally finding the right location for the store. Yes, that must be it.

Mercy drifted over to the sales counter while the mother browsed and the kids wreaked havoc. Since there was little they could hurt or that could hurt them (despite the place being an obstacle course for Dana), no one paid the children any mind.

"Let me guess," she said. "That was C.J."

"Why would you think that?"

"Because your face wasn't darker than your dress five minutes ago."

"Bite me."

That merited a cackle. "He ask you out?"

"No, goofball—he has another place to show me."

"Miss?" the mother asked. "How much is this play kitchen?"

"It should be tagged," Mercy said with a smile. "Let me

see if I can find it for you." Then, over her shoulder to Dana as she edged toward her customer, "I've got a real good feeling about this one."

"Oh, for pity's sake, Merce—"

"The property, the *property*," Mercy said, saucer-eyed. "Why, what did you think I meant?"

Then she cackled again, and Dana thought, *With friends like this...*

Dana was so quiet, so expressionless. C.J. listened to her sandals tapping on the dusty wooden floor as she wordlessly walked from room to room in the quasi-Victorian, her expression telling him nothing.

"The Neighborhood Association would be thrilled to have you in the area. Plus, it's close enough to Old Town to pull in a nice chunk of the tourist traffic. And I think the other businesses around would complement yours—"

She shushed him with a swat of her hand.

It was beastly hot in the house, which smelled of musty, overheated wood and dust and that damned perfume; several strands of her hair hung in damp tendrils around her neck.

And he stared. As if he'd never seen damp necks and tendrils before. So he looked out a grimy window, thinking maybe it was time to bring the electronic little black book out of retirement. Except the thought made him slightly nauseous.

The tapping came closer, stopped. He turned; she was smiling. *Beaming.*

"It's perfect! When can the others see it?"

"Whenever you like."

She clapped her hands and let out a squeal like a little girl, her happiness contagious. And C.J. hoped to hell his inoculations were up to date.

A few minutes later, after they'd returned to their cars,

C.J. said, "See, what did I tell you? When it was right, you had no trouble at all making a decision."

Her laugh seemed to tremble in the heat. "True. In fact..." Her gaze met his over the roof of his car. She glowed, from the heat, from excitement, from what he guessed was profound relief. "I feel downright...empowered."

C.J. opened his car door, letting out the heat trapped inside. "And what," he asked without thinking, "does an empowered Dana Malone do?"

Her grin broadened. "She offers to cook her Realtor dinner."

Nothing to lose, Dana reminded herself as perspiration poured down her back in such a torrent she prayed a puddle wasn't collecting at her feet. As she watched C.J.'s smile freeze in place, the undeniable beginnings of that *Oh, crap* look in his eyes.

"But before you get the wrong idea," she said over her jittering stomach, "this is only to thank you for all your patience with me, especially since I know how busy you are and you probably eat out a lot, or stick things in the microwave—"

"Dana," he said gently, looking wretched. "I'd love to, really—"

And here it comes.

"—but I don't think...that would be a good idea."

Despite having steeled herself for the rejection, embarrassment heated her face. Still, she managed a smile and a light, "Oh. Well, it was just a thought. No harm, no foul." Except after she opened her own car door, she wheeled back around. "Although you could have at least *lied* like any other man, and told me you already had plans or something."

"And if you'd been any other woman," he said softly, "I probably would have. But you deserve better than that." He drew in a breath, letting it out on, "You deserve better than *me.* Marriage, babies…not in my future, Dana. But something tells me you very much see them in yours."

Her eyes popped wide open. "Who said anything about…? It was just *dinner,* for heaven's sake!"

Now something dangerously close to pity flooded his gaze. "Would you have extended the same invitation if I were involved with someone? Or if you were?"

"Um…well…" She blew out a breath, then shook her head.

His smile was kind to the point of patronizing. "I'm a dead end, Dana. Don't waste your effort on me."

She glanced away, then back, her mouth thinned. "I'm sorry, it was stupid, thinking that you'd…be interested. Especially after everything Trish said."

His head tilted slightly. "Trish?"

"Lovett. My cousin. She worked for you for about six months, oh, a year ago? And she said…never mind, it's moot now."

"Dana," C.J. said, a pained look on his face, "trust me, it's better this way."

Their gazes skirmished for a second or two before she finally said, "Yes, you're probably right," then got into her sweltering car and drove off, repeating "*No* isn't fatal" to herself over and over until, by the time she got home and called Cass with the good news about the store, she was almost tempted to believe it.

Way to go, dumb ass, C.J. thought as he sat at a stoplight, palming his temple. In less than a century, man had invented cell phones, the Internet and microwave pizza. And yet after fifty thousand years, give or take, no one had yet to figure out how to let a woman down without hurting her.

But what else could he have said? That, yeah, actually he would have killed for the privilege of spending a little more time in her company? To see that dimpled smile, to hear her laugh? To simply enjoy being with a woman without an agenda?

Except…she did have one, didn't she? Maybe a bit more soft-edged than most, but no less threatening. Or sincere. And how fair would it have been, to accept her offer, to give her hope, when he knew it wouldn't go any further? That selfish, he wasn't.

And then there was the little sidebar revelation about Trish being her cousin. Uh, boy…he could just imagine what would hit the fan if Dana knew everything about *that* little side trip to insanity.

C.J.'s brow knotted. So why *didn't* Dana know? Then he released a breath, realizing that whatever Trish's reasons for keeping certain things to herself, if she hadn't told Dana by now, she probably wouldn't. And there was no reason for her to ever find out, was there?

A car horn honked behind him: while he'd been on Planet Clueless, the light had changed.

And even if she did, he thought as he stepped on the gas, what difference would it make? Once this deal was finalized, he'd have no reason to see or talk to Dana Malone ever again.

Which was a good thing, right?

In a bathroom flooded with far too much morning sunshine, Dana blearily stared at herself in the mirror. She pulled down a lower lid—yeah, the bloodshot eyes were a nice touch. Not to mention the still slightly visible keyboard impression in her right cheek. Charming.

She shakily applied toothpaste to brush, only to realize she wasn't sure she had the oomph to lift the brush to her mouth. From the living room, her pair of finches chirped away, merrily greeting the new day, momentarily tempting her to go find a hungry cat. But if she'd been up until nearly 4:00 a.m., at least she hadn't spent it brooding. Much. Since here she was, still alive (sort of), she guessed her "*No* isn't fatal" mantra had worked. And anyway, she'd only have to see C.J. once, maybe twice more, right? If that. So. Over, done, let's move on.

She shoved the brush into her mouth. And naturally, right at the pinnacle of sudsiness, the phone rang.

Dimly, from some tiny, marginally awake corner of her brain, it registered how early it was. She spit and flew back into her bedroom, fumbling the phone before finally getting it to her ear.

"Hel—"

"Dana?"

A few more brain cells jerked awake. "Trish?" She glanced at the caller ID. Blocked call. Shoot. "Where are you—?"

"I just wanted to make sure you were going to be at the shop at nine. That's what you said, right? Nine? I mean, are you going to be there any earlier?"

As usual, she sounded borderline crazed, but in a controlled sort of way.

"I usually get there around ten 'til. Trish what's going on—?"

Click.

The girl *really* needed to get herself some phone manners. Sheesh.

An hour or so and a half bottle of Visine later, Dana pulled into the far side of the empty parking lot in front of the shop. It was her day to open up, a good thing since she wasn't yet ready to face humanity. Or Mercy's inevitable squinty assessment of Dana's putty-knife makeup application. She was, however, supposed to be facing Trish, who was nowhere in sight. But then, reliability had never been her cousin's strong suit.

Bracing herself, Dana took a deep breath and swung open the car door. Instant oven. Already. Yech. And it always took an hour for the store to cool off after being closed up all night. Double yech.

Her purse gathered, she slammed shut her door and crossed the parking lot, noticing the drooping petunias in the oversized planters by the front door. If they didn't get water soon, she thought as she shoved her key into the lock, they'd turn into twigs. Lord, her slip was already fused to her skin. Knowing she had thirty seconds to deactivate the alarm before it went off, she shoved open the door—

Behind her, something sneezed.

The key still in the lock, the door swung open as whatever it was sneezed a second time. She turned, letting out a half-shrieked, "Ohmigod!"

The baby peered at her from underneath the nylon hood of the car seat, its face tinted blue from the reflection. It stared at Dana for a long moment, then offered a big, basically toothless, drooly grin.

Dana was far too stunned to grin back. But not too stunned to immediately scour the neighboring parking lots, her hand shielding her eyes from the morning sun glinting off the top of a beige sedan as it disappeared down the street. She stepped off the sidewalk—

Brrrrannnnnnnnnnnnnnnnnnnnnngggggggg!

Dana yelped and the baby started to yowl like a banshee as the alarm blared loud enough to wake the dead. On Mars. She grabbed the car seat and roared into the store, thunking the seat onto the counter so she could dump out her purse to find the key to deactivate the alarm. Ten seconds later, she'd killed it, but not before nearly wetting her pants.

In the ensuing silence the baby's howls seemed even louder. Dana unlatched the ridiculously complicated harness and hauled the little thing into her arms, then paced the jammed sales floor, almost more to calm herself than the infant. After a bit, the wails had softened to exhausted sobs, and Dana no longer felt as though her heart was going to pound out of her chest. She dropped into a rocking chair, the infant clutching the front of her dress, now adorned with baby tears and drool.

"No…" she breathed. "No, God, no…this can't be happening…."

Trish surfaces out of the blue, asks when Dana's going to be at the shop; lo and behold, a blond baby appears, smelling of cheap perfume and cigarettes. As she assumed the baby didn't wear cheap perfume or smoke, it didn't take a real big leap of faith to figure out who *did.*

She got up, deposited the baby—dressed in a miniature football outfit, so she was guessing boy—into a nearby playpen and stormed back outside, startling a couple of pigeons.

"Well, Patricia Elizabeth Lovett," she muttered to the air, "you've outdone yourself this time."

Since said Patricia Elizabeth obviously wasn't going to jump out from behind a Dumpster and yell, "Surprise! Had you there for a minute, huh?" Dana's only option was to go back inside and figure out what to do next. As she turned, however, she noticed the shopping bag. A quick glance inside revealed a small stack of clothes, six or seven disposable diapers and three filled bottles.

How thoughtful.

Dana snatched up the bag so hard one of the handles broke, nearly dumping everything into the gasping petunias. That's when she noticed the note. Of course. There was always a note, wasn't there?

She dumped the bag on the counter, saw that the baby seemed happy enough gurgling to his own hands as he lay on his back, then tore open the envelope.

Her eyes flew over the one-page letter, picking up the essentials. "…*tried it on my own…knew how much you loved and wanted kids…it'll be better this way…full custody…hope you'll forgive me...Ethan's really a little doll, you'll love him...birth certificate enclosed..."*

It was *so* Trish. On a sigh, Dana unfolded the birth certificate, if only to find out how old this kid was.

"WHAT?"

The baby lurched at the sudden noise, then started to cry again. Nearly in tears herself, Dana threw the letter and birth certificate on the counter and went to pick him up. None of this was the baby's fault, she reminded herself as she hauled the infant out of the playpen and cuddled him in her lap. None of it. Least of all who his daddy was.

Cameron James Turner, the paper said.

Cameron James Turner, of "fatherhood isn't part of my future" fame.

"Well, guess what, buddy?" Dana hissed under her breath as she grabbed a bottle off the counter and stuck it in her new little cousin's mouth. "Fatherhood sure as hell is part of your *present*."

Chapter Four

Dana thanked the police officer for coming so promptly, assured her she'd be in touch if she heard anything or needed her, then showed her out. Not that the visit had been exactly productive. Or even illuminating. Turned out there wasn't a whole lot anybody could do, seeing as Trish had left Ethan with family and all. Technically, it wasn't abandonment. Of course, the officer had said, if Dana really felt she couldn't take care of the baby, there was always foster care…

Uh-huh. Sharp sticks in eyes and all that.

Mercy took the baby from her as Cass—whose own son was sawing logs in a cradle in the back—slipped an arm around her shoulders.

"For crying out loud," Dana said, "how could anyone be so selfish? *Ooooh!*" Her palm slammed the counter, dislodging a teddy bear from its perch by the register. She caught it, only to squeeze the life out of the thing. "If Trish showed her face right now—" the bear's floppy limbs flailed as she shook it "—I swear I'd slap her silly. What an air-brained, self-centered, addlepated little *twit*."

"Familial love is such a wonderful thing," Cass wryly observed.

Ignoring Cass, Dana stuffed the bear back into its chair. "What am I supposed to do now?" She shook her head, watching six-month-old Ethan play with Mercy's hair. Her own, as usual, was coming undone. "How am I supposed to take care of a baby on my own? I live in this itty-bitty apartment, and hello? I work full time? What on *earth* was Trish thinking?"

"Maybe your parents could take over during the day," Mercy suggested, but Dana wagged her head emphatically.

"Neither one of them is up to full-time babysitting at this point in their lives."

Then both of her partners went ominously silent, instantly putting Dana on the alert. "What?"

"What about C.J.?" Mercy asked, wincing a little as she dislodged curious little fingers from the three-inch-wide gold loops dangling from her ears.

"Oh, right. Mr. Family Man himself." When they both blinked at her, she sighed and 'fessed up about the day before. Okay, she might have done a little judicious editing of the conversation—they didn't need to know about the dinner invite—but she definitely left in the "He doesn't want kids" part.

"Be that as it may," Cass said, assuming the role of Voice of Reason. She folded thin, bare arms over a button-front blouse already adorned with a telltale wet spot on one shoulder. "C.J. doesn't strike me as the kind of man who'd blow off having a kid. So my guess is Trish left town without telling him."

Dana hadn't thought about that. Still, she wasn't exactly in a charitable mood. "And if she did?"

Mercy leaned against the counter, setting the baby on the edge, protectively bumpered by her arms. He yanked off her turquoise satin headband and began gnawing on it; she didn't seem to notice. "Hey, if he knew about the baby and refused to take responsibility, you better believe I'd be first in line to string him up by his gonads. But if he didn't—and remember, you're not absolutely sure Ethan *is* C.J.'s—then I think you're gonna have to wait and see. Give him a chance."

"You weren't there, you didn't see the look on his face…" Dana began, then shook her head, her mouth pulled tight. She reached for Ethan, her eyes burning for reasons she had no intention of thinking about too hard. "I think it's pretty safe to assume I got me a baby to raise."

The bell jangled over the door; with a grunt of annoyance, Mercy left to help the pregnant woman slowly picking her way through the store. Cass, however, stroked Dana's arm for a second, then grasped Ethan's chunky little hand.

"Honey, I understand what you're saying. But you really have no idea how C.J.'s going to feel once he sees his son. Look at him—he's adorable. How could he not fall in love with him?"

At that, the baby turned all-too-familiar blue eyes to Dana and grinned as if to say, "Hey! Where ya been, lady?" Amazement and terror streaked through her, so powerful, and so sudden, she could hardly breathe. Dana nestled the infant to her chest, rubbing his back and sucking in a sharp breath. *I've been given a baby,* she thought, only to then wonder…was this a dream come true?

Or the beginning of a nightmare?

She gave Cass a wan smile. "Hand me the phone, wouldja?"

Hours later, Dana watched Mercy scan the tiny one-bedroom apartment, her features a study in skepticism. Between her Firebird and Dana's Jetta, they'd managed to haul a portacrib, playpen, baby swing, a case of powdered formula, two jumbo packs of disposable diapers, clothes, rattles, wipes, bedding and at least a million other "essentials" Mercy insisted Dana would probably need before sunrise. In the middle of all this, Ethan lay on his back in the playpen, grunting at the birds. Mercy's eyebrows knotted a little tighter.

"You sure you're gonna be okay?"

"Uh-huh," Dana squeaked out. "Besides, I don't want any witnesses when C.J. shows up."

"Damn. I always miss all the fun."

Dana managed a weak, but nonetheless hysterical, laugh. All afternoon she'd ping-ponged between hope and profound skepticism. Maybe prejudging the man wasn't in anybody's interest, especially Ethan's, but she wasn't so naive as to expect him to take one look at his kid and suddenly switch tracks.

"Sweetie," Mercy said gently, "why don't you call your mom? Let her come help you out."

"I will, I will. Soon. But one does not spring potentially life-altering news on my mother without a plan. The woman has turned worrying into an art form."

"I hear ya there. At least let me set up the portacrib—"

Dana took her friend by the arm and steered her toward her door. Not that it wouldn't make sense to let her stay. Most of Mercy's sisters were spittin' out babies like popcorn. No matter when one visited the Zamora household, it was awash in little people. But while Mercy's presence would have been a great help in many ways, Dana wouldn't have been able to think. And thinking was the one thing she most needed to do.

And she really didn't want any witnesses when C.J. arrived. Not because she was going to kill him—she didn't think—but because Ethan's sudden appearance had turned a nonrelationship into…well, she didn't know what, actually. But so much for never having to see the guy again.

Thirty seconds and a heartfelt hug later, Dana was finally alone.

With a baby.

She zipped to her bedroom, rummaging through her bottom drawer for a pair of old shorts, and a faded UNM T-shirt, changing into both at warp speed. The gurgling, drooling six-month-old pushed himself up on his elbows when she walked back to the living room; Dana squatted down in front of the playpen as if inspecting a new life form. Yesterday, she had no idea this child even existed. Now she was responsible for him, maybe for a few days, maybe for the rest of her life.

The thought slammed into her so hard she nearly toppled over. *One day,* she figured she'd adopt a child or two, when she was ready, both financially and emotionally. At the moment, she was neither. She'd always assumed she'd have some prep time for accepting a child into her life. As, you know, part of a couple?

So much for that idea.

A particularly ripe odor wafted to her nostrils. A by-product of the earlier grunting, no doubt.

"Let me guess. You messed your pants."

Ethan grinned and cooed at her, lifting his head at exactly the right angle for Dana to get a good gander at his eyes. Lake-blue, flecked with gold around the pupils, exactly like you-know-whose. On a sigh, she stood and hefted the smelly little dear out of his cage and over to the sofa, where she changed his diaper with surprising aplomb and less than a dozen wipies.

"Now I bet you're hungry, right?"

In answer, Ethan stuck his fist in his mouth and started

gnawing on it with the enthusiasm of a lion ripping into fresh wildebeest. Dana picked up the much sweeter smelling child and plopped him back into his car seat, which she figured was as safe a place as any to try to shovel food down his gullet. But what food, she wondered, might that be?

"Next time you dump a kid on me, Trish," she muttered, ransacking the paper bag full of little clanking jars Mercy had helped her pick out at Albertson's on their way home, "don't forget the dag-nabbed feeding instructions!"

She yanked out a jar, holding it up to the baby hunk with the killer eyes. "Carrots?"

Ethan gurgled, then let out a loud "Bababababababa" while waving his arms. Then he chortled. Not giggled. Chortled.

Dana sort of chortled back, popping open the jar. "Carrots it is, then."

Except carrots, it wasn't. It was like trying to shove a video into a malfunctioning VCR—it slid right back out.

She opened another jar, held it up. "Peaches?"

That got a slightly more forceful rejection.

"O-kaaay…maybe orange stuff isn't your thing. How about green?"

Green beans went in… and green beans oozed out, accompanied by the quintessential "*Get real, lady,*" expression.

Dana quickly discovered that baby food didn't exactly come in a wealth of colors. Or tastes. But she gamely tried creamed corn, chicken (that, she couldn't get past the baby's lips), squash, pears and beets.

Pears and beets went down. And down and down and down, until Dana wondered if babies, like puppies, would simply stuff themselves until they got so full they threw—

"Oh, *gross!*"

—up.

At least four times more food came back out as had

gone in. Krakatoa had nothing on this kid, she mused while frantically trying to catch the maroon-and-pear colored mess that kept spewing forth from those little rosebud lips.

Three saturated napkins later, Ethan chortled again. Not seeing the humor this time, Dana did not. And she was hot and getting hungry herself. Not only that, but it was beginning to sink in with alarming speed that no one was going to come take this vomiting bundle of joy away in an hour or two. And what if he didn't sleep through the night?

With a little groan, Dana let her head clunk onto the tabletop, not realizing how close she was to a pair of enterprising little hands.

"Ye-ouch!" Her own hands flew to her head, prying five tiny and amazingly strong fingers from her hair, which was now liberally infused with regurgitated Gerber 1st Foods. Well, hell. Somebody, somewhere, probably paid big bucks for this look. She got it for free.

Rubbing her scalp—man, the kid had a grip—she regarded her little charge, now in deep conversation with the Tiffany-style lamp over the table. She skootched over, out of Clutcher's way, and laid her head down again.

So many questions and thoughts swarmed in her brain, she couldn't sort them out, let alone act on any of them. For tonight, her top priority was keeping the child alive. She was off all day tomorrow, and Ethan had to sleep *sometime,* right?

Dana lifted her head far enough to prop it in her palm, reaching out to the baby with her other hand. Ethan grabbed Dana's fingers and tried to stuff them into his mouth. The two little teeth on the bottom made their presence known really fast, but she felt ridges on top, too.

"You getting yourself some new teeth, big guy?" she said with a tired smile.

Ethan chortled.

Dana's heart did a slow, careful turn in her chest. She stood and scooped the baby out of his car seat, cuddling him on her lap. Ethan settled right in, tucking his head underneath Dana's chin, and her heart flopped again, more quickly.

This was all too unpredictable for her taste. Her cousin might change her mind, C.J. might want…actually, God knew what C.J. might want.

She cursed under her breath, noting that more no-nos had slipped past her lips in the past several hours than in the entire thirty-two years that had preceded them. Insecurities and turmoil and all the unanswerables swirled and knotted together into a nebulous anger no less fierce for its vagueness. Her eyes stung as she realized how furious she was, at Trish, at C.J. (yes, even though he probably didn't know about the baby), at fate.

At herself.

All her life, she realized tiredly, she'd let people push her around. All her life, she'd been the one voted most likely to say "sure" when she really wanted to say "I don't have time" or "I'm not comfortable with that idea" or even, simply, "I don't want to." Suddenly, she was a kid again, hearing her mother's gushing to some neighbor or teacher or saleslady who'd admired Dana's impeccable manners. "Oh, Dana's never given us a single moment's worry," she'd say. "Always does what she's supposed to do, never gives us any lip. Just a perfect little angel!"

"Just ask Dana—she won't mind…"

"You can always count on Dana for a job well done and a smile to go with it…"

"You know, I've never heard Dana complain, not even once…."

"Dana won't be a problem. She'd go along with whatever we decide to do. Won't you, Dana?"

She pushed herself off the sofa, hugging Ethan, realizing there was nowhere to go. So she stood in place, jiggling the baby, fuming and muttering and cussing—but not so Ethan could really hear her—over the finches' agitated twittering.

Okay, that's it—Dana Malone's doormat days were o-*ver.* No more swallowing her anger when someone pissed her off. No more smiling when she really felt like popping someone upside the head. No more Ms. Nice Lady. She was *mad,* dammit, and God help the next person who got in her way—

The doorbell rang.

She marshaled all her newfound fury into one hopefully emasculating glare and marched to the door.

The way her topknot hung by a thread over her right ear was C.J.'s first clue that something was very, very wrong.

The baby slung on her hip was the second.

Her voice mail had been short, and not exactly sweet. *"Meet me at my place anytime after six,"* she'd said, then left her address, finishing with, *"And believe me, it's not what you think."*

"You…wanted to see me?"

Wordlessly, Dana spun around and stomped back inside the apartment, which he cautiously took as permission to enter.

His first horrified thought, when he saw the room, was that she'd been burgled. After he swallowed his heart, however, he realized the damage seemed superficial. In fact, it was all baby stuff. A swing and playpen fought for space between a peach-colored armchair, a glass-topped coffee table; diapers—both clean and dirty, from what he could tell—littered the pastel, Southwest design sofa; an infant car seat took up half the blond dining table, the rest of which was covered by no less than a dozen open jars of baby food and a mountain of dirty napkins or paper towels or something.

She'd gone into the kitchenette, where she dampened a cloth to wipe off the squirming baby's cheeks. Said child giggled, somehow snatched the wet rag out of Dana's hand and tossed it with unerring accuracy smack into her face.

A finely honed survival instinct told C.J. to proceed with extreme caution.

"Babysitting?" he asked.

"Funny you should say that." Dana caught the cloth as it fell, slapping it onto the counter. Hot little flames sparked in her eyes. "Trish breezed back into town today."

C.J. literally felt the blood drain from his face.

"Oh?"

"Yeah. She brought me a present. Now, it's a very nice present, to be sure, but heaven knows I wasn't expecting anything like this. Nor did I realize I wasn't going to be given any say in whether or not I even *wanted* this present."

He looked at the baby, who flashed him a wide, gummy smile, then back at Dana. Somehow, even her *hair* seemed redder. Okay, *Trish in town* probably equaled *Trish told Dana.* But she'd have hardly asked him to come over about that, for crying out loud. And what did the baby have to do with anything?

"I'm sorry," C.J. said, "but am I missing something?"

Her mouth set, she swept past him on her way from kitchen to living room, bending awkwardly with the child still balanced on her hip in order to pull something out of her handbag. Then she marched over to him and smacked a triple-folded sheet of paper into his palm.

Acid etched at the lining of his stomach as he unfolded the paper, burst into flame when he read it. The first word out of his mouth was particularly choice.

"Yeah. That was about my reaction, too," Dana said. "Well?"

"Well, what?"

"Did you and my cousin…"

"You mean, she didn't tell you?"

"She didn't *tell* me squat."

Still staring at the paper, C.J. pushed out a sigh. "Once, Dana. Right after she'd quit. And we both knew it was a mistake."

He couldn't quite tell if that was disappointment or flat-out, go-to-hell-and-don't-come-back hatred that was making her eyes so dark. "And does the date correspond to that *once?*"

"Yes. But…" He shook his head, as if doing so would make it all go away. "This can't be right."

"Why not?"

He lifted his eyes to Dana's. "Because I had a vasectomy. Five years ago."

Silence stretched between them, painful and suffocating. Until, on a soft little "Oh," Dana dropped onto the sofa with the baby on her lap.

The baby, C.J. thought, with eyes exactly like his.

But then, lots of babies had blue eyes. Tons of babies. Millions, even.

And somewhere, some deity or other was grinning his— or, more likely her—ass off.

"Wow," Dana said. "You weren't kidding about not seeing babies in your future."

C.J.'s mouth pulled tight. "That had been the plan. But—"

"Oh, geez, sorry to have come down so hard on you. I should have realized… Especially knowing my cousin…" She frowned. "What?"

"I think I need to sit."

"Uh…sure. Make yourself at home."

C.J. shoehorned himself into a half-blocked club chair across from the sofa and stared again at the birth certificate. At the letters that formed, of all the crazy things, his name. Yeah, as screwups went, this one was in a league of its own.

He supposed Trish could have been lying, otherwise why wouldn't she have surfaced sooner? Still, something deep in his gut told him she wasn't.

"C.J.?"

He let out a humorless laugh, then collapsed back into the chair, meeting her gaze. "You really believe me, don't you? About Ethan. Not being mine."

"Um…yeah. Shouldn't I?"

"No. I mean, yes, I'm telling you the truth. But for all you know, I could be some bastard who'd say anything just to get out of accepting responsibility."

"Are you?"

"A bastard?" he said with a weak smile.

"Trying to duck responsibility."

He shook his head.

"I didn't think so," she said, and he hauled in a huge breath.

"The thing is…I've been a bad boy."

She smirked. "I don't think you want to go there."

"No, I mean…" He exhaled. "The procedure's ninety-nine percent effective. About the same as the Pill. Which your cousin told me she was on, by the way. Why are you shaking your head?"

"Trish couldn't take the Pill, she had bad reactions to the hormones."

C.J. stared at Dana for a moment, then scrubbed the heel of his hand across his jaw. "I'll have to get back to you on *that* piece of information. But as I was saying—"

"Ninety-nine percent."

"Yes."

She was quiet for a long time. Then: "Bummer."

In spite of himself, he felt his mouth pull into a smile. "See, I'm supposed to have things checked every so often. To make sure…"

"I get the picture," she said, flushing slightly. "I take it you—"

"Oh, I did. Every six months for the first two years. No worries, they said."

"But they were wrong?"

"Well, *something* sure as hell was."

She made a funny noise, like a balloon beginning to leak air. "No wonder you look kind of sick. So you really didn't know?"

His own anger, at Trish, at circumstances, but mostly at himself, erupted. "Of course I didn't know! How could I know about something that wasn't supposed to happen, for God's sake?"

She hauled the baby up onto her shoulder, as if shielding him. "Sorry. I had to ask. Because you're right. For all I know—which isn't a whole lot, obviously—maybe you are a master at sidestepping consequences and I'm a fool for believing otherwise."

"You're not a fool, Dana. You're nobody's fool."

"Unlike some people in this room," she said, and he shut his eyes, his head on the back of the chair.

"I suppose I had that coming."

She snorted softly, then said, "Hold on a minute. Did you tell Trish you'd been…fixed?"

"It didn't come up. What I mean is," he said quickly, pushing his head forward to look at her again, "since she volunteered that she was taken care of first, there didn't seem to be any reason to mention it."

"Or to use a condom?"

"You know, I think I liked things better when I thought you were a shrinking violet." She glowered at him. "No, Dana, we didn't use anything else. Since we'd both recently had insurance physicals, there didn't seem to be any point. Especially since I thought, oddly enough, we were doubly safe."

"One chance in a hundred is still pretty slim odds," Dana said, nuzzling the baby's soft, flyaway hair, and C.J. forced himself to take a good look at this kid who may well have beaten the odds, just for the dubious honor of being his son. For a moment, the room spun, as though the earth had shifted under his feet.

"Oh, God," he said on a rush of breath. "What the hell do I know about taking care of a kid?"

Dana had wanted so badly to hold on to her anger, to not feel sorry for the obviously shattered man in front of her. Staying angry with him gave her some focus for her own turmoil, at least. But the shock contorting his features tore her apart. She'd been left with the child, true—but at least she'd always wanted children. C.J., on the other hand, had every reason to feel duped. By everybody.

Still and all, he was a big boy. A big boy who should be more than acquainted with the actions-have-consequences concept by now. Take enough swings at the ball, sooner or later you're gonna break a window.

Even, apparently, one made out of safety glass.

However, in answer to his question, she now swept one arm out, indicating the disaster-stricken apartment. And herself. "And does this look like the living space of someone who *does* know what she's doing?"

"But you're such a natural with kids."

A slightly panicked laugh burst from her mouth. "Loving them and keeping them alive are not the same thing. I'm an only child, never had any little siblings or anything to practice on. I never even babysat, because I was too busy being the nerdy straight-A student. So I don't have anything more to go on than you do."

"I somehow doubt that," C.J. said, and there was no

mistaking the bitterness edging his words. But now was not the time to pursue it. Especially when he asked, "Why do you think your cousin lied about being on the Pill? Why would she have taken that chance?"

Dana lowered Ethan onto his tummy in the playpen, then sat on the sofa in front of it, laying her cheek on her folded arms across the padded top. "Logic has never exactly been Trish's strong suit," she said, watching the baby. "Who knows? Maybe she…" She gulped down the pain. "Maybe she wanted to get pregnant."

"That's nuts."

"No, that's Trish."

"Then why didn't she tell me about the baby, for God's sake?"

She shifted to look at him. "Because this wasn't about you, it was about whatever was going on in my cousin's head at the time. Although those I'd-rather-eat-scorpions-than-become-a-father vibes you give off probably didn't help. And no, it wouldn't even occur to her to fight that. Staying power isn't exactly her strong suit. Heck, sitting through a two-hour-long movie is a strain."

C.J. pushed out a groan. "And you have no idea where she is?"

"Not a clue. I did talk to the police, however," she said, filling him in on the events leading up to her becoming Ethan's caretaker, including her chat with the officer that morning.

"You think she'll come back?"

Dana leaned to one side to see if his face gave more of a clue than his voice as to what he was really thinking, then stood up, retrieved the note. Handed it to him with a, "For what it's worth."

She watched him read it, watched his expression grow more solemn.

"C.J., until you know for sure that Ethan's yours, maybe

you shouldn't get yourself anymore tied up in knots than you already are."

Haunted eyes met hers. "And if he's not?"

"Then I'll deal," she said quietly. "Somehow."

He held her gaze in his for several seconds. "And if he is, then so will I." He handed the note back to her, his gaze drifting to Ethan. "What a crappy thing to do to a kid," he said, the steeliness underlying the softly spoken words sending a shudder up her spine. "No way am I turning my back on my own son, Dana. I'm not hurting financially, he'll have everything he'll ever need. But if she wanted you to have custody…" He shook his head, letting the sentence trail off unfinished.

Several seconds passed before she could speak. But no way in hell was she going to just sit here and nod and go, "Okay, sure, whatever." That Dana didn't live here anymore. "*Excuse me?* What happened to 'no way am I turning my back on my own son'? I didn't shove that birth certificate in your face in exchange for your checkbook, you big turkey!"

"But Trish left him with *you!*" he said, and a raw anguish she hadn't seen before blistered in those deep blue eyes. "Not me."

And with that, comprehension dawned in the deep, muddled recesses of her brain.

Dana sucked in a steadying breath and said, "C.J., my cousin is so many sandwiches short of a picnic she'd starve to death. But she certainly knew I'd recognize your name, and that I'd contact you. So in her own weird way, I don't think she deliberately meant to shut you out."

"Never mind that that's exactly what she did," C.J. said coldly, and Dana thought, *Ah-hah.*

"In any case," she said, "we'll deal with Trish later. Maybe. But right now, this is about Ethan. And if he is yours, damned if *I'm* letting you off the hook like she did."

C.J. flinched as though she'd poked him with a cattle prod. "Dammit, nobody's letting anybody 'off the hook!' Believe me," he said, his mouth contorted, "nobody, *nobody*, knows more than I do that this is about a helluva lot more than money. But pardon me for needing more than fifteen minutes to get used to the idea of being somebody's father!"

The last word came out strangled. His throat working overtime, C.J.'s head snapped toward Ethan, sprawled on his tummy in the playpen. The baby had been contentedly gumming a teething ring; now he lifted his face to them, his drooly grin infused with a trusting curiosity that twisted Dana's heart.

She shifted her own gaze to C.J., thinking, *This is not a bad man.* Screwed up, maybe, but not bad. And expecting him to turn on a dime was not only unfair, but unrealistic. Especially when she remembered how she'd felt after receiving her own life-altering news not all that long ago. It takes time to regain your balance after getting walloped by a two-by-four.

At that, Dana rammed her fingers through her hair; it finally succumbed to the inevitable and came completely undone. "Look," she began again, more gently, "this is a really bizarre situation, and I don't know any more than you do what the next step's going to be. I mean, it all hangs on what you find out, right?"

"Yeah. I suppose."

"All righty then. So. Ethan and I are good for now. And you…" she pushed herself away from the playpen to take C.J. by the arm and steer him toward her door "…need to go home."

Genuine astonishment flashed in his eyes. "You're throwing me out?"

"What I'm doing, is giving you some time to adjust. Trust me, you'll thank me later."

At her doorway—which he did a remarkable job of

filling—he twisted, his eyes grazing hers, rife with emotion. "Later, hell. I'm thanking you now."

"Whatever." Then, with a half-assed shove, she turned him back around. "But if you don't leave immediately," she said, so tired she was beginning to wobble, "I'll have to sic the birds on you."

C.J. looked over her shoulder at Ethan for a full five seconds, gave a sharp nod and left. Dana leaned back against the closed door, watching the small person happily smacking the bottom of the playpen, and thought, *Well, this has been one swell day, hasn't it?*

Back home, C.J. turned on the air-conditioning, ignored his mail, which Guadalupe had left neatly stacked on the kitchen island, and changed into a pair of holey jeans he couldn't imagine any woman putting up with. From the center of the bed, the cat did the one-eyed stare routine and it hit C.J. with the force of a tidal wave that his unencumbered bachelor days were, in all likelihood, history. Because while he'd be an idiot not to get proof that Ethan was his, he'd be a lot more surprised to find out the baby wasn't.

C.J.'s stomach growled. His bare feet softly thudding against the uneven, cool tiles, he stalked to the kitchen and threw together a sandwich without paying much attention to the contents. One set of nitrates was as deadly as another, right?

Ignoring the air-conditioning, he cranked open the kitchen window over the sink, breathing in the scent of fresh cut grass from his neighbor's yard that instantly suffused the still, stuffy room. Steve jumped up onto the sill, mashing his ears against the screen and chattering to the delectable whatever-they-weres incessantly chirping in the juniper bushes under the window. Still standing, C.J. attacked the sandwich, somehow swallowing past the grapefruit-sized lump in his throat as an image of Dana sprang to mind, barefoot in that matchbox of an apartment, her burnished, baby-food-streaked hair floating around her face.

The hard, unforgiving look in her eyes when she'd greeted him at the door, Ethan firmly parked on her hip. Now there, he thought as he took another bite of the sandwich, was someone with all her nurturing instincts firmly in place.

Unlike him. Who wouldn't know a nurturing instinct if it bit him in the butt.

A plan, he thought. He needed a plan. Plans solved problems, or at least reduced them to manageable chunks. When in doubt, just bully your life into order, was his motto. So, still chewing, C.J. marched into his office. Steve followed, complaining; C.J. tromped back to the kitchen, filled the cat's bowl, returned to the office. Sat down. Rammed both hands through his hair.

Thirst strangled him. Seconds later, ice cold beer in hand, he sat down again, yanking open desk drawers until he found a legal pad and a pen. He slapped the pad on his desk, to which Steve promptly laid claim. C.J. threw the beast off; he hopped right back up and settled on top of the phone, glaring. C.J. glared back, then picked up the pen, stared at the paper.

Nothing. Not a single, solitary, blessed thought came to him. But then, how the hell was he supposed to make a plan without all the particulars? Instead, all he saw were two sets of eyes, one blue, one glinty gray green. A child for whom he might very well be responsible, and a woman he had no business getting anywhere near. And, if he got the test results he expected, the two were inextricably linked.

As he would then be to them.

Because while he really wouldn't turn his back on his own child—no matter how unlikely the situation in which he now found himself—neither would he, could he, take the baby away from Dana if her cousin didn't come back. Not that she'd let him, he thought on a wry smile. Poleaxed as she undoubtedly was, she was also clearly already superglued to the kid.

Envy sliced through him, along with a sense of longing so sharp, so unexpected, it took his breath away.

The pen streaked across the room, dinging off the wall. What if he couldn't do this, couldn't be what both woman and child needed him to be? Not that he wouldn't give it his best shot: Even going through the motions would be better than letting a child grow up believing he was a mistake. A burden. But what if that wasn't enough? Would they both end up hating him? The boy, when he realized his father had been faking a connection he'd never really felt? And Dana. Oh, God, Dana. Could he deal with the inevitable disappointment in her eyes?

So what are you going to do about it, lamebrain?

Seconds later, C.J. found himself standing in one of the two guest bedrooms. The one he'd left empty, since guests had never been an issue.

As Steve writhed around his ankles, his questioning meow seeming to ask what the hell they were doing in here, C.J. stood frozen in the center of the room, visualizing a crib in one corner. And in that crib, a chubby little boy with blue eyes leaning over the side, smiling, arms outstretched…

…trusting in his father's unconditional love.

C.J. shut his eyes and waited until the dizziness passed.

Chapter Five

At 8:00 a.m., the phone rang. Wedged in the corner of the sofa with twenty pounds of guzzling baby in her lap, Dana could only glower from across the room as some chick with this godawful Southern accent told whoever to leave a message.

"Hey, it's C.J. I'm on my way over."

Click.

She muttered something unseemly, realizing she wouldn't be able to use the no-no words for long with a baby around. Not only did the apartment look worse than it had yesterday, but she was still unwashed and in her Mickey Mouse sleep-shirt. And despite the Glade PlugIns rammed into every available outlet, she strongly suspected the place reeked of beet-infused baby doo.

Mercy said six-month-olds generally slept through the night. Unfortunately, no one had informed His Highness of that fact. The kid not only peed like a herd of goats, but was

apparently one of those "sensitive" types who didn't tolerate
wet diapers very well, stay-dry linings be damned. Dana cal-
culated she'd had roughly three hours sleep over an eight-hour
period. Again. The last thing she needed was company.
Especially sexy male company who would probably waltz in
here looking ready for brunch at the country club. Whereas
she, on the other hand, looked like week-old roadkill.
Probably smelled like it, too.

She jiggled the bottle, determining Ethan had maybe five
minutes yet to go. It occurred to her she had no idea where
C.J. lived. With any luck, Taylor Ranch, clear on the other
side of the—

Bzzzzzzzt went her doorbell.

—city.

Cell phones, she decided, were the instrument of the devil.

"Who is it?" she yelled, as if she didn't know.

"Dana? Honey?"

Apparently, she didn't.

"Dana?" Her mother's voice came through the door, thin
and anxious. "It's just me, honey, I thought I'd drop by before
I went on to church. You okay in there? Why aren't you
opening the door?"

There was only one person she'd rather see less than C. J.
Turner at that moment, and that person was standing on the
other side of her door.

"Just a sec, Mama!" Dana heaved and grunted her way out
of the deep-cushioned sofa. Ethan never broke his rhythm.
"I'm not, um, dressed."

"Oh, for heaven's sake, honey, I've seen you undressed
before…*oh*…"

The last *oh* was the kind of *oh* people say when they think
they've caught you at an awkward moment. Which was true,
God knew, but, alas, not *that* kind of awkward moment.

"Hang on, almost there…" Swinging Ethan to one hip, she looked down into his fathomless blue eyes. "Okay, you're about to meet your great-aunt Faye." Formula dribbled out of the corner of the baby's mouth, making tracks down his chin. Dana bunched up the hem of the already baptized sleepshirt and wiped away the trickle. "Now, she really loves babies, but don't be surprised if she acts a little peculiar there for a bit. Just hang loose, and we'll all get through this. Okay?"

And exactly who was she trying to reassure here?

"Dana? It's gettin' hot out here in the sun, honey…."

She plastered a smile to her face and swung open the door. "Hey, Mama! What brings you here?"

Her mother's eyes zinged straight to the baby, then drifted over Dana's shoulder to inside the apartment. "I, uh, made coffee cake," she said, sounding a little distracted, "and figured I'd better not leave it around or your father'd eat the whole…dang thing." There was a small, anxious pause, then, "Honey?"

"Mmm?"

"Why are you holding a baby?"

"Because he can't walk yet?"

In a flash of pale rose polyester, Mama pushed her way past Dana into the apartment. "Looks to me," she said, her voice gaining altitude with each syllable, "you've got any number of places you could put him—it is a him, isn't it?—"

Dana nodded.

"—down…oh, my word!" Her hand flew to her mouth. Dana somehow caught the foil-wrapped paper plate before it landed on the carpet and set it on the dining table. She cringed as realization bloomed in her mother's eyes.

The hand fell, and words gushed forth. "Oh, sweet heaven, tell me that isn't Trish's baby! But it has to be, doesn't it? He's the spittin' image of her when she was a baby! That's why she suddenly left town, isn't it? Because she was pregnant? Why she called, wanting to know all about what you were doing and all? Because she had a baby? Well, say something, Dana, for goodness sake!"

"As a matter of fa—"

"Oh, my stars, he looks *exactly* like her! That chick-fuzz hair, and those fat little cheeks… Except for those blue eyes. Where did those blue eyes come from?"

"Anybody home?"

Both women snapped their heads around to the man of the hour, standing in the doorway. He held up a McDonald's bag, as if in explanation for his presence.

"Breakfast?"

Ethan let out a series of gleeful grunts, as if he recognized C.J., who wasn't, Dana realized, dressed for brunch in any country club she'd ever heard tell of. A gray sleeveless sweat-shirt, ratty jeans, well-worn running shoes. Far cry from dress shirts and business suits. And yet, he had the nerve to still look good. Probably smelled good, too, fresh from the shower, she guessed, judging from the way his damp hair curled around his ears.

Yeah, heckuva time for the hormones to kick in.

"And who might *you* be?" Dana's mother shrieked, effec-tively smashing to paste all hormones foolish enough to venture forth this fine Sunday morning.

C.J. thrust out his free hand, laying on the charm thick enough to suffocate the entire Northeast Heights. "C. J. Turner, ma'am." Dana saw her mother's eyes pinch in concentration as she tried to place the name. "And you must be Dana's mother," he said, grinning. "There's no mistaking the resemblance."

Faye's eyes popped wide open, arrowing first at C.J.— "The Realtor Trish worked for"—then to Dana—"the one who's showing you places for the shop?"

Wouldn't be long now. "The very same."

"Well, what's he doing here this early on a Sunday morning? And why is he bringing you breakfast?" Her eyes zipped up and down his body, settling on his eyes. His very blue eyes. With gold flecks around the pupil. Just like Ethan's. "Dressed like tha—" The word ended in a gasp as Faye slumped against the edge of the table, clutching her chest.

The woman had truly missed her calling.

"You…and Trish…and…and…" Faye jiggled her index finger at C.J.'s face, her jaw bouncing up and down for several seconds before she got out, "Blue eyes…*your* blue eyes. The baby…you…and Trish…and…oh."

And still, he managed to give her mother the perfect smile, a little abashed, a little nervous, appropriately contrite. "Yes, Mrs. Malone," he said calmly, "there's a strong chance I'm Ethan's father."

Shock gave way to blazing indignation, of the kind peculiar to Southern women whose kin have been wronged. "Lord have mercy, boy—you must be at least ten, twelve years older than Trish! What were you thinking? She was barely more than a *child!*"

"Oh, come on, Mama." Bouncing Ethan on her hip, Dana grimaced at her mother. "You know as well as I do Trish hasn't been a child since she hit puberty. Or it hit her. And C.J. already told me how it happened, so you can't put all the blame on him—"

Sparking eyes shot to hers. "What do you mean, he already told you?" Dana's face flamed. She was eight years old again, caught sneaking off to her girlfriend's house before she'd cleaned her room. "Yesterday," she said in a somewhat steady voice. "Which is when, uh, Trish left Ethan with me."

"So you spoke with her?"

"Well, no, not exactly. You know all those old movies

where somebody finds the baby in the basket on the doorstep? It was kind of like that."

"Oh, for the love of…" Her mother shut her eyes, shaking her head, but only for a second. Presumably recovered, she said, "Wait a minute—she left him with *you?* Instead of with—" her eyes shot to C.J., then back to Dana "—him? And why didn't you tell me?"

"Because I couldn't deal with having a baby dumped in my lap *and* your overreacting, too!"

"Don't be ridiculous, I've never overreacted in my life!" Faye quit clutching herself long enough to press her fingers into shut eyelids. "But I'm so confused. Was this a secret or something? Did you know about this?" she lobbed at C.J., then to Dana, "Did *you?* I mean, what did Trish say when she dropped the baby off? And where is Trish, anyway?"

Not before a shower and breakfast, Dana decided, could she deal with this. And since C.J. looked as though he'd had the luxury of at least one of those things already—and probably more than three hours sleep, to boot—he was more than welcome to have first crack at her mother.

It was a rotten thing to do, but hey. In all likelihood, he was family now. The sooner he weathered his first Faye Malone interrogation, the better it would be for all concerned.

"Tell you what—" With a sweet smile, Dana handed the baby to a very startled C.J. "Why don't you play with Ethan while I go jump in the shower before the city slaps me with a condemned notice? And you can get acquainted with my mother, while you're at it." She grabbed the McDonald's bag out of C.J.'s hand, extracted coffee and an Egg McMuffin. "Good choice," she noted, then got her fanny, as well as her unconfined 38 D's, the hell out of there.

Holding an active six-month-old, C.J. immediately discovered, was like trying to hang on to a stack of greased phone books. Every part of the child—and there seemed to be an amazing number of those—was hell-bent on veering off in a different direction from all the other parts. After nearly dropping the kid three times in as many seconds, he settled for securing him to his hip under his left arm, his hand braced across the baby's chest. That finally settled, he dared to look up at Dana's mother, who was glowering at him with all the sympathy of a highway patrolman who's clocked you at eighty in a fifty-five-mile-per-hour zone.

Talk about curveballs. Here he'd been all revved up to discuss possible options with Dana, only to be confronted with this fire-breathing she-dragon ready to chew him up and spit him back out in itty-bitty pieces. Her daughter's quick vanishing act didn't seem to faze her. Nor did the fact that two minutes ago, they'd never laid eyes on each other.

"One question," Mrs. Malone said, crossing her arms. "Why are you doubting my niece's assertion that you're the father?"

After he explained, as obliquely and quickly as he could, she regarded him shrewdly for several seconds, then blew out a breath.

"I think I need to sit down," she said, doing just that. "And you do, too, before you drop that baby. Oh, for heaven's sake," she said, leaning over, "this isn't nuclear physics...."

After several seconds of fussing and adjusting, the child was finally seated on his lap to her satisfaction. Then she leaned back, squinting. "So if there's a good chance the baby *isn't* yours," she said, more calmly, "why are you here?"

"Because I don't feel right about leaving Dana to shoulder the burden alone."

"I see. And if it turns out he isn't?"

At that moment, the baby grabbed one of C.J.'s hands, doubling over to gnaw on his knuckle. Without thinking, C.J. shifted to keep the little guy from falling on his noggin, then lifted his eyes to Mrs. Malone's. "Guess I'll deal with that moment when it comes."

Faye gave him a strange, inscrutable look, then shook her head. "I cannot believe that girl just *left* the baby. Then again," she said on a sigh, "knowing Trish, I can. Well…" She slapped her hands on her thighs. "I guess, for once, they'll have to do without me at church."

With that, she sprang from the couch, then began picking up and straightening out as if being timed, only to stop suddenly in front of the balcony door, hugging her elbows. "I owe you an apology, Mr. Turner," she said, her voice tight with humiliation and frustration. "It's not you I'm mad at. My niece has always been headstrong. Always determined to do whatever she wanted and damn the consequences. Even her own mama finally gave up on her, when she was fourteen, sent her to Dana's daddy and me to see what we could do with her."

She turned to him, her mouth set, her eyes hidden behind the window's reflection in her glasses. "Obviously, it wasn't enough. But it's true. By this age, Trish is nobody's responsibility but her own. Whatever the outcome, it's a little late to be accusing anybody of leading my niece down the primrose path. Heaven knows, if she walked in here right now?" Her hair, darker than Dana's, tangled in her collar as she shook her head. "I'd be tempted to throttle the living daylights out of her. Dumping her baby on Dana like that, not having the decency to even tell you about the child…nobody in this family has *ever* done anything like this."

She snatched an empty baby bottle and a rolled-up diaper off the coffee table. "But this family sticks together, Mr. Turner," she said, wagging the bottle for emphasis. "That child's gonna know he belongs, that he has kin that care about him, no matter what his scatterbrained mama might have done."

"I couldn't agree more," C.J. said. "Which is why, if Ethan really is mine, I want him to come live with me."

Three feet from the living room, Dana froze in her tracks.

Her wet hair hanging in trickly little snakes down her back, soaking the fabric of her camp shirt, she cautiously peered out into the living room. Her mother's back was to her, partially blocking her view of C.J. Not that she needed to see his face to picture his expression.

"You don't exactly sound overjoyed about this," Mama said.

"It's hard to sound much of anything when you're still in shock. But it's a no-brainer, wouldn't you say?"

Dana ducked back into the shadows to lean against the wall, too stunned to think clearly, let alone join the fray. Which would probably not be a wise thing until she figured out which side she was on. Shoot, at this point, she didn't even know what the sides *were*. Her mother, however, didn't miss a beat.

"Then why d'you suppose Trish left the baby with Dana and not you?"

It got so quiet, Dana peeked around the corner to make sure everyone was still there. She could see C.J. clearly now, cradling Ethan to his chest, one strong hand cupping the fuzzy little blond head in a protective, masculine pose that set her insides to bubbling.

No instinct for fathering, her foot. Only then his quiet, "Probably because I didn't exactly give her the impression I wanted children," made Dana wince.

"And now you do?"

"Now…I'll *do* whatever I have to. If he's mine."

"Well, he *is* ours," her mother said in that tone of voice that always raised the hair on the back of Dana's neck. "So why not leave him where you know he'll be loved? Without reservation?"

Showtime, Dana thought, lurching into the living room as if pushed. "Okay, Mama, this is really none of your business—"

"Nonsense," her mother replied, completely unperturbed. "This is about *family.*"

"I realize that, but this is a bizarre enough situation without having to deal with outside interference."

"Interference?"

"Yes, interference. As in butting in, an activity at which you excel."

"Well, I never—"

"Yes, you do. Every opportunity you can get. C.J. and I haven't had two minutes to discuss our options—"

"Do you *want* him to take the child?"

She knew what her mother was really asking. And it had nothing to do with C.J. "You mean, because here's a shot at getting the grandbaby I can't give you?"

Her mother flushed. "No, of course not—"

"For goodness' sake, I didn't even know about Ethan forty-eight hours ago! How dumb would it be to start thinking about him as my own this early in the game? Besides which, we already talked about this, how I can always adopt. You'll have your grandchild, Mama," she said, tears prickling behind her eyelids. "Someday. When the time's right. But at the moment, I only want what's best for Ethan."

"And how is it best for the child to send him to live with a man who doesn't even want children?"

"Mrs. Malone," C.J. said quietly, getting to his feet, "I appreciate your concern, which is more than valid. But until I know for sure I'm Ethan's father, there's really nothing to discuss."

"And anyway," Dana said, "Trish is a completely unknown factor in all this. For all we know she might well come to her senses and want her baby back. Until then," she said with a daggered, determined look in C.J.'s direction, the equally determined expression in his eyes making her own sting even harder, "this kid's going nowhere." She looked back at her mother. "But I wouldn't dream of keeping Ethan from his daddy, whoever that turns out to be."

A war raged in her mother's eyes: anger at being dismissed—for that was what Dana was doing—tangling with an unwavering love, that primal maternal desire to see everything work out. To keep her own child from getting hurt. And that, when all was said and done, tamped down Dana's own annoyance and frustration.

She walked over to the dining table, picked Faye's handbag off the table and handed it to her. The older woman hesitated, looking like the last guest at a party who can't decide how to make a graceful exit, then took the bag.

"If you hurry, you won't even miss the first hymn," Dana said quietly.

Defeated—though for how long, was anybody's guess— Faye simply nodded and headed to the door. Then she turned, worry brimming in her eyes. Dana touched her arm. "It's gonna be okay."

"You're sure?"

"Oddly enough, yeah. I am."

Her mother smoothed away a strand of hair from her daughter's face, squeezed her hand and left. Dana shut the door, leaning her head against it, staring at her bare feet for a moment. "Well," she said to the doorknob, "that went well, don't you think?"

"You can't have children?" C.J. said softly behind her.

Her head jerked around, her insides constricting at the kindness in his eyes. "Nope. Stork took me off his delivery route more than a year ago."

"God, Dana...I'm so sorry. Of all people for that to happen to." He released a sigh. "Talk about not being fair."

She nodded toward the now dozing infant slumped against C.J.'s chest. "You should know."

He gave her the oddest smile, and something kicked in her stomach, a premonition that she wasn't going to like what she was about to hear. She walked over to C.J. to remove the slumbering infant from his arms and lower him into the playpen. The man followed, close enough to feel his heat, for that soap-and-male scent to reach right in and yank her idiot libido to attention.

"I have no intention of taking Ethan away from you, Dana. Especially now."

Hanging on to the side of the playpen, she pressed the heel of her hand to one temple, deciding the heat was making her fuzzy-brained. "Then why did you tell my mother you were?"

"No, what I said was, I wanted him to live with me."

She twisted around. Moved over a bit. Frowned. "Is this where I point out that you're not making any sense?"

His laugh sounded...strained. "No. This is where I ask you to move in, too."

"Get *out*," Mercy and Cass both said simultaneously when Dana got to that point in the story.

After reaching a deal with the owner of the new place, the partners returned to Cass's (since the store was always closed on Mondays) to discuss the hows and whens of the relocation.

Only Dana's insane weekend was proving a much more interesting topic than floor plans and moving company selection. Go figure.

"Yeah, kinda stopped me dead in my tracks, too," Dana said, then frowned at the box of gooey, glistening, probably-still-warm glazed donuts Mercy had just plopped in the middle of the tempered glass table out on Cass's patio. "And you're blatantly setting temptation in my path why?"

Curls glistening, the tube-topped elf settled her tiny fanny on the cushioned faux wicker chair. "Not to worry, these have half the sugar of the regular ones."

Dana's frown deepened. "Oh, you're talking serious crime against nature. Donuts with half the sugar is like sex without…you know."

"And sex without 'you know'," Mercy said, delicately selecting a long john and taking a huge bite, "is better than no sex at all." She wagged the mangled treat at Dana. "He's actually making noises about you moving in before he even knows for sure Ethan's his?"

On a heavy sigh, Dana snatched one of the donuts from the box and morosely bit into it, surprised to discover it wasn't half-bad. As opposed to her life, which was rapidly going down the tubes. She took another bite before mumbling, "He even started talking schedules, believe it or not."

"And like most men," Cass said drily, "he'd no doubt decided that since he'd come up with *a* solution, it had to be *the* solution."

"Yeah, that pretty much covers it." Dana licked guilt-free glaze off her fingers, then popped the plastic top off her skinny latte. "Guy looked like he'd just bagged the mastodon single-handed." If scared out of his wits, Dana silently amended. "Because, he said, it would be the best solution for Ethan. If…well, if things work out that way. Apparently his outrage over Trish's little stunt trumps whatever issues he has about being a father. Oh, for heaven's sake!" she said when she realized they were both giving her say-it-isn't-so looks, "I didn't *agree* to move in with him. Years of dealing with my mother's unilateral decisions notwithstanding, I'm not about to blithely go along with one made by a man I barely even know. Especially when it involves sharing the kitchen at seven in the morning."

Mercy winced in sympathy, while Cass muttered something about God saving them all from men's honor complexes.

"Hah!" Mercy said. "I could name names…." She rolled her eyes.

"So can I," Cass said. "Blake pulled the same number on me, remember? My second husband hadn't even been dead a month and there my first husband was, asking me to remarry him. To *save* me."

"Yeah, except you needed saving," Dana said. "Alan had left you in debt up to your butt, you were pregnant, you had like a million people dependent on you—"

"Hardly a million, Dana."

"Okay, so three. Four, counting the baby. Plus, you and Blake did still have a son together. A teenaged son at that. Oh, and another thing…" She selected a second donut, because she could. "Blake really, really wanted you back. I don't think honor had a lot to do with it, frankly."

"Chick's got a point," Mercy said.

"Still," Cass said with a daggered looked toward Mercy, "why do they insist on equating 'rescuing us' with 'doing something'?"

"Because they're hardwired that way," Mercy said. "The good ones, anyway. Protecting their womenfolk and children is what they do. And sometimes," she went on before Cass, who Dana knew had suffered from her father's obsessive overprotectiveness, could object, "we rescue *them*. Even if they don't know it." The brunette shrugged tawny shoulders. "Basically, I don't see the harm in a little well-placed macho protectiveness, but that's just me."

"In any case," Dana interjected, "that's not what's going on here. This isn't about rescuing *me*, it's about doing right by a six-month-old. And it's not as if I'd be giving up my apartment or anything." Wide-eyed, she looked from one to the other. "Oh, God…I really said that, didn't I?"

"Hey," Mercy said, taking a sip of her rudely unskinny latte with gobs of whipped cream, "if it were me, I'd be over there so fast it'd make his head spin." When both Cass and Dana gawked at her, she shrugged. "The guy's loaded, right? So we're probably not talking some crumbling old adobe in the South Valley. And let's face it, sweetie…" She leaned over and patted Dana's hand. "You live in a shoebox. Besides, if the man wants to help take care of the kid, why not?"

"Because nothing's settled yet?" Dana said.

"And the longer he has to mull things over before the paternity issue *is* settled, the more chances he has to change his mind. Trust me, honey. Giving a man time to think is never a good idea."

Dana's gaze swung to Cass, who lifted her shoulders. "I'm afraid I have to cede that point to her. And you do live in a shoebox. Of course," she said, swirling the remains of her coffee around in her cup, "you could always move back in with your parents."

"Like hell," Dana said, and Cass smiled.

"So when will C.J. know for sure whether he's the father?" she asked.

"In a few days, depending on the lab's turnaround. He had an appointment for first thing this morning. He, uh, decided to go ahead and submit…samples for both tests now, rather than wait on the…you know, before initiating the paternity test. As a matter of fact, I have to take Ethan when we finish here to let them swab the inside of his cheek for the DNA sample. What?" she said at Mercy's head shake.

"I think the word you're looking for is *semen?*"

Cass choked on her coffee while Dana blushed. "We're practically strangers," she said in a whisper. "Talking about his…"

"Swimmers?" Mercy supplied.

"…just seems a little…personal at this point."

"And yet, somehow, you're not still a virgin. Amazing."

"So still no word from Trish?" Cass asked. Bless her.

"Nope. But C.J.'s got her social security number from her employee records, he said he might have someone see if they can find her that way. He wants some answers. So do I." Her eyes burned. "I never realized how much I hated being taken advantage of before this happened. And you know what's most annoying about this whole thing? The unsettledness of it. So what happens if I take care of Ethan for a few months, or a year? Or more? And then Trish waltzes back and decides she's changed her mind? Not only have I put my own life on hold during the interim, but how is this good for Ethan? It kills me to think that right when everybody starts thinking in terms of permanent, Trish'll have a change of heart and we'll all the get rug yanked out from under us."

Dana caught herself, flushing with embarrassment. Because her outburst hadn't been only about Ethan, although it was true—withholding part of herself from the child, in case she lost him, wasn't even an option. She simply wasn't made that way. Withholding part of herself from C.J., however, was another issue entirely. Yes, falling for him would be beyond stupid, but, like every other woman in the known universe, *stupid* was not as alien a concept as she might have wished.

And if she did end up moving in with him, maybe sharing living space would knock those stars right out of her eyes. With any luck, he put on all that charm and suaveness like one of his thousand-dollar suits, shucking them the minute he got back home, revealing the real throwback lurking underneath the public persona. Maybe C.J.'s living alone was actually a blessing to womankind the world over.

Okay, so it was a long shot. But you never knew, right?

Then Lucille, Cass's former mother-in-law, tottered out

onto the patio in platform sandals, clutching a squirmy, Onesie-clad Jason to her nonexistent bosom. "Somebody wants his mommy," the blazing redhead said as Cass quickly took her infant son from his grandmother. "And yours," she said to Dana, "is still sacked out in the middle of my bed like somebody slipped him a mickey. Hey, donuts! Don't anybody tell Wanda," she said, reaching over and snagging one, "or my tuchus is in a sling for sure."

But Ethan *wasn't* hers, Dana thought with a prick to her heart; only half listening as her partners finally got the business discussion back on track. Because for all Trish's tenuous grasp on reality, she'd still clearly taken good care of her baby. Yeah, she'd freaked, as Trish was wont to do, but still, that it had taken her six months to reach her breaking point said a lot.

Namely, that in all likelihood she would change her mind. Maybe tomorrow, maybe months from now. But eventually she'd come back for her child, leaving Dana with nothing but memories…and an ever-widening hole in her heart. And then, to make matters ten times worse, there was C.J.'s offer to consider.

If he turned out to be Ethan's father.

If Trish didn't return.

If Dana decided there was no better way to handle the bizarre situation. For Ethan's sake.

*If, if, if…*the tiny words pelted her like hyper BBs.

One day, she thought, it'll be for real.

One day, she thought, scarfing down another donut, *maybe I'll finally get to live my own life, instead of being a place-holder in everybody else's.*

If. If.

If.

Chapter Six

C.J. stared through his office window at the mottled Sandias on the other side of the city, backlit by masses of foamy, billowing white thunderheads. He checked his watch for the hundredth time, but it was still too early.

Today. Today, he'd know for sure.

The first lab result—which showed that, yep, his little guys had indeed, against all odds, found their way back into the game—had left the door open for the second. He'd been reasonably able to concentrate up till now, but the closer he got to D-Day, the more toastlike his brain became. Every time his phone rang, his stomach jolted. He'd even spaced on an appointment with a new client earlier, something he *never* did.

Not since his MBA days, when he'd sweated out that last, excruciating final in Statistics, had he gone through this kind of wait-and-see hell. Only a damn sight more was hanging on the outcome of *this* test.

Worst of all, C.J. still had no idea how he felt about any of it. Or was supposed to feel. Not that the idea of being responsible for this innocent little dude still didn't make his stomach knot, but the initial constant howl of outrage had at least throttled down to the odd, intermittent burst of irritation. After all, he'd been warned this could happen, that he needed to be diligent about checking. That he hadn't was nobody's fault but his. So if he'd dodged the bullet, by rights he should be profoundly relieved.

Except…

C.J. glared at the cloud-shaped shadows scudding across the face of the mountains. So what was up with the kick to his gut every time he saw the baby—which had only been a couple of times, given both his and Dana's impossible schedules and Dana's justified resistance to getting too cozy before the results came back? Never in a million years would C.J. have guessed that, in the end, some idiotic biological imperative could override more than twenty years of what he'd been completely convinced he'd wanted. Or, in this case, not wanted.

But there it was, jeering at him from the sidelines: an unwarranted, and completely illogical, anxiety that Ethan might *not* be his.

Val appeared in his doorway, hands parked on hips. "Okay. You want to tell me what in tarnation is up with you today?"

C.J. swiveled his gaze to her don't-even-think-about-messin'-with-me one. And part of him wanted nothing more than to come clean to this woman who'd become far more than an office manager over the past few years. But until he knew for sure, he wasn't keen on letting any more people into the loop than absolutely necessary. Even Val, increasingly difficult though it was to keep her out.

"Sleepless night," he said. Which was true. And not only because of the whole tenterhooks thing about his possible paternity, but because every time he'd start to drift off, Dana's horrified reaction to his suggestion that they live together would romp through his thoughts. Not that he blamed her. Why in God's name he'd thought it made perfect sense at the time, he had no idea. Why he still thought so, he understood even less.

Especially considering the serious train wreck potential of having Dana Malone living under his roof.

"Never affected your work before," Val said, her power-saw twang slicing through his musings. "Sleepless nights, I mean."

He glowered at her. "And how would you know whether I've had sleepless nights or not? I don't exactly advertise it."

"Other than the fact that on those mornings you grunt instead of talk, you guzzle coffee like somebody declared a shortage, and your ties never go with the rest of your clothes? I've seen subtler billboards. Still and all, I've never known you to let your private life—if you even have one, which I sometimes doubt—affect your work. So I repeat…what's going on?"

C.J. gave his office manager a long, steady look. "First off, there's a reason it's called *private,* Val." She gave an unrepentant snort. "And secondly, *I* repeat, nothing's going on. So sorry to blow your theory."

"You haven't blown anything. Because sure as I'm standing here you're lying through those movie star teeth of yours. And you do know there will be hell to pay when I find out the truth."

Refusing to rise to the bait, he said instead, "Thanks for covering with the Jaramillos, by the way."

"No problem. Just remember it when it's time for my salary review. And when you come out of that fog you're not in, that market analysis you're gonna ask for is already on the computer. As are the month-end sales figures. We're up ten percent over last year, by the way, so you shouldn't have any trouble finding money for that raise you're gonna give me. You want more coffee?"

"God, yes. But you don't have to—" Her raised eyebrows over her glasses cut him off. "Thank you," he said on a rush of air.

"You're welcome," Val said, turning to leave.

"Don't know how I'd live without you," he called to her retreating back, chuckling at her fading, "That makes two of us," from down the hall. A half minute later, she appeared with a huge mug of steaming coffee, his mail and a pink While You Were Out Slip, all of which he took from her.

"You took this message five minutes ago," he said, frowning at her scrawled time notation beside the unfamiliar name and number. "Why didn't you put it through?"

"Because I'm screening your calls today, that's why. Said she's got a house up in High Desert to go on the market, some friend of hers recommended you."

He handed her back the slip. "I've got more listings than I can handle, pass her on to Bill. What?" he said after a moment when he realized Val was still standing there, gaping at him.

"Since when do you pass up a listing for a million-dollar house? She gave me the address and the square footage, I checked the comps," Val said to his unanswered question. "Maybe even a million-two." She firmly put the slip back on his desk. C.J. picked it up again, held it in front of her.

"And the whole reason I took on the other agents was to give me at least half a shot of seeing forty. And Bill could use the finessing practice. *What?*" he said again at the twin lasers piercing him from those beady eyes of hers.

"*Nothin's goin' on,* my fanny," she muttered, snatching the slip and once again hotfooting it out of his office. A few minutes later, she buzzed him to announce she was going to lunch and that all the calls were being forwarded to his office, and to ask, did he need anything before she left?

"No, I'm good," he said, although he wouldn't mind

putting in an order for an auxiliary brain right about now. He cursorily checked his mail, which included an invitation to yet another charity function, then forced himself out of his chair and down the hall to the small room where they kept employee records, finally addressing a task he'd been putting off for days.

Minutes later, he was back at his desk, Trish's social security number scrawled on a Post-it note, making a phone call he'd never in his wildest dreams envisioned himself making. And not only because he'd once dated the P.I., years ago when she'd been a rookie cop who'd pulled him over for speeding.

"You say this chick left the baby with a friend of yours?" Elena Morales now said, clearly unable to suppress the curiosity in her voice.

"Yeah. The mother's cousin, actually."

"I see. And you're worried this gal won't come back?"

"No, actually, I'm worried she will. That is to say…" C.J. rubbed the space between his brows, realizing he must sound like a primo nutcase. "It's complicated. And I'd like to see as few people hurt as possible."

"The baby's yours, C.J., isn't he?" Elena said quietly.

"Very possibly," he admitted. "I'll know soon."

"Wow," Elena said, the single word positively drenched in amused irony. "Sounds like somebody's finally grown up."

C.J. grimaced. Even in her early twenties, Elena had wanted more than C.J. had been willing, or able, to give her. From what he understood, she'd found it, with someone else, shortly after they'd split. "I was twenty-five when we dated, Lena. Thinking back, I probably shouldn't have been allowed out in public, let alone anywhere near another human being."

She laughed. "Oh, don't be so hard on yourself. It's over, it's done, and I seem to recall we had a lot of fun. For a while, anyway." He could hear the smile in her voice. "Besides, regrets are a waste of energy. I'm just saying, I'm hearing something now I never heard then."

"And what might that be?"

"I'm not sure. Like maybe you actually give a damn? That you're *involved.* Anyway. I'll get on this, and I'll let you know as soon as I find something. Or the woman herself."

But instead of feeling more settled now that he'd taken at least some control of the situation, he felt more discombobulated than ever. Involved? Try trapped. In a situation not of his choosing, and yet undeniably a result of his own idiocy. If he'd only listened to his urologist…if he hadn't given in to Trish's entreaties…

If, if, if.

The phone rang; without checking the display, he punched the line button.

"Turner Realty—"

"Mr. Turner? It's Melanie from Foothills Lab. We have the results of your DNA test…."

This, there was no keeping from her mother. Not that she hadn't been tempted.

"But why, Dana? Why do you have to go *live* with the man?"

As she was saying.

"Because, Mama," Dana said, mindlessly tossing enough clothes into a suitcase to get her through the week, "now that there's no question that C.J.'s the father, his custodial rights far outrank mine. No matter what Trish wants," she added, cutting her mother off. "And, you know, considering his initial aversion to fatherhood, maybe everybody should see his willingness to do right by his kid as, you know, a *good* thing?"

"What's this?"

Dana turned to find her mother fingering through one of the many spiral notebooks Dana kept around the house, confusion etched in her features when she glanced up. "You're still writing?"

"Yes, Mama, I'm still writing," Dana muttered, practically grabbing the book from her mother and tossing it on top of the clothes. She'd started scribbling down ideas for a story as a way to dodge the depression that had threatened to take her under a year ago, only to find the outlet far more fulfilling than she would have ever expected. And increasingly habit-forming, despite all the other demands on her time. She'd only mentioned it to her mother once, however.

"Oh. I thought you'd given up on that. I mean, isn't it kind of pointless?"

"Ma? Hello?" She zipped up the bag. "Bigger fish to fry right now?"

Her mother huffed and seamlessly shifted gears again. "So why can't you share custody? Ethan could go to his father's house one night, yours the next—"

"Because C.J. knows less about taking care of a baby than I do? Because it's going to be hard enough for him to bond with his son without shunting him back and forth between our houses? Because my place is too small? Because Trish left him with *me*."

Dana headed to the living room, her mother's, "You could move back in with us, you know," following in her wake. Grabbing the birdcage cover, she tossed her mother a brief, but pointed, *not-in-this-lifetime* glare in response. "It's an option, honey," her mother said, wilting slightly.

"One which I entertained for about two seconds and immediately rejected." Dana tossed the cover over the cage, earning her a squawk from Ethan, who'd been holding a lengthy conversation with the finches from his playpen. When she caught the *just-kill-me-now* set to her mother's mouth, however, she let out a long breath, then put her hands on the older woman's arms. "Look, I know this isn't ideal. But what can I tell you, crazy circumstances call for inventive solutions. And this is the only way I can figure out how to do what's right by everybody. Including not violating Trish's wishes."

Worry still crowding her mother's eyes, she reached across to lay her hand on top of Dana's. "But you don't even know what she's gonna do, honey. And I hate the idea of you gettin' in over your head. It's happened before, you know, more than once. Now, don't be put out with me," she added when Dana pulled away to gather up the rest of her writing journals and laptop from her desk, tucking them into a canvas totebag. "The way you always see the good in people is a wonderful thing, it truly is. But while I'm sure C.J. intends to do his best by his child, that doesn't mean—"

"—that he's even remotely interested in taking us as a package," Dana finished over the sting of her mother's words.

"Well. It's just that you're so tender-hearted, you know—"

"That doesn't mean I'm blind," Dana said, reeling on her mother, her arms clamped over her midsection. "Or stupid." Faye's eyebrows lifted. "Okay, fine. To put an end to your pussyfooting around the subject, I don't suppose there's any point in pretending I'm not attracted to the man."

"See, that's what worries me—"

"Well, stop it. Right now. Because I am also very well aware that C. J. Turner isn't interested in me that way. Besides, even if he was looking to settle down, which he's made plain he isn't, I can't see that we have anything in common other than Ethan. So see, Mama, I have thought this through. Long and hard. So you're going to have to trust that I'm made of sterner stuff than you're apparently giving me credit for."

"And if your heart gets broken? Again?"

"Not gonna happen." Dana looked steadily at her mother, knowing full well it wasn't only Dana's potential attachment to

C.J. she was worried about. She tapped down the twinge of apprehension that echoed through her and said, "Now if you want to be helpful, you could pack up Ethan's diaper bag for me."

A request that, amazingly enough, derailed the conversation.

Two hours later, however, standing in the stone-floored entryway to C.J.'s more than spacious house, holding a babbling Ethan and gawking through the living room's bank of floor-to-ceiling windows at the mountain vista scraping the periwinkle sky, her only thought was, *I am so screwed.*

And only partly because of the excruciating awkwardness of the situation, the way C.J. and she were suddenly acting with each other like a couple on a forced blind date. Nor was it—she told herself—because she was in any danger of falling for the guy. His house, however…

Slowly, she pivoted, taking in the twelve-foot ceilings, the stone floors, the archways leading in a half-dozen directions. Not that her parents' three-bedroom, brick-and-stucco ranch house was exactly a shack. But compared with *this*…

This, she could get used to. Unfortunately.

"You hate it," she heard behind her.

She turned to see C.J., in jeans and a faded Grateful Dead T-shirt, carefully setting the birdcage into a small niche right inside the living room. "Not at all. Why would you think that?"

"There's not exactly a lot of furniture."

True, other than the floor-to-ceiling bookshelves crammed to the gills, the decor was a bit on the spartan side. But the oversized taupe leather sofa and chairs, the boldly patterned geometric rug in reds and blacks and neutrals underneath, got the job done. "It's okay, I like it like this."

"Really?"

"Really."

His eyes swung to hers. Tonight, an odd whiff of vulnerability overlaid the cool confidence, that aura of success he normally exuded. In fact, if she weren't mistaken, there was the slightest shimmer of a need for approval in his expression. Although she imagined he'd chop off a limb rather than admit it.

"I'm here so seldom, I never got around to…" He made a rolling motion with his hand. "You know. The stuff."

She smiled, his obvious discomfiture settling her own nerves a hair or two. "Accessories, you mean?"

"Yeah. All those little touches that make a house a real home. Like your apartment."

What a funny guy, she mused, then said gently, "It's not the stuff that make a house a home, C.J. It's the people who live there."

He nodded, then apparently noticed she was about to drop the baby. "Um…well, I suppose I should show you where you and Ethan are going to sleep."

"Good idea. Although…" She hefted the baby toward him. "Here, he's gettin' heavier by the second."

"Oh…sure." After only a moment's hesitation while he apparently tried to figure out the best way to make the transfer, C.J. gingerly slipped his hands under the baby's armpits, giving her a relieved smile once the baby was securely settled against his chest, rubbing his nose into the soft gray fabric of his daddy's shirt. C.J.'s eyes shot to Dana's. "Does he need a tissue or something?"

Dana laughed, even as her insides did a little hop-skip at the mixture of tenderness and panic on C.J.'s face. "No, I think that means he's sleepy. We'd better get the crib set up pretty soon so we can put him down."

"Crib. Right. Follow me."

C.J. loped down the hall leading off the foyer, Ethan clearly enjoying the view from this new, and much higher, vantage point. Dana trotted dutifully along behind, catching glimpses of a simply furnished dining room, a massive kitchen given

to heavy use of granite and brushed steel and a family room
with a billboard-sized, flat-panel TV.

"I thought we could put the baby in here," he said, as she
followed him into a large, completely empty bedroom with
plush, wheat-colored carpeting and a view of the golf
course…and the pool. Of course. "And then *this* room," C.J.
said, barely giving Dana the chance to register that he'd already
bought a beautiful wooden changing table and matching chest
of drawers, "is yours." She double-stepped to catch up.

"Oh!"

Not at all what she'd expected, given the masculine mini-
malism in the rest of the house. And certainly the cinnabar-
hued walls were a shock after the inoffensive real-estate
neutrals in her own apartment. But the rich color, the honeyed
pine headboard on the high double bed, the poufy, snowy-
white comforter and masses of pillows, immediately brought
a grin to her lips.

"Blame the decorator," he said behind her.

"*Thank* the decorator, you mean," she said, unable to resist
skimming a hand across the cool, smooth surface of the comforter. She could sense him watching her; she didn't allow
herself the luxury of contemplating what he might be
thinking. That he'd been invaded, most likely.

"Well," he said. "That's good, then. Okay. Well. Here," he
said, handing back the baby. "I'll go bring in the rest of the stuff."

Jiggling Ethan, she stuck her head into the adjoining
bathroom, shaking her head at the expanse of marble and the
multiheaded shower stall that looked far grander than
anything that utilitarian had a right to look. "Heck, you can
even see the entire city from the john," she murmured to the
baby, who had decided prying off her nose would be amusing.
"Is that weird or what?"

But then, so was this whole setup. Moving in with a man

she barely knew wasn't exactly something she did on a regular basis. Heck, moving in with *any* man wasn't something she did on *any* kind of basis. But still. As weird setups went, this was about as classy as they came.

Once back in the bedroom, she stopped dead at the sight of the gargantuan, charcoal-gray cat sitting smack dab in the middle of the bed. Pale green eyes—curious, bored—assessed her with unnerving calm. C.J. had a cat? A cat who undoubtedly made walls tremble when he walked through the house. A cat who— the thing yawned, sucking up half the air in the room—probably lived for catching and eating things. Like mice. Chihuahuas.

Tasty little finches.

With another yawn, the beast fell over on his side and began to clean one paw. "You are so not sleeping with me," Dana said, then carted the baby out of the cat-infested room and back to his own, where C.J. had set up the portacrib in a corner close to one window.

"Do we need to change him or something?" C.J. asked.

"Nope. Already did that before we left the apartment, so he's good. Okay, sweetie," she whispered to the tiny boy, nuzzling his corn-silk head before lowering him into the crib. "It's night-night time. Get that white blanket out of the diaper bag, would you? Yes, that's it," she said to C.J. Except instead of reaching for it, she said, "On second thought, why don't you give it to him?"

"Me? Why?"

"Because it's his 'lovey.' It makes him feel secure. So he'll start associating feeling safe with you."

"Uh, gee, Dana. I don't know…."

"C.J.," she said firmly. "The idea's to make *him* feel safe. Not you."

Those blue eyes, gone a soft gray in the twilight, grazed hers for a moment before he nodded, then lowered the blanket into the crib. The baby grabbed it and keeled over, his eyes shutting almost immediately. C.J. stood as though paralyzed, gripping the railing.

"Good God," he breathed, his voice littered with the shrapnel of confusion, amazement, shock. "There's a *baby* sleeping in my house."

"Now you know how I felt the past two nights. Except he didn't do a whole lot of sleeping. Come on, we can finish up in here later."

But when she got to the door, she turned to find C.J. still rooted to the spot, his gaze glued to the now-sleeping infant.

She opened her mouth to call him again, only to tiptoe away instead.

Hours later, C.J. lay in bed, his hands linked behind his head, staring at the ceiling. Had he ever had—what had Dana called it? A "lovey?"—when he'd been a baby? Somehow, he doubted it. Although, from what she'd said when he asked her about it over pizza a little later, most babies had something they use to soothe themselves when they were by themselves—a blanket, a stuffed toy, a small pillow.

Actually, she was a font of information, especially for someone who insisted she knew nothing, really, about taking care of babies. With a pang of sympathy, he wondered how long she'd been studying up, in anticipation of being a mother herself someday. How cheated she must have felt to have had that particular opportunity ripped from her. And yet, when he'd questioned her about it, there'd been no bitterness in her voice that he could tell. Just acceptance.

Grace, he thought it was called.

C.J. hauled himself upright, his abs having plenty to say about how long it had been since he'd even set foot inside the state-of-the-art exercise room next to his bedroom. Still, there was no denying the wonder in Dana's eyes when she looked at Ethan. Or the longing. And watching the two of them, the way they seemed to mold themselves to each other, he'd felt...ashamed. Inadequate.

And, again, envious.

He forked his hand through his hair three times in rapid succession, it finally registering that the cat had abandoned him sometime during the night. At the same time, a tiny sound came from the baby monitor next to his bed—his nod to gallantry, since Dana had been clearly dead on her feet. In the dark, C.J. stared at it, not breathing.

There it was again. Not exactly distressed, he didn't think, but definitely a call for attention. Sort of a questioning gurgle. On a sigh, C.J. got up, adjusted the tie on his sleep pants and plodded to the other end of the house, flicking on the hall light to peer into Ethan's room. The wide-awake baby inside turned his head toward the light, then flipped over onto his tummy, giving C.J. a broad grin through the mesh of the portable crib. A second later, C.J. caught wind of the reason behind the baby's wakefulness.

Uh...

He scooted down the hall toward Dana's room, both surprised and relieved to find her door open. A shaft of light from the hall sliced across the bed, where she lay sprawled in a tangle of sheets and nightgown, making cute little snuffling sounds. With an unmistakable "What the hell?" expression, the cat's head popped up from behind the crook of her knees.

From the other room, Ethan made a noise that sounded like "Da?"

"Dana?" C.J. whispered.

Nothing. Out like a light. Although the cat *prrrped* at him. And Ethan let out another, more insistent, "Da?" Or maybe it was "Ba?" Hard to tell.

Resigning himself to the inevitable, C.J. released another breath and returned to the baby, who was now lying on his back, thoughtfully examining his toes with a scrunched-up expression that made C.J. chuckle in spite of...everything. Ethan swung his head around, his entire face lighting up in a huge, nearly toothless smile of welcome. Or maybe gratitude.

And way deep inside C.J.'s gut, something twinged. Like unexpectedly pulling a previously unused muscle.

"I suppose you need your diaper changed," he said, turning on the light. Ethan, now beside himself with anticipation, started madly flapping his arms and kicking his legs, which wasn't doing a whole lot for the smell factor.

Okay, he could do this. Just as soon as he figured out what the hell half the things in the diaper bag were for. C.J. rummaged around in the bag for a few seconds, pulling out some kind of pad thing that looked reasonable to spread underneath the kid on the changing table, followed by a diaper, powder, wipes and lotions. There. That should do it. Then he sucked in a huge breath, hauled Mr. Stinky out of the crib and over to the table, and got to it, trying to picture his own father doing this for him. Somehow, he wasn't seeing it.

A minute or so and roughly half a container of wipes later, he heard Dana's huge yawn behind him.

"Now you show up," C.J. muttered, stashing the last of the wipes inside the gross diaper and cramming the whole mess into what he hoped was a bag for that purpose. But, judging from Ethan's kicks and little squeals, the kid was clearly enjoying being sprung from the nastiness so much C.J. hadn't had the heart to put the clean diaper on him yet.

"Sorry," she said on another yawn. "I was really out. Uh, C.J.?"

He twisted around and thought, simply, *Uh, boy.* Heavy-lidded eyes. Masses of sleep-tangled hair in a thousand shades of red, brown, gold. Pale shoulders, nearly bare save for the skinny little straps holding up that nightgown. A plain thing, nothing but yards of thin white fabric skimming her unconfined breasts, falling in deeply shadowed folds to the tops of her naked feet, revealing toenails like ten little rubies. Except for where it clung just enough, here and there, to stir all sorts of unrepentantly male thoughts and musings and such. C.J. mentally shook his head. "What on earth have you been feeding this kid?"

"Food. C.J., really, this isn't a criticism, but you might want to—"

"Oh, crap!" he yelled as a warm stream hit him square in the chest.

"—not let the air get to his…him like that."

C.J. yanked one of the wipes from the container and started swabbing himself off. "Don't you dare laugh."

He heard her clear her throat. "Wouldn't dream of it." The gown billowed at her feet as she crossed the room. "Go get cleaned up," she said, laughter bubbling at the edges of her words. "I'll finish up here."

When C.J. returned a minute later, she was bent over the crib, babbling at the baby, her voice soft and warm as a summer breeze, radiating enough femininity to drown a man in all things good and bad and everything in between. When she smiled up at him, he frowned. She misinterpreted.

"Oh, don't be such a grump," she gently chided. "It's just a little baby pee. Isn't it, sweetie?" she cooed to Ethan. "You were just doin' what comes naturally, weren't you?"

C.J. grunted, appreciating the irony of his son, the by-product of *his* doing "what comes naturally," returning the favor. "Glad you're having such fun at my expense."

Dana handed Ethan's blanket back to him, then padded back toward the door, signaling to C.J. to follow. "They say," she whispered, "if you don't play with them when they wake up in the middle of the night, they're more likely to go back to sleep. Otherwise they'll think it's party time. And if it makes you feel any better, he got me good the first night I had him, too."

"Yeah?"

"Oh, yeah." She started down the hall as C.J. flicked off the light. "I looked like I'd been in a wet T-shirt contest—" Her eyes squeezed shut for a moment, and one hand shoved her hair back from her face. Which probably wasn't the brightest move in the world on her part in that lightweight gown. "Wow, I'm suddenly *starved.* What I mean to say is…how about I meet you in the kitchen and we can see what you've got. In your refrigerator, I mean."

C.J. folded his arms over his bare chest, thoroughly enjoying the moment. Especially the part involving the play of the hall light over all those folds and things. Dear God, the woman had more curves than a mountain road. And C.J. wouldn't have been human—let alone alive—had he not entertained at least a brief thought involving the words *test drive.*

"Oh, I can tell you what I've got," he said evenly, even as *You are so screwed* blasted through his skull. Because if they kept meeting up at night like this, with her dressed like that, he was gonna have a helluva time remembering she was here strictly for the baby's sake. And only temporarily, at that.

Ah, hell. Not the doe eyes. Anything but the doe eyes.

"Leftover pizza," he said, and she flinched slightly and said, "What?"

"What I've got. In the refrigerator. Leftover pizza."

"Oh," she said, then smiled brightly. "Fine. Let me grab my robe and I'll be right there."

"You want it hot?" C.J. said to her back as she scurried away. When she spun around, those eyes ever wider (how *did* she do that?), he grinned. Because, dammit, he was having fun. And okay, because he wanted another glimpse of her before she covered everything up with a robe. "The pizza," he said.

Their gazes sparred for a moment or two before she said, in a voice that managed to be sweet and sultry at the same time (and he really wanted to know how she did *that*), "Don't put yourself out on my account. I'm perfectly capable of…taking care of myself." Then *she* grinned. With her head tilted just…so.

A doe-eyed, sweet-sultry voiced smart ass. Yeah, he was in trouble, all right.

Chapter Seven

"Okay," Dana said, peering into C.J.'s destroyer-sized refrigerator at the box of leftover pizza, three cans of beer and quart of milk staring balefully back at her. "Somebody's gotta do some serious shopping tomorrow. This is pitiful. And so—" she hauled out the box of pizza "—clichéd."

Speaking of pitiful. And clichéd. What was up with that little do-si-do between them out in the hallway a few minutes ago? Not to mention her reaction to it? Okay, so it had been a while, but…yeesh.

She stuck a piece of mushroom-and-olive pizza in the microwave, stole a surreptitious glance at the beard-hazed, bed-headed hunk somehow sprawled on a barstool, his elbows propped behind him on the bar, and thought, *This will never do.* Well, actually, he'd do quite nicely, she imagined, but *there,* she was definitely not going. Unfortunately, *here,* she already was, which was why she was having all these wayward, albeit intriguing, thoughts at two-thirty in the morning.

"So we'll go shopping," C.J. said on a yawn, then gave a lazy, not-quite-focused grin. "There you are, you rotten beast," he said to the cat, who had wandered into the kitchen and was now sitting in the middle of the floor like the world's largest dust bunny. "So what's with throwing me over for the first beautiful woman to cross your path?"

Dana's gaze hopped from the cat back to C.J. Such a simple sentence to produce so many questions. And, as if sensing the most profound of those questions, C.J. shrugged and said, "You and Ethan are our first overnight guests."

"And how long have you been here?"

"In this house? Two years, give or take. I was previewing it for a client and decided to buy it myself."

"I don't blame you, it's really spectacular."

"What it is, is an investment. In five years, it'll be worth twice what I paid for it, easily." The muscles in his face eased, though, when he said, "Funny, though, how I wasn't even looking for a house." He tore off a tiny piece of cheese and threw it either to or at the cat, Dana couldn't tell "Anymore than I was looking for a cat. But I opened the door one stormy night, just to smell the rain, and this soaking wet *thing—*" another piece of cheese rocketed through the air "—ran inside. And never left. Right, Steve?"

"Steve?"

C.J. shrugged. "It seemed to fit, what can I say?"

The microwave dinged. She retrieved her pizza and leaned against the counter to eat it standing up. "You don't strike me as a cat person."

"I'm not." He tossed Steve a piece of pepperoni. Dana could hear the cat's purr from clear across the kitchen.

"You could have taken him to the pound, you know."

"Not once I'd named him."

"Of course."

He chuckled. "You—" he stabbed the air with his pizza crust for emphasis "—don't like cats."

She smirked. "I think it's more that they don't like me."

"Why would you think that?"

"I've had, at various times in my life, three cats. They've all run away."

"Don't take it personally. Cats are just like that sometimes."

"My point exactly. At least with birds you put them in a cage, and there they stay."

"Unless they get out. And birds aren't real good at coming when you call."

"Oh, and cats *are?*"

"When it suits their purpose, sure. But Steve's the perfect roomie. Food, water, a patch of sunlight, access to my bed," he said with a slanted grin, "and he's good. And best of all, there's none of that messy emotional stuff to weigh us down."

"Ah. One of those no-strings, you-just-sleep-together relationships."

"Like I said. Perfect."

"Are you deliberately trying to annoy me or what?"

"Nope. Just tellin' it like it is. Although, as I said, Steve dumped me for you tonight."

She blinked, his earlier words finally sinking in. "What?"

"You didn't notice? When I peeked in on you—"

"When you what?"

"I thought the baby might've awakened you, so I looked in to check. Anyway, there the cat was, plastered right up against you, happy as a clam. Not that I blame him." He grinned, heat lazily flickering in half-hooded eyes.

Dana huffed. "You're doing it again, aren't you?"

"What can I tell you, it's late, my defenses are down."

Even if other things aren't.

Bad enough that the unsaid words practically rang out in the cavernous room without Dana's having no idea whose unsaid words they were.

Brother.

"So, shopping," he said, scattering the unsaid words to the four winds. "What time do you have to be at work?"

And so it began. The great baby-and-work shuffle. Because their momentary sharing of living space notwithstanding, it wasn't as if either of them could drop everything to stay home with a baby. The situation was still more expedient than living separately, perhaps, but far from ideal.

"Nine. Or thereabouts. I have to drop the baby off at my mother's first."

"Yeah, I'll be gone by eight, so I guess the morning's out." Then his forehead knotted. "I thought you said your parents couldn't take care of him?"

"What I said was, I didn't think they *should* be saddled with taking care of a child at their ages. Especially since they've finally gotten to the point where they can load up the RV and hit the road whenever the mood strikes. As hard as they've both worked all their lives, they deserve time to themselves. When I suggested looking into day care, however, my mother had a hissy and a half."

"I bet she did. Your mother's a real—"

"Piece of work?" Dana said around a mouth full of blissfully gooey cheese.

"I was going to say, a real she-wolf when it comes to her family."

"Same thing," Dana muttered, and C.J. chuckled. But she'd caught, before the chuckle, a slight wistfulness that had her mentally narrowing her eyes.

"I take it, then," C.J. said, his hands now folded behind his head, "a nanny or an au pair wouldn't be an easy sell, either?"

"Let a *stranger* look after her own great-nephew? Not in this lifetime. Trust me, you do not want to get her started on the evil that is day care."

His gaze was steady in hers. Too steady. "But sometimes there's no alternative."

"Yeah, well, you know that and I know that, and God knows millions of children have come out the other side unscathed, but this is my mother we're talking about. As far as she's concerned—" she finished off the slice of pizza and crossed to the sink for a glass of water, only to find herself completely bamboozled by the water purifier thingy on the faucet "—a child raised by anybody but family is doomed to become warped and dysfunctional. Okay, I give up—how the heck do you get water out of this thing?"

She heard C.J. get up, sensed his moving closer. He took the glass from her hand, flipped a lever and behold, water rushed into it. Amazing.

"Thanks," she muttered, taking a sip as he returned to his seat.

"Maybe she has a point," he said softly, and Dana started. "Who?"

"Your mother. After all, I was raised by nannies and look at me."

As if she could do anything else. He'd donned a T-shirt to go with his sleep pants, but for some reason it only added to the whole blatantly male aura he had going on. And while she was looking at him, she set the glass on the counter and crossed her arms. "Your mother worked?"

A small smile touched his lips. "No. She died in a crash when I was a baby."

"Oh, God, I'm so sorry—"

"Don't you dare go all 'oh, poor C.J.' on me. I never knew

her, so it's not as if I ever missed her. We're not talking some great void in my life, here. Okay?"

She nodded, thinking, *Uh-huh, whatever you say,* then said, "What about your father?"

The pause was so slight, another person might have missed the stumble altogether. "He made sure I had the best caregivers money could buy," he said. "All fifteen of them. You want another slice of pizza?"

"Fifteen?"

"Yep. Pizza?"

"Uh, no, I'm good," she said, and he rose to put the rest back in the fridge. Somehow, she surmised the fifteen-caretakers subject was not on the discussion list. For now, at least. "Still," she said to his back, "I've known warped people in my time. Trust me, you don't even make the team."

"Thanks for the vote of confidence," he said, shutting the door, then shifting his gaze to hers. "But I'm hardly normal, am I?"

"And is there some reason you waited until *after* I'm living in your house to mention this?"

He smiled, then said, "You do have to admit, reaching my late thirties without ever having been in a serious relationship is pushing it."

"So what?" she said with a lot more bravado than she felt. "Lots of people are slow starters. Or…or prefer their own company. That doesn't make you weird."

Even if it did make him off-limits, she reminded herself. Especially when he leaned against the refrigerator, his arms crossed over his chest and said, "I'm not a slow starter, Dana," he said quietly. "I'm a nonstarter. A dead end. Remember?"

The occasional rapacious glance aside. Yes, he might be willing to take responsibility for his own child, or a nondemanding stray cat, but that was it.

Which she knew. Had known all along. *Remember?*

"And just to set your mind at ease," she said, "I learned a long time ago it's easier to grow orchids in the Antarctic than to convert a die-hard bachelor into husband material. And lost causes ain't my thang. Because, someday? You better believe I want 'all that messy emotional stuff.' And the strings. Oh, God, I want strings so bad I can taste them. But only from somebody who wants them as badly as I do. So you can quit with the don't-get-any-ideas signals, okay? Message received, C.J. Loud and clear."

His eyes bore into hers for a long moment, then he said, "So we'll go shopping after we get off work tomorrow night?"

"Sure," she said, then left the kitchen, Steve trotting after her, hopping up onto her bed as though he owned it. She and the cat faced off for several seconds, she daring him to stay, he daring her to make him get down. Finally she crawled into bed, yanking up the cover. "Mess with my birds and you're toast."

The cat gave a strained little *eerk* in reponse, then settled in by her thighs, absolutely radiating smugness.

No wonder C.J. hadn't taken the thing to the pound.

Sunlight slapped Dana awake the next morning, along with the alarm clock's *blat...blat...blat.* Like a sheep with a hangover. Groaning, she opened one eye to discover that she'd apparently hit the snooze button.

Three times.

Covers, and a very pissed cat, went flying as she catapulted from the bed and hurtled toward Ethan's room, not even bothering with her robe since C.J. had said he'd be gone by eight, and—sad to say—eight had long since passed.

"Hey, sugar," she sang, sailing through the door, "you ready to get up...?"

No baby.

She scurried across the room to check the crib more

closely, because that's what you do when you're not firing on all jets yet and the baby entrusted to your care isn't where you last left him, only to spin around and make tracks toward the kitchen, hoping against hope C.J. had lied about leaving at eight and/or that wherever he was, Ethan was with him.

But no. Oh, she found Ethan, who greeted her from his high-chair with a joyful "Ba!" But instead of a tall, good-looking man in his prime, there, beside the baby, stood (at least, Dana thought she was standing, she wasn't quite sure) a short, squat, black-haired woman whose prime, Dana was guessing, had predated color television. But before she could get the words, "And you are?" out of her mouth, the phone rang. Whoever-she-was picked it up, said, "*Sì,* Mr. C.J., she is right here," and held it out to Dana with what could only be called a beatific, if curious, smile.

"Hey," C.J. said, "did I happen to mention Guadalupe?"

Dana's gaze slid over to the smiling woman. "I take it that's who answered the phone?"

"That would be her. She comes in to clean for me twice a week. It completely slipped my mind that today was her day. I briefly explained things to her when she came in this morning. I would have awakened you before I left, but Steve looked like he'd remove a limb if I tried."

With a flickering smile at Guadalupe, whose steady stream of Spanish Ethan was apparently eating up as enthusiastically as his rice cereal, Dana carted the portable phone out of earshot. "Never mind that I nearly had a heart attack when I went to get Ethan out of his crib and he *wasn't there,*" she whispered into the phone. "A little warning might've been nice. And how the heck does one *briefly* explain the sudden appearance of a baby and a strange woman in your house?" She put up a hand, even though he couldn't see her. "Unfamiliar, I mean."

After a barely perceptible pause, she heard, "You have no idea how tempting it is to say, no, you were right the first time."

"And where I come from, bantering before coffee is a hanging offense."

A soft laugh preceded, "In any case, I simply told her the truth, that Ethan's my son and you're his cousin, that neither of us knew of his existence two weeks ago, and that we're trying to figure out the best way to handle a very complicated situation. She seemed to take it in stride. But then, taking things in stride is what Guadalupe does. You'll see." He paused, as though catching his breath. "I really do apologize for the brain cramp. Are you okay?"

"Yeah, *now.* Five minutes ago was something else again. Look, thanks for calling, but I'm running seriously late—"

"Right, me, too, I've got an appointment in ten. See you tonight, then."

And he was gone. Dana told herself the sense of watching an un-subtitled foreign movie was due to the combination of severe caffeine deprivation and leftover heart arrhythmia from the earlier shock.

She returned to the kitchen, where Guadalupe was busy wiping down a squealing Ethan, who wasn't taking kindly to having his attempts at pulverizing a blob of cereal on his high chair tray thwarted whenever Guadalupe grabbed his little hand to clean it. The older woman flicked a brief, but chillingly astute, glance in Dana's direction.

"So," she said. "Mr. C.J. says you are not the mother?"

Dana shook her head. "No. His mother's my cousin."

"She as pretty as you?"

Warmth flooded Dana's face at the out-of-left-field compliment. She sidled over to the coffeemaker and poured herself a huge cup. "Trish is…very different from me," she said, dumping in three packets of artificial sweetener, some half-and-half. "Lighter hair. Tallish. Skinny."

One eyebrow lifted, Guadalupe went for the other little hand. "So how well do you and Mr. C.J. know each other?"

"Not very, really. Oh, let me take the baby, I need to get him dressed to go to my mother's."

"I can get him dressed, just leave out what you would like him to wear. And while you shower, I fix breakfast, no? I bring eggs, chorizo, the green chile for Mr. C.J.," she said when Dana opened her mouth. "There is plenty extra for you. Is *muy bueno*, you will like. So, go," she said, shooing.

Fifteen minutes later, Dana returned, face done, hair up, body clothed in a silky loose top and a drapey, ankle-length skirt in jewel tones that coordinated with the plastic fruit gracing her high-heeled, Lucite mules. The baby was dressed and in his car seat, ready to go; from the tempered glass breakfast table, a plate of steaming, fragrant eggs and sausage beckoned. Her brain said, "*Stick with the coffee,*" but her stomach said, "*Who are you kidding?*"

After depositing her purse on the island, she clicked across the stone floor, sat at the table. Lifted fork to mouth. Groaned in ecstasy.

"Is good, no?" Guadalupe said, smiling, from the sink.

"Delicious. Thank you."

"*De nada.* You cook?"

"I love to cook. But I've never gotten the hang of Mexican."

"I teach you, if you like. I teach all my daughters, now my grandchildren. Twenty-seven," she said with a grin, and Dana nearly choked on her eggs.

"Goodness. Y'all must have some Thanksgivings."

The old woman threw back her head and laughed, her bosoms shaking. "*Sì*, last year we had three turkeys and two hams, and enough enchiladas to feed half of Albuquerque. Done?" she asked, when Dana stood, whisking away her empty plate before she had a chance to carry it to the sink.

"Well, this little guy and I better hit the road," she said, moving toward the seat, which Guadalupe had set by the patio door in a patch of filtered sunshine. But the old woman touched her arm.

"I know I am a stranger to you, but I have worked for Mr. C.J. for many years, I am good with children, you could leave *el poco* angel with me…."

"Oh…I'm sorry, I can't. Not because I don't trust you," she hastily added at the woman's hurt expression, "but my mother would kill me. Because it's very possible that Ethan's as close as she's going to get to a grandchild. At least for the fore-seeable future."

Confusion clouded the dark eyes for a moment, replaced by an understanding sympathy so strong Dana was glad for the excuse to squat in front of the baby's seat. Steve shoved himself against her calves, mewing for attention.

"Hey, guy," Dana said softly, crouching in front of Ethan, who gave her a wide, trembly smile when she came into focus. "Ready to go? You are?" she said, laughing, when the baby started pumping his arms. "Well, come on then, your Auntie Faye's waitin' on you…."

Just like that, the unfairness of it all squeezed her heart so tightly, she could barely breathe. Clutching the sides of the seat, waiting for her lungs to get with the program, she heard behind her, very gently, "What will you do when your cousin comes back for her *niño?*"

Dana stood, hefting seat and baby into her arms. "There's no guarantee that she will."

"But if she does?"

"Then I suppose we'll cross that bridge when we get to it."

"And if the bridge is one you do not wish to cross?"

Balancing the seat against one hip, Dana grabbed her purse off the counter and slung it over her shoulder. "Thanks again for breakfast, it was great," she said, making herself smile. "Will you be here this evening when we get home?"

Heat flooded Dana's cheeks at the slip. *We* and *home* in the same sentence? After one day?

A little presumptuous, yes?

Guadalupe's eyes narrowed, but all she said was, "I usually leave at three, there is not much to clean in a house where only one person lives. But anytime you need me to take care of this precious child," she hastily added, "I will be more than happy to stay. You have a good day, Miss Dana, okay?"

Yeah, well, Dana thought as she lugged His Highness out to her car, she'd do her best.

During a lull between appointments, C.J. brought Val into his office, shut the door and told her about Ethan. Not surprisingly, the further into the story he got, the higher went her eyebrows, until he half thought they'd crawl off her face altogether.

"The Trish who worked *here?*" she said at the appropriate point in the narrative. "What the hell were you thinking, boy?"

"Could we please not go there, Val? The past is past."

"Actually, it looks to me like the past just came up and bit you on the butt, if you don't mind my sayin' so."

"If I did, I wouldn't have told you. But wait. There's more."

There went the eyebrows again. "You mean, you can top a six-month-old son you didn't know about?"

"I don't know about topping, but…" His desk chair creaked when he leaned back in it. "You remember Dana Malone? The woman who was in here a couple of weeks ago?"

"Sure do. Cute little thing. Big eyes. What about her?"

"Trish is her cousin. And she kind of…left the baby with her. Granted her guardianship, actually. In writing. So she's kind of…living with me. Well, they are. Dana and the baby."

Three, four seconds later, Val blinked at him, then lifted her hands in an I-don't-even-want-to-know gesture. Then she sighed. "I *knew* there was somethin' goin' on, I just knew it, the way you were acting mush-brained all last week. And didn't I tell you I'd find out?" When he didn't answer—because, really, what could he say?—she finally sank into the chair across from his desk, her eyes brimming with concern. "So what are you going to do?"

"Find Trish. Solidify custody arrangements. After that…" He shrugged. "Take it day by day, I guess. Although I guess I'll be cutting back my hours, so I can spend time with…with my son."

"Boy, those are two words I never thought I'd hear come out of your mouth."

His mouth stretched. "You and me both."

"Couldn't you get one of those au pairs or something?"

C.J.'s stomach turned, even as he grimaced. "I suppose I'll have to look into it eventually. But it has to be the right person. And I have to get the idea past Dana's mother first.

"And what about the gal? Dana? How's she fit into all of this? Long-range, I mean?"

"Hell, Val. Right now, I'm doing well to plan out the next ten minutes. I can't even begin to wrap my head around 'long range'."

Any more than he'd been able to wrap his head around that bantering business this morning. Because bantering was not something he did, as a general rule. Oh, he could hold his own in a serious discussion with the best of 'em, as long as the conversation stayed on safe topics. Like politics or religion. And as long as it was conducted from behind nice, thick impersonal walls.

But Dana had no walls. Dana, in fact, was the antiwall.

Dana not only made him banter, she made him want to banter. To indulge in playful, affectionate exchanges, like some happy couple on a sitcom.

And all this after less than twenty-four hours in his house.

He started at Val's touch on his arm. "There anything I can do?" she asked gently.

"Other than promise me you won't start sending out your résumé?" He shook his head. "Nope. Not a damn thing. I'm all on my own with this one."

For the rest of the day, work crowded his thoughts, albeit with an occasional detour into the personal when he spoke with Elena (no, she hadn't found anything yet, but it had only been a day, after all), and when the papers his father had promised finally arrived, prompting C.J. to realize he should probably tell the old man he was a grandfather, at some point. Not yet, though. Not until he'd come to terms with the whole thing himself. And one by one, he told the other agents he'd be turning over more clients to them. And why. If they were shocked, none of them let on. Not too much, anyway.

At six, he left. Just like that. Packed his briefcase and walked out the door. Not to see a property, or a client, but his own child.

And Dana, he thought with a tingle of anticipation that made him frown. It was okay to like her, he reassured himself as he steered the Mercedes across town, thinking how strange it was to be heading home while it was still this light, this early. But was it okay to look forward quite so much to being with her, to hearing her laughter, to being the brunt of her gentle teasing? Wasn't it cheating, the one-sidedness of it?

It had been wrong, and selfish, to bring her here, he thought as he parked his car beside hers, already in the driveway. Even more wrong to have put her in such a tenuous position, he chided himself as he walked into the house, heard those silly birds of hers, then her laughter, blending with the baby's from several rooms away.

He found them in Ethan's room, where she was changing the

baby's diaper, still dressed from work, he assumed, in some floaty skirt and top, a pair of crazy shoes that made him smile. Made him…other things. She looked up at his entrance, her smile dimming slightly, and a brief, bright spark of annoyance flashed in his brain, that she should feel wary of him. That she needed to continue being wary, for her own good.

As if sensing C.J.'s entrance, Ethan twisted himself around, grinning. Trusting. After a moment of stillness, all four limbs struck out simultaneously, pumping the air in pure, joyful abandon.

"Somebody's sure glad to see his daddy," Dana said

Oh, God. This was what it was like, having someone to come home to.

Having someone giddy with happiness that you'd *come* home.

Giddy. Not wary.

"Oh, shoot," Dana said. "I brought home a whole bag of clothes for him from the shop, but I left them in the other room."

"Stay there, I'll get them."

Grateful for a moment to regroup, C.J. sprinted down the hall and into Dana's room, glancing around for the telltale bright blue Great Expectations bag, at last spotting it on a chair beside a little writing desk the decorator had called "too, too precious for words." In grabbing the bag, however, he bumped the desk, startling the open laptop on top of it awake.

To a word processing program she hadn't shut down.

Chapter Eight

He hadn't meant to read the text that appeared on the screen, but eyes will do what eyes will do, and before he knew it, he'd scrolled through five or six pages of some of the driest, funniest stuff he'd read in ages—

"Ohmigod…no!" He turned to see Dana striding across the carpet, a diapered Ethan clinging to her hip. "Nobody's supposed to see that," she said, slapping closed the computer, her cheeks flushed.

"You wrote this?" he asked.

"Yes, but—"

"But, nothing. It's good, Dana. No, I'm serious," he said when she snorted. "The old Southern lady going on and on about her ailments…" He chuckled. "Priceless. You should be published."

Her blush deepened. "Yeah, well, it's not that easy."

C.J. took the baby from her, a little surprised to see how

quickly he'd grown used to the squirmy, solid weight in his arms. How quickly, and completely, the instinct to protect this tiny person had swamped the initial shock and panic and anger. "Have you even tried?" he said, laying the baby on the bed, then holding out his hand, indicating to Dana she needed to give him something to put on the kid.

"Um…well, no. I mean, I can't, it's not finished yet."

"Then finish it," he said, taking the little blue sailor outfit from her and popping it over the baby's head. Getting arms and legs into corresponding openings was a bit trickier, however, so it took a while for him to realize Dana had gone silent behind him. When he turned, her eyes were shiny. And, yes, wide.

"You really think it's good?" she asked.

"I really do. And for what it's worth, I'm not a total philistine. I minored in contemporary American lit in college. So I know my stuff."

"Oh. Wow. I'm…"

"…extremely talented. Really."

She blinked at him for another few seconds, then said, "So. Are you ready to storm Smith's?"

Ah. He'd embarrassed her. She'd get over it. What *he* wouldn't get over, he realized as they all trooped out to his car, in which he'd installed the Cadillac of baby seats in the back, was that he'd never championed anyone before. Had never met anyone he'd wanted to champion.

What a rush. A breath-stealing, heart-stopping, panic-inducing rush.

Once in the store, he gave her free rein, offering little comment as she filled the cart with vegetables and fruits and roasts and fish and whole grain breads, with things he had no idea what to do with, other than to consume them once they'd been cooked. A perk he hadn't even thought about, when he'd asked her to move in. And one he couldn't help feeling a pang of guilt about now. Not a huge pang—he couldn't remember the last time he'd had roast pork—but a twinge nonetheless.

"Your cooking for me wasn't part of the arrangement."

After a smile for the baby when he grabbed for C.J.'s hand with the obvious intention of gnawing on his onyx ring, she said, "I'm not cooking for you. I'm cooking for myself." She snagged several boxes of Jell-O off the shelf, tossing them into the cart. "May as well toss in a little extra while I'm at it."

"So I take it you know your way around a kitchen?"

"People who love to eat generally love to cook." She held up a small jar. "How do you feel about capers?"

"Just don't put them in the Jell-O."

"Deal."

And so it went, their conversation. Careful. Circumspect. He talked about work, she intermittently grilled him about his food preferences. He'd have had to be blind to not notice that she didn't look his way unless she absolutely had to, that her smiles were fleeting, rationed. Strike what he'd thought before about her not having any walls, because there was definitely one up between them now, transparent and flimsy though it may have been. Not that she was a whiner. In fact, it was the way she seemed to curl around her obvious bad mood, swallowing her true feelings, that annoyed him so much. He didn't like this Dana, he wanted the other Dana back, the one who'd tease and flash that dimpled smile for him.

Periodically piercing the annoyance, however, was the swell of pride whenever someone stopped to admire Ethan. Which happened approximately every twenty feet. And Ethan took to his role as the charmer with equanimity, bequeathing wrinkle-nosed, two-toothed grins on everyone who spoke to him. After one gushing elderly couple continued on their way,

C.J. looked at the baby and said, "How could anyone walk away from such a perfect kid?"

That was enough to earn him a sideways glance, at least. And a smirk. "Says the man who's lived with the child for one night. Believe me, he has his moments—"

"Ohmigosh, aren't you just the cutest little thing?" yet another admirer said, cooing at the baby as though she'd never seen one. "Oh, would you look at those two little teeth! How old?" she asked Dana.

"Six and a half months."

"Aw, that's such a wonderful age. Enjoy it, honey—it goes so fast. I had four, they're all parents of teenagers themselves now, but it still seems like yesterday. And look at you, expecting again already, bless your heart! Well, bye-bye, sweetie," she said to Ethan with a fluttery wave, then trotted off.

The whooshing in C.J.'s ears nearly obliterated the piped-in seventies oldie bouncing off the freezer cases. At last he turned to Dana, his heart cracking at the stoic expression on her face.

"You want me to go beat her up?"

"That's very sweet," she said with a fleeting smile, "but I think I'll pass. And anyway, better she think I'm pregnant than I'm nothing but a lazy slob without the willpower to starve myself down to a size eight."

"One isn't better than the other, Dana."

"Maybe not. But I'm used to it. Come on," she said quietly, nudging the cart toward the checkout. "It's getting close to Ethan's bedtime."

If she'd been subdued before, she was downright uncommunicative on the ride back to the house, his every attempt to draw her out meeting with little more than a monosyllabic reply.

Oh, man, not since he was a kid had he felt this...this extraneous. Not that he hadn't been well aware of his inability to connect with another human being except on the most basic of levels, but if this didn't drive it home, boy, he didn't know what did. Because, whether he understood it or not, whether he liked it or not, he did genuinely care about this woman, about what she was feeling. He hated seeing her hurt. But even more, he hated not knowing what to do to make it better.

When they got back to the house, he offered to get Ethan ready for bed while Dana started their dinner. He wondered, as he carted his sleepy son down the hall, how he thought some biological connection was going to make him any more able to fix the inevitable hurts for his child than for Dana. With that, the resentment demons roared back out onto the field from where he'd tried desperately to keep them benched, fangs and claws glinting in the harsh light of C.J.'s own fear.

Ethan lay quietly on the changing table during the diaper-changing process, gnawing like mad on his fist, watching C.J. with those damn trusting eyes, and hot tears bit at the backs of C.J.'s. He hadn't wanted this, he thought bitterly, stuffing plump little legs into a pair of lightweight pajama bottoms. Hadn't asked for it—

The baby clung to him like a little koala when he picked him up, and C.J. clung right back, his hand cradling his son's head, his cheek pressed against one tiny shell of a little ear.

How the hell was he supposed to be something he didn't know how to be?

He lowered Ethan into his crib, unable to resist the tug to his emotions when the kid grabbed his blanket, his eyelids drooping almost immediately. "'Night, Scooter," he whispered, slightly startled when the nickname popped out of its own accord. Then he stepped into Dana's room to grab the baby monitor off her nightstand, his emotions assailing him a second time at the basic here-ness of her—a pair of shoes, carelessly kicked underneath the chair, her lingering scent. The laptop, firmly closed, like an old woman with secrets.

* * *

Standing barefoot at the island, tossing a salad, Dana glanced up when C.J. entered the kitchen. Her forehead creased in concern. "Everything okay?"

"What? Oh…sure. I just…" He smiled, shook his head. "It's nothing," he said, setting the monitor on the counter. "Work stuff."

Her expression said she didn't believe him for a minute, but all she said was, "I fake-baked a potato in the microwave for you, but I thought we could do the steaks out on the grill?"

C.J. grabbed a beer from the fridge, then allowed a rueful smile. "Guess this is as good a time as any to tell you I've never used the damn thing."

"Get out! What kind of red-blooded American male are you?"

"One who eats out a lot."

Dana huffed a little sigh that eased his mind somewhat—at least his ineptitude as a backyard chef was giving her something to focus on besides herself. Undeterred, she picked up the salad bowl and the monitor, commanding him to bring the steaks, adding it was high time he learned this basic suburban survival skill. When they got outside, she shook her head in amazement at the built-in grill tucked into a low wall on one side of the patio.

"Heck, compared with my daddy's little old barbecue, this is like going from a motorboat to a yacht. So maybe you should go sit way over there, so you won't see me make a fool out of myself, trying to figure this thing out."

But for all her concern, the steaks turned out fine. And as the sun set, the temperature dropped and a light breeze picked up, there they were, just two people enjoying dinner out by the pool.

Yeah, right.

"So if you can't cook," she said, dangling a tiny piece of steak for Steve, whose purr C.J. could hear from five feet away, "what *can* you do?"

"Well, I make a great deal of money. Does that count?"

"Maybe," she said, her eyes sparkling for the first time that evening. "Of course, it depends on what you do with all that money."

"Meaning, do I horde it like Scrooge? No. Although I do have quite a bit socked away in various retirement funds. The thought of ending my life living in a cardboard box does not appeal."

"No," she said softly. "It doesn't."

"But then, the thought of anybody else living in a cardboard box doesn't appeal, either. So I support a lot of local charities. For the homeless, the food bank, things like that. In fact…" He took a pull of his beer, thought *What the hell.* "I've got a fund-raiser to go to a week from Saturday, and—"

"Oh, I can stay with Ethan, no problem."

"—*and* I was wondering if you'd like to go with me."

She stared at him for a second or two, then jumped up and began clearing their dishes.

"Dana? What the—? It wasn't a trick question!"

Plates balanced in both hands, she turned. "Wasn't it? I mean, why ask me now? Tonight?"

He stood, as well, taking the plates from her. "Look, if you don't want to go, just say so."

"It has nothing to do with whether or not I'd like to go."

"Then what is it?" When she didn't answer, he sighed. "This wouldn't have anything to do with that woman in the store, would it?"

She snatched up their water glasses and headed inside. "You tell me."

"You think I'm inviting you because…what? I feel sorry for you? Dana, for God's sake." He followed, setting the plates by the dishwasher. "It was a simple invitation, no ulterior motives behind it."

"C.J., get real. Nothing's *simple* between us."

"Point taken. But I swear, I only asked you because I hate going to these things alone, and I thought you might enjoy getting out…and I'm just digging myself in deeper, aren't I?"

She emitted a desiccated little sound that might have been a laugh, then looked at him. "You're not exactly winning any major points," she said, but without a lot of steam behind it. "What happened to the charmer who's supposed to know exactly the right thing to say?"

"Is that what you think I am? A charmer?" When she shrugged, he reached out, taking her hand. "Fine, so maybe playing the game is what's gotten me through so far. You say what people want to hear, they generally do what you want them to do."

"And you're proud of this?"

"I've never deliberately misled anyone, Dana. Or used anyone for my own purposes. There are ways of working it without hurting people. Still, to answer your question…no. I don't suppose I am particularly proud of how I've lived my life. But what I'm trying to say is…the baby…" He stopped, shutting his eyes for a moment, trying to make the words line up, make sense. When he opened them again, it was to meet that cautious, careful gaze. "I look at Ethan, and I realize a large part of who I was won't cut it anymore. I don't really know yet what that means, what I'm supposed to do, or who I'm supposed to be. But I do know you're somehow part of that revelation."

She flinched. "Me? How?"

"Because when I'm with you, I don't want to be who I was before, either. I mean, before tonight, I can't remember ever being angry enough on someone else's behalf that I wanted to hurt another human being. Not that I'm going to go off the deep end and start beating up little old ladies—"

"Good to know."

"—but my point is, since Ethan came into my life, I suddenly…care. About how someone else might feel."

She tilted her head. "Empathy?"

"Yes! That's it! I mean, yeah, I've always felt I needed to help people who were down on their luck, or who'd gotten a raw deal, but never on a personal level before. And tonight, the more I realized how hurt you were, the angrier I got."

Her eyes narrowed. "And yet you weren't inviting me to this charity thing because you felt sorry for me."

"No, dammit, I invited you because I *like* you! Because I want to beat people up for you! And that's not all!"

"It…isn't?" she said, looking slightly alarmed.

"No! Because I grew up in a house where nobody talks to anybody, and it sucks. Which is why I've always preferred to live alone. But Ethan's here, and you're here, and if you need to vent, I'm not going anywhere. In the meantime, get out of here, go write or whatever you want to do while I clean up."

"Lord have mercy," she said after a long moment, "but you are one strange man."

"Yeah, well, if you felt like somebody'd just removed your brain, rearranged all the parts and crammed it back inside your skull, you'd be strange, too."

She blinked. "Maybe…I'll go sit out by the pool for a while, then."

"Fine."

She walked to the door, hesitated a second, then turned back around. "Okay, I'll go with you. To the charity thing."

"Taking pity on the *strange* man, are we? Hey, don't do me any favors."

"I'm not. Like you said, it's been a while since I've been out."

And she left. Fifteen minutes later, however, he was finishing the washing up when he heard the muffled double-shushing of the patio door opening, then closing. C.J. watched as she padded over to the fridge, pulling out a jug of orange juice. After pouring herself a small glass, she slid up onto one of the barstools.

"See," she began quietly, "the skinny people of the world look at people like me and think, What's wrong with her? Why can't she control her weight? They never stop to think that, you know, maybe I have tried every diet known to man, maybe I've even gone to doctors about it, maybe I do exercise and eat right ninety-five percent of the time." Her mouth pulled into a tight smile. "That maybe I would have done anything to stop the other kids from calling me Fatty when I was a kid. Except it doesn't always work that way. For some of us, it's not just a matter of eating less, or exercising more, or having willpower."

"You're not fat, Dana," he said, meaning it.

"Oh, but according to every chart out there, I am. I weigh thirty pounds more than I 'should' for my height. Which, by the way, is thirty pounds less than I weighed about five years ago, when I finally realized scarfing down a pint of Ben & Jerry's every time I got stressed was a bad idea. Then again, the thought of never again eating real ice cream, or a piece of cheesecake, or mashed potatoes with gravy, or a cheese enchilada…" She shook her head. "Now *that's* depressing. But God forbid I go into a restaurant and order something besides a piece of broiled fish and a salad, hold the dressing. People look at me like I'm a criminal."

"That's their problem, honey. Not yours."

"And most of the time I do know that. But every once in a while it gets to me, what can I say? Just like the other thing. Not being able to have kids. And with all this about Ethan…you happened to catch me at a bad time."

"Lucky me," he said, and she smiled. Not a big one, but enough to see the dimples. God, he loved those dimples.

"Okay, your turn," she said, her expression brightening. "If

I have to open up, so do you. So what's your story…oh, shoot," she said as Ethan's reedy cry came through the monitor. Her gaze touched his. "Coin toss?"

"No, that's okay, I'll go," C.J. said, barely managing to keep from jumping off the stool. "And anyway, it's late, and I've got a seven-thirty breakfast meeting tomorrow, so maybe we should call it a night, anyway."

Still smiling, Dana shook her head. "You are so transparent, C. J. Turner," she said quietly. "But you know something? You can run, but you can't hide. Maybe from me, but not from yourself. And one day, you're gonna have to face whatever you don't want to face. And deal with it, too."

But as C.J. tromped down the hall to see what was up with his son, it occurred to him that "one day" was already there.

"Sorry I'm late," Dana shouted to Mercy over the Friday-night crowd chatter in the little bistro by the university. "Traffic tie-up on the freeway."

"It's okay, there's a fifteen-minute wait." Mercy held up a small pager. "They'll call us when the table's ready. Outside or bar?"

"Your call."

"This was a grèat idea, by the way," Mercy yelled over her shoulder as they pushed their way through the throng. "If a surprise."

"Yeah, well, it occurred to me that C.J. needed some one-on-one time with Ethan," Dana yelled back. "And I needed the night off."

"So naturally you decided to spend it with someone you already see five days a week," Mercy said, slithering up onto a bar stool. "Makes total sense."

"Says the woman who pounced on the idea like a cat on a grasshopper."

Shortly thereafter, as Dana reluctantly sipped a glass of white wine and Mercy tackled a margarita larger than her head, her partner nodded appreciatively at Dana's outfit, a low-cut blousy top tucked into a long, tiered skirt. "The cleavage is seriously hot."

Dana glanced down. "Not too much?"

"No such thing, *chica*. Really, you should take the girls out more often, they look like they could use the air. Well, look at *you*, Ms. Techno Babe," she said as Dana set her cell phone on the bar. "Welcome to the twenty-first century."

"C.J. insisted I needed one. Because of the baby."

"And you love it already."

Dana smirked. "And I love it already."

After a chuckle into her drink, Mercy poked Dana's wrist with one long fingernail. "So. Have you slept with the guy yet?"

"Honestly, Merce. You really do have a one-track mind, don't you?"

That got an unrepentant grin. "I live to yank your chain, you know that. But seriously. How's it going? It's been, what? Nearly a week, right?"

Dana took a small sip of her wine, flinching when some man brushed against her as he got up onto his bar stool. "Not quite. Five days. Seems longer."

"Is that good or bad?"

"I'm not sure. In some ways it's a lot easier than I thought it would be. I mean, we've worked out a pretty good routine, C.J.'s been a real trouper about taking care of the baby…"

"But?"

"But…" Dana frowned at the slightly trembling liquid in her glass. "No matter how gracious C.J. is, I'm still a guest." She lifted her eyes to Mercy's dark, sympathetic gaze. "And the question is, for how long?"

"Because of Trish, you mean?" Dana nodded. Mercy fingered the rim of her sombrero-sized vessel. "So you haven't heard anything yet?"

"The investigator C.J. hired keeps running into dead ends, apparently. As though Trish dropped off the baby, then the planet—"

"Hey," said a reasonably good-looking suit who'd popped up out of nowhere. His gaze bounced off Dana's breasts, then zeroed in on Mercy in her bright red spaghetti strap top and matching, flippy skirt. "Can I buy you ladies a drink?"

"Thanks," Mercy said, "but we're fine."

"Hey, you know, maybe it'd speed things up if we shared a table—?"

One French-manicured hand shot up. "No. Thank you." She faced Dana again, pointedly turning her back to the guy. "So. You were saying?"

As the poor schlep trundled off, his wounded ego trailing behind like a strip of toilet paper, Dana smiled and said, "We don't *have* to hang out tonight. I mean, if something better comes along…"

"Better than you? Never happen. Besides, when have you known me to pick up a strange guy in some bar?" At Dana's raised brow, she huffed out, "Recently?"

Dana chuckled, then sighed. "But what does it say about us that, here we are, two women in our thirties, spending our Saturday night with each other?"

"That we're comfortable enough with who we are to do that?"

"Or bored out of our skulls."

"Yeah, that, too…oh! I'm blinking!" Mercy said, snatching the pager off the bar, then her drink. "Although you know," she said as the hostess signaled them over, "at least *you* had an option. *You* could have stayed home with Mr. Gorgeous, flashing your girls at him instead of me. But no… Thanks," she said with a bright smile for the hostess as they slid into their booth. Then she leaned across the table. "You're here. With me. Instead of there. With him."

And Dana leaned over and said back, "And maybe there's a reason for that."

"One can hope."

Dana rolled her eyes, then told her about the whole "You make me want to beat people up" speech, which didn't exactly elicit the reaction Dana had hoped.

"*Dios mio,* you little idiot!" Mercy's dark eyes glittered in the dim light from the puny little votive in the center of the table. "This is *huge,* like something right out of a movie, when the guy suddenly realizes he can't live without the girl! We're talking *When Harry Met Sally,* or *As Good as It Gets.*"

"Oh, this is definitely as good as it gets, all right."

Mercy's eyebrows collided over her cute little nose. "Not following."

"Merce, all this is, is C.J.'s coming to terms with being responsible for another human being. Meaning Ethan. I watch him, and I can tell being with his son is opening him up to all sorts of emotions he's never dealt with before. Never *let* himself deal with before. And it's as if…" She glanced away, trying to find the words, then looked back at her friend. "You know what it's like, when you first fall in love, how the whole world seems brighter? And suddenly you love everybody, because what you're feeling is too overwhelming to focus on a single person? That's all that's going on here, trust me. Only it's with Ethan, not me."

After a couple of seconds of introspective frowning, Mercy said, "So you think he said all that because, what? You happened to be in the vicinity? Like the victim of a gas cloud?"

"Basically, yeah. Nothing's going to come of this, Merce," she said firmly when the brunette pushed out a sigh.

"Well, it sure as hell won't as long as you go out with me, or spend the night in your own apartment."

"But that's what it's going to come down to eventually, anyway. Or did you think I was going to live with C.J. until Ethan graduates from high school? It was only ever supposed to be temporary, so the last thing either of us needs is to get too used to the other's company."

"I see. And you're not just saying this because you're afraid of getting hurt?"

Dana's eyes snapped to Mercy's, irritatingly astute under those perfectly arched brows. "I'm saying this because I'm a realist."

"And?"

"And...I'd be a fool to believe the man's done a complete about-face in less than three weeks, baby or no baby. Accepting his responsibilities as a parent doesn't mean he's changed his mind about anything else."

"So this *is* about protecting yourself."

She snorted. "Can you blame me?"

"No," Mercy said gently. "But people do change, honey."

"I know they do," Dana said. "Because I have. Or at least, I'm trying to. And it's going to take a lot more than a single impassioned declaration for me to let my guard down—"

She clamped shut her mouth, focusing on the flickering little flame between them. And Mercy, bless her, did nothing more than reach across the table to quickly squeeze Dana's trembling fingers.

Somehow, though—probably because of the mutual, unspoken moratorium imposed on the subject of C.J. and/or anyone's love life—she actually enjoyed the rest of the evening. For the most part they talked business, since the move into the new space was imminent, so by the time they went their separate ways a little after nine, Dana was beginning to feel at least a little less crazed.

In fact, she even thought she might get some writing done before she went to bed, only to remember she'd left her laptop and all her notebooks at C.J.'s. She was half tempted to forget it, except it seemed a shame to blow off her muse simply because she didn't feel like trekking all the way back to C.J.'s.

Praying he wouldn't notice her return, Dana let herself in and started toward "her" room, only to be waylaid by Steve, plaintively meowing and head-butting her shins as though he hadn't seen her in three years. Or been fed, more likely. Honestly. She followed the cat into the kitchen, where, as she suspected, Iams abounded in his food dish.

Which is when she heard C.J.'s voice coming in low, angry bursts through the slightly open patio door.

Chapter Nine

Dana froze, knowing she should hotfoot it out of there, and yet…she couldn't. Not that she could really hear what C.J. was saying—or wanted to!—but simply because it was such a shock, hearing those sounds come out of that man.

The sounds of a man having his heart shredded, basically.

Then suddenly the door slid open and he was there, barely ten feet in front of her, his cell phone clamped to his ear, a hundred emotions roiling in his eyes. Not the least of which was irritation at her unexpected presence.

Blushing furiously, Dana pointed toward her room and hurried away, even more hurriedly stuffing her laptop and notebooks into a canvas tote. Although if her muse hadn't run for the hills by now, she'd be very surprised.

Naturally, she had to peek in on the baby on her way back down the hall. In the charcoal light, she saw him lift his head, heard him burble at her.

"Hey, little guy." She set down the tote by the door and crossed the room, fighting the urge to pick him up. Bad enough she'd come in instead of walking away, letting him get back to sleep. Still, since she was here anyway, she bent over and sniffed. Nope, nothing but baby powder and tear-free shampoo.

"'Night-night, sugar," she whispered, handing him back his blanket, which earned her a quavering, sleepy smile. Oh, heck, how could she not touch him? So she cupped the silky head, only to practically jerk back her hand, as though she'd been tempted to take something that didn't belong to her.

On a sigh, she crept back out, snatching her tote bag along the way, hoping against hope to make her escape without running into C.J.

"Dana?"

So much for that.

His voice drained of its earlier fury, her name floated out from the darkness in the living room. Then, like an apparition, the man himself appeared. Wrecked was the only word for his expression. Exhaustion, and something else Dana couldn't quite identify, slumped his shoulders, fettered his smile. "What are you doing here? I thought you weren't coming back tonight."

She lifted the bag. "Left my writing stuff here. I'm sorry, I didn't mean to—"

"It's okay. You just surprised me, that's all."

"Sorry," she repeated. "So…how'd it go with Ethan?"

The smile relaxed, a little. "I gave him a bath. Or he gave me one, I wasn't quite sure which. He asked where you were."

"He…? Oh. You almost had me there for a second."

C.J. slid his hands into his khaki pockets, his eyes fixed on hers. "You aren't going to ask who I was arguing with?"

"Why would I do that?" she said, slightly confused. "It's none of my business."

"It's not an old girlfriend, if that's what you're thinking."

"I'm not thinking anything. Really."

Actually, her brain was processing so many possibilities she half expected it to short out. But if he was hinting that maybe he was ready to talk…well. He'd have to do more than hint. Because almost every time she'd handed him an opening the past few days, he'd clammed up. So, tough.

Never mind that everything inside her was screaming to give him one more chance, one more opening. To be the sounding board she suspected he'd never had, or at least not for a long time. But torn as she was, the new Dana—the older, wiser Dana—had finally learned there were some roads best left unexplored.

At least, until she was sure she'd come out okay on the other end.

C.J. closed the space between them, taking her bag. "I'll carry this out to the car for you."

"You don't have to—"

"Hush, woman, and let me be the man."

The cat barreled past her when the door opened, streaking into the night. They walked to her car in silence; C.J. opened her door, setting the bag in back.

"Thanks."

"*De nada.*" Was she hallucinating, or was he focusing entirely too much on her mouth? Then he lifted his hand, and she held her breath…

…and he swatted away a tiny night critter fluttering around her face.

Then, with what sounded like a frustrated sigh, he gently fingered a loose curl hovering at her temple.

"I'm a mess, Dana."

"So I noticed."

He dropped his hand. And laughed, although the sound was pained. "And here I always thought Southern women bent over backward to be diplomatic."

"Clearly you've been hanging out with the wrong Southern women."

"Clearly," he said, his expression unreadable in the harsh security light. Then, gently: "Go, Dana. For both our sakes…go."

Only, after she slid behind the wheel, he caught the door before she could close it. "That was my father," he said. "On the phone."

Her breath caught. "Oh? Um…I'm sorry?"

"Don't be. I finally got some things off my chest. Someday, I'll tell you the whole sordid story. If you really want to hear it, I mean."

Afraid to speak, she simply nodded. He pushed her door shut; her throat clogged, Dana backed into the street, put the car into Drive, drove away. Noticed, when she glanced into her rearview mirror, C.J. still standing in the driveway, hands in his pockets, watching her until she got all the way to the end of the street.

"Oh, Merce," Dana whispered to herself. "Now *this* is huge."

"No news yet?" Val asked from the doorway to C.J.'s office.

He swiveled in her direction. "What? You're bugging the phones now?"

"No, I was on my way to the kitchen and your voice carries. And when you're the youngest of seven you get real good at deducing what's going on from only one side of the conversation." She waltzed in and plopped down across from him. "So what'd she say? That private investigator gal?"

"Not much. But if Trish is working off the books somewhere, or hasn't used a credit card recently, it might be harder to track her down."

"Well, the child couldn't have just vanished. She's bound to turn up, sooner or later."

"That's what worries me."

"I don't understand, I thought you wanted to get things settled. Legally. So there'd be no question."

On a weighty sigh, C.J. leaned back in his chair, tossing his pen on his desk. Frankly, he doubted things would ever feel settled again. With Trish, with Dana…

Oh, God, Dana. The more he was around her, the less he could figure out if she was the best thing, or the worst thing, to happen to him. If she'd had any idea how close he'd come to kissing her the other night…

And then what? Take her to bed? Lead her to believe things were headed in a direction he couldn't, wouldn't go? That much of an idiot, he wasn't.

At least, he hoped not.

He stuffed his thoughts back into some dark, dank corner of his brain and once again met Val's quizzical, and far too discerning, gaze. "If Trish doesn't reappear soon," he said, "the law's on my side. I'd get custody free and clear. It's the limbo that's killing us."

"Us? Oh. You and Dana?"

He let his gaze drift out the window. "Until we know what Trish is really up to, we can't make any permanent arrangements. Which we very much want to do. Need to do. For Ethan's sake."

The older woman eyed him for several seconds, then rose. "Well, I truly hope it all works out. For everybody. And soon. So…subject change—you ever decide who to take to the charity dinner Saturday night?"

Despite the permanent knot in his chest these days, C.J. chuckled. "It's not the prom, Val. And I'm taking Dana."

"'Bout time you did *something* right," she said, and waltzed back out.

Big whoop, he thought. One measly thing out of, what? A hundred? A thousand? Not that he didn't want to do the right thing, or *things*, it was just that he still wasn't sure what, exactly, that was.

Two showings, an office meeting and a closing later, he walked through the garage entrance into his house to be assailed by the mouth-watering aroma of roast pork, the pulse-quickening beat of bluegrass fiddle. Tugging off his tie, he followed his nose to the kitchen, where Dana—oblivious to his arrival—was stirring something in a pot on the stove, her white-shorted fanny wiggling in time to the music. In one corner, safely out of harm's way, Ethan sat up in his playpen, gnawing on a set of plastic keys. The instant he caught sight of C.J., though, the keys went flying. With a huge grin, the baby lifted his arms, yelling "Ba!"

Dana whipped around, her hand splayed across her stomach. As usual, several pieces of her hair had escaped her topknot, curling lazily alongside her neck, the ends teasing her collarbone and the neckline of her loose tank top. She laughed. "Somebody needs to put a bell on you, mister! You're home early!"

Home. The word vibrated between them, like a single note plucked on a violin, clear and pure and destined to fade into nothingness. A word C.J. had never associated with this house. Or any other place he'd ever lived, for that matter. A concept he'd never associated with *himself,* he realized as he set down his briefcase and scooped up his baby son, who began to excitedly babble about his day.

C.J. stood there, literally soaking up his baby's slobbery smile. At that moment, he felt as though he'd stepped into some family sitcom, where no matter what tried to rip apart the characters during the course of the episode, family ties always triumphed in the end. Except real life wasn't a sitcom, and the habit of a lifetime wasn't going to be fixed in twenty-two minutes.

"What's all this?" he asked, deliberately derailing his own train of thought.

"Nothing 'all this' about it. Business was slow so I took off early, figured I might as well throw the pork in the oven. We're eating in the dining room, by the way."

He glanced toward the room in question, saw the table set with place mats, cloth napkins, candlesticks. A *centerpiece,* for God's sake.

"I never eat in the dining room," he said.

"Then it's high time you did," she said.

Honest to Pete, she'd had no agenda behind dinner beyond feeding everybody. Roasts were no-brainers, for heaven's sake. As were boiled potatoes and steamed asparagus. Okay, so maybe the gravy was a little tricky, but not if you'd been making it since you were twelve.

And really, she hadn't been trying to impress him or anything with the table setting, she'd just thought it seemed a shame, never using the dining room. The man needed to start appreciating his own house, that's all.

So the look on his face when he'd walked in, smelled the cooking, seen the table, taken that first bite of pork…was icing on the cake. Seriously.

His chuckle when she handed him a dessert dish of Jell-O topped with a fluffy mountain of whipped cream, however… priceless.

They'd progressed to the family room, ostensibly to watch a film. She'd raided her parents' stash of DVDs, hauling back everything from old Hepburn-Tracy flicks to Clint Eastwood westerns, vintage Woody Allen to *Indiana Jones,* eighties-era chick flicks to over-the-top disaster movies. But the slim, colorful cases lay fanned out on the coffee table, temporarily forsaken. Instead, C.J. sat cross-legged on the floor in front of the fireplace with Ethan in his lap, halfheartedly fending off the baby's attempts to steal his whipped cream, and Dana thought, *Yeah, it's like that.*

Or could be, anyway.

"I'd forgotten how good this is," he said.

"Isn't it crazy?" she said, spooning a big glob into her own mouth. "Mama always used to make Jell-O for me when I was feeling down in the dumps."

He lifted one eyebrow. "So it's a comfort food, then?"

"Well, the whipped cream is the comfort food, actually. But squirting whipped cream directly into your mouth is really pathetic."

"Or efficient," he said with a grin. "Go away, cat," he said to Steve, who kept trying to bat at the whipped cream. C.J. held the dish up out of the cat's reach. "Mine. Mine, mine, mine." Ethan's eyes followed the dish, followed by a squawk. C.J. gave her a helpless look, and she giggled.

"Oh, go on, let him have some."

C.J. blew out a sigh, but lowered the dish anyway. Only the poor cat couldn't figure out how to attack something that wouldn't stay still, his head bobbing along with the quivering whipped cream. C.J. laughed, and Ethan chortled, and the cat finally stalked off, thoroughly put out.

"So how's the writing coming?" C.J. asked. Then frowned. "What?"

"Oh, nothing. It's just that I hate that question."

"Oh. Sorry. Why?"

"Because I never know how to answer it. I know you mean well, but—"

"It's okay, I understand. Well, actually, I don't, but if you don't want to talk about it, you don't want to talk about it." He fed another bite of Jell-O to the baby, then said, "One question, though—does anyone else know you're writing?"

"Not really. Well, my parents do," she said on an exhaled breath. "My mother thinks it's silly."

His forehead creased. "Has she read any of it?"

"I doubt that would make a difference. It's all a little too pie in the sky for her. Offends her practical sensibilities."

"Because it's a risk, you mean?"

"I suppose. She had enough trouble dealing with me going into business with Mercy and Cass, instead of getting a nice, secure accounting job with some well-established firm." A smile flickered over her lips. "She worries."

His dessert finished, C.J. set the dish up on the coffee table, then turned Ethan around to face him. Laughing, the baby dug his feet into the carpet and pushed up, clutching the front of C.J.'s shirt.

"Hey, look at you, hot stuff!" he said, clearly delighted, only to immediately suck in a breath. "Oh, God—when do they start walking?"

"Whenever they're ready. Around a year, maybe later. He has to crawl first, though. At least, so I gather."

And will I even be in the picture when that happens?

The thought pricked the haze of contentment she'd let herself be lulled into, propelling her to her feet to gather dessert dishes, which she carted back into the kitchen. C.J. followed, the baby in his arms.

"Hey. What's wrong?"

"Nothing. Really," she said with a forced smile when he frowned at her. "Just one of my moods again." Then, because melancholy always led to masochism, she said, "So how exactly did you end up with my cousin, anyway?"

Clearly startled, C.J. pushed out a short laugh. "Where on earth did that come from?"

"I'm a chronic scab-picker, what can I tell you?"

He held her gaze in his for several seconds, then sighed.

"Trish had quit, maybe a week before, I don't really remember. I was the only one in the office when she came in to pick up her last paycheck, except I had a little trouble finding it since Val had put it someplace 'safe.' Anyway, by the time I did, your cousin seemed very distraught. So...I asked her if she wanted to go get a drink." His mouth pulled flat. "And things...took their course."

She opened the dishwasher, started loading their dinner plates. "I see."

"I'm not proud of it, Dana," he finished softly. "It shouldn't have happened. But I didn't take advantage of her, if that's what you're thinking. Even if I did take advantage of...the situation. Just so you know, however," he said, shifting the baby in his arms, "I don't do that anymore. Start something I have no intention of finishing, I mean." He smiled tiredly. "It gets old."

"Yes," Dana said carefully, once again all too aware of the warning in his words, no matter how mildly they'd been delivered. "I can see how it would. Well. Thanks. For being honest with me."

"It's the least I can do," he said, and she thought, *Geez, story of my life or what?*

"Like hell you can wear that," Mercy said, her face a study in horror.

Dana looked down at the black charmeuse tunic and ankle-length skirt, still in its transparent shroud from the cleaners, she was holding up to her front. They'd just locked up for the night, leaving only a couple of spotlights on in the front of the store, and Dana had—in a clearly misdirected moment—decided to show her partners what she was wearing. "What's wrong with it?"

"You'll look like a leech?"

"Don't be ridiculous. It's even got sparklies. See?" She wiggled the bag in front of Mercy, who recoiled.

"Okay, a leech with a Cher fixation."

Dana looked to Cass, who was also going to the shindig. Under duress, apparently. Blake had insisted it would "do her good" to get out and mingle, although, according to Cass, all she really wanted to do was stay home and sleep.

"What are you wearing?" Dana now asked the blonde.

"Some red jersey number I've had forever."

Mercy blinked. "As in, the slinky little thing you wore to my sister's wedding? The one with no back? And not a whole lot of front, either, as I recall?"

"That would be the one."

Mercy gave Dana a pointed look.

"These hips don't do slinky, Merce," she said. "They do…softly draped."

"Yeah, well, your hips need to break out of their rut. Hold on." Mercy vanished into the back to return a second later with something…*not* softly draped. Or black. But not, at least, slinky, either. "Which is why I brought this. The color will go great with your hair, don't you think?"

"Where did you get that?" Dana asked. "And why is it here?"

"From Anita, and because I consider it both an honor and my duty to save you from yourself. Anyway, 'Nita's more or less your size. But instead of hiding her body, she *celebrates* it." She thrust the dress at Dana hard enough to make her lose her balance. "If that doesn't work, there are others. And ditch the bra, there's one built right into the dress."

"You might as well humor her," Cass said at Dana's glare. "You know she'll only make your life miserable otherwise."

On a sigh, Dana snatched the dress out of Mercy's hand and tromped to the bathroom to change. Five minutes later, upon glimpsing herself in the narrow, full-length mirror on the back of the bathroom door, she let out a shriek.

"Let us see, let us see!" she heard from the other side of the door.

"No way! For God's sake, I'd put somebody's eye out in this thing! No! Don't open the door!"

Too late. There stood her partners, one grinning like a loon, the other gasping.

"Get your butt out here," Mercy said, grabbing Dana's wrist and yanking her through the door, "so we can get the full effect."

"Yeah, *full* is right," Dana mumbled, then swung a pleading glance in Cass's direction. "Tell her I can't possibly wear this."

After a pause, during which Dana assumed Cass was working to get back her voice, the blonde said, "Honey, don't take this the wrong way, but I have never, ever seen you look better."

"See, Merce, what did I tell y—" Dana's eyes cut back to Cass. "*What* did you say?"

"You look unbelievably gorgeous. I swear."

"These go with it," Mercy said, handing Dana—who was too busy gawking open-mouthed at Cass—a small silver box, already open. Inside lay a pair of outrageously ornate chandelier earrings that, sad to say, immediately made Dana's mouth water.

"Ohhhh," she said on a soft sigh, almost not caring when she caught Mercy conspiratorially poking Cass in the arm.

He couldn't take his eyes off of her in that dress.

Neither could any other straight man in the room. Including Cass's husband Blake, who'd been trying so hard all through dinner *not* to stare at Dana's breasts. C.J. almost felt sorry for the poor bastard. But who could blame him? Dear God, they were magnificent.

She was magnificent. And if C.J. found himself occasionally battling the urge to deck every guy whose eyes lingered a little longer over that magnificence than he would have preferred…

Man, this protective business really packed a wallop.

Not that Dana needed protecting. Except, perhaps, from him.

His reaction, when she'd come out of her room, knocked him clear into next week. The dress, in some shiny fabric the same lush, deep blue of the sky just before nightfall, was truly a marvel of engineering, both lovingly and aggressively displaying Dana's no-holds-barred curves to perfection. But it was the woman inside the dress who'd set his pulse rate off the charts, the tilt of her chin that said *Yes, I know* exactly *how I look in this dress,* warring with the remnants of insecurity in her eyes, that made him want to do things to her, *for* her, he had no right to do. That he'd told her as considerately as he could he *wouldn't* do.

So, yes, he'd given her an appreciative whistle, but he'd otherwise played it cool. Careful. Not letting on how much he ached to trail his fingertips along the line of her jaw, down her neck, across the swells of those flawless, oh-God-just-kill-me-now breasts.

He tore his gaze away to scan the ballroom, recognizing probably half the people there. Including more than one woman he'd dated over the past decade. All of them beautiful, stylish, classy. Some of them at least momentarily intriguing. Or so he'd thought at the time. And yet, he couldn't remember ever anticipating being with any of them the way he did with Dana, simply preparing a meal together, or giving Ethan a bath, or just sitting out by the pool, shooting the breeze.

As if hearing his thoughts, she glanced over, a quizzical smile playing over her lips, and the thought of her leaving nearly made him dizzy.

Dinner over, the band started to play a run-of-the-mill pop

standard that got people up and moving, but not too fast. C.J. suddenly felt, if not old, at least close enough to middle age to give him pause. The other couples at their table, including Cass and Blake, all headed toward the dance floor; C.J. smiled over at Dana.

"Shall we?"

"Uh, thanks, but no. I am, without a doubt, the world's worst dancer."

"I don't believe that. I've seen your moves in the kitchen."

She laughed. "Sorry, you'll have to take my word for it.... What are you doing?" she said on a tiny squeal when he stood, took her by the hand, and led her out on the dance floor anyway. "I told you—"

"Hush," he said, settling one hand at the small of her back, tucking one of hers against his chest. Stupid move, but whatcha gonna do? "It's a slow dance, all we have to do is stand here and sway. Even you can sway, can't you?"

"And you're not afraid people will get the wrong idea?"

"Because we're swaying?"

"Because of the position we're in while we're swaying."

"Can't sway without touching," he said, pulling her closer to avoid colliding with another couple. "It's in the rulebook."

"And what rulebook would that be—?"

"C.J.! My goodness, I've been trying to catch your eye all night!"

Damn. And he'd been doing everything in his power to avoid hers.

"Cybill," he said smoothly, even as Dana jerked out of his arms, bumping into the person behind her. Grabbing her hand to keep her from bolting (which earned him a brief but potent glare), C.J. turned, meeting the other woman's glossy, predatory smile with a cool one of his own. Her nipples blatantly on display in a shimmery, silvery gown that looked more like something she'd wear to bed than a charity function, she was a mere illusion of womanhood, he realized, reeking of designer perfume and desperation.

"You are *such* a bad man," Cybill said on a breathy laugh, completely ignoring Dana. "Pawning me off on that Bill person when I called your office and specifically asked for you."

C.J. frowned. "I'm sorry, I don't remember getting a message."

"Oh, this was a couple of weeks ago. Silly me, I should have used my maiden name, I forgot you wouldn't have known my married one, which I only use for the children's sake." A cool, spindly hand landed on his arm. "Bill said you'd been really tied up, but I said I'd be more than willing to wait—" a brief glance speared in Dana's direction "—until things had, um, calmed down." Her smile veered back to C.J. "I'm in no hurry."

He wondered now how he'd ever found Cybill and her ilk even momentarily appealing. Women who, for whatever reason, felt they were somehow entitled to whatever they wanted.

"I'm very flattered," he said, "but unfortunately I don't see my schedule easing anytime in the foreseeable future. And I can assure you, you're in excellent hands with Bill." He placed his hand at the base of Dana's spine, gently tugging her to him. "You remember Dana Malone, don't you?"

Recovering quickly from C.J.'s less-than-subtle brush-off, the woman blinked once, then turned her puppetlike smile on Dana. "Of course I do. A *client* of C.J.'s, isn't that right? Did you two happen to run into each other here?"

Offended for Dana at the presumption, he casually roped one arm around her shoulders, knowing he'd pay dearly for the unspoken *What the heck are you doing?* practically vibrating from her as a result. "No, actually. We came together."

Her smile frozen in place, Cybill said, "Well, isn't that

nice?" Then, to Dana, "And don't you look absolutely adorable in that dress! I'd never have the nerve to wear something that…revealing."

"I suppose it helps to have something to reveal," Dana said sweetly.

C.J. managed, barely, to choke down the laugh. "Well, point to you," Cybill said with a watery laugh of her own, the twin spots of color on her thin-skinned cheekbones completely ruining the makeup he guessed she'd spent hours perfecting. She lifted her hand, as though to touch him again, only to apparently think better of it. "I'll call you," she said.

Unbelievable. "You'd only be wasting your time," he said, as kindly, but as firmly, as he knew how. Something like defeat flickered in her eyes for a moment before, on a tiny nod, she spun around and took off across the dance floor.

Just as Dana did the same thing in the opposite direction.

She heard his "Dana! Dana, wait…!" behind her as she slalomed around a half dozen couples toward Cass and Blake, who were standing at their table, checking the room with concerned looks on their faces. But suddenly, she'd had it. With the evening, with C.J., with…everything.

"Oh, good," Cass said when Dana got to the table, "we didn't want to disappear without telling you we were leaving, but I've got to get back and feed Jason. So much for my wild partying days—"

"Could I get a ride with you guys?"

"What? I mean, of course, but—"

Dana let out a small, startled yelp when C.J. grabbed her hand, pulling her around to face him. "Honey, I apologize, I know that was rude—"

"Yeah, it was." She yanked her hand from his, snatched her evening bag off the table. Despite his crowding her, she managed to face him, holding the bag up between them like a tiny, jeweled shield. "I'm leaving with Cass and Blake."

"If you want to go, I can take you home."

"And where exactly is that, C.J.? No—*what* is that?"

For several painfully awkward seconds, C.J.'s gaze swam in hers. Until he finally said, on a clearly frustrated breath, "Damned if I know." Only then he narrowed his gaze at her, throwing her completely off guard with, "But that's not what this is about, is it?"

Dana started when Cass touched her arm. "How about we meet you out front in five minutes?" she said, then left without giving Dana a chance to protest. Taking his cue, C.J. cupped Dana's elbow and led her outside. *Don't touch me,* she wanted to scream, but she'd already caused enough of a kerfuffle for one night. Despite their attempts at keeping their voices low and civilized, people had begun to stare.

Once outside, a valet who barely looked old enough to drive pounced on them; C.J. waved him away. Dana vaguely wondered where her ride was, deciding they must have gone for a short, discreet drive to give C.J. and her time to talk.

Except she didn't want to talk, she wanted to stew. She wanted to be left alone to berate herself for being the wussiest of the wusses, for not even having enough willpower to resist falling for someone she knew—knew!—would never fall for her. Hell, would never even be *attracted* to her.

But alas, being alone was not meant to be. At least, not until she got through the next five minutes. Or maybe four, if she was lucky.

"I take it this means you're going back to your place?" C.J. asked.

She nodded. They'd left Ethan with her parents; her mother had said it made no sense for them to disturb the baby by picking him up late, that they might as well let him stay until morning.

"Dana," C.J. said softly, "look at me. Please."

The last thing she wanted to do. But God forbid she came across as childish and petulant. When she finally twisted her head, he said, "Look, you can spend the night wherever you want. As long as you tell me what the hell is going on."

She looked away again. "I'm not sure I can."

"You? At a loss for words?"

"It's not the words, it's…" She walked over and sat on a low wall flanking the entrance, farther away from the clutch of valets, laughing and talking under a drooping old cottonwood. Even now, she was still more than half-tempted to keep her feelings to herself, to at least hang on to some semblance of dignity. But what was the point? Heaven knew how long their lives would be entwined because of Ethan. Did she really want to spend the next, oh, twenty years or more pretending?

The very thought made her queasy. So she looked up and said, "I thought I could do this, but I can't."

"Do what?"

"Whatever it is we're doing. Trying to figure out where the boundaries are, mostly."

"I'm sorry…I thought…" C.J.'s pricey loafers scuffed the mica-glittery pavement as he came closer. "I thought we were doing okay," he said on a sigh, sitting beside her.

"Yeah. I did, too."

She could feel his gaze on the side of her face. "So what happened?"

There she stood, on the very edge of the cliff. But instead of jumping, she backed up and said, "Good Lord…what on earth did you ever see in that woman? She has all the substance of a saltine."

"Hey, don't knock saltines. There may not be much to them, but at least you always know what you're getting."

Dana snorted. "Is that what's bothering you? Cybill? Because I thought it was pretty obvious it was all one-sided."

"No, not her, precisely. What she represents."

"I don't understand."

"The kind of woman you're used to being with. To…" *Just spit it out, sister.* "To taking to bed."

C.J.'s brows shot up. "They weren't all like Cybill, believe me—" He shut his eyes, a look of extreme consternation flattening his mouth. "That didn't come out quite the way I intended. Okay, yeah, I've dated more than a few women along the way. But I didn't sleep with all of them. Hell, I didn't sleep with *most* of them."

"And yet you did with my cousin," she said, earning her a flash of guilt in response. "Dammit, C.J.," she said softly. "Even Trish had one night with you. Which is more than I'll ever get, isn't it?"

The silence that followed told her everything she needed to know. Thank God, then, the Carters' SUV glided to the curb just at that moment. Dana stood up and walked over to the car, cringing when C.J. opened the back door for her, claiming her hand before she could duck into the backseat. He was close enough for her to smell his cologne, the fruity tang of wine on his breath. Close enough for her to see the *"I'm sorry"* in his eyes. A brief, tortured smile flickered on his lips. "You're not a saltine, Dana. You're more like…"

"Cracked wheat?"

He blew out a breath, looking away, then met her gaze again, shaking his head slightly as if not quite able to decide what to make of her. "I'll pick Ethan up from your parents' place tomorrow morning," he said. "You might want to warn them."

Then he walked away, handing his ticket to one of the valets. He glanced over, his eyes touching hers once more, but this time she couldn't even begin to decipher what was going on behind them.

"Sweetie? Are you okay?" Cass asked the moment Dana sank into the butter-soft backseat.

"I'm fine."

Two beats. Maybe three. Then, "Wanna spend the night with us?"

The mere thought of all those people in residence at the Carters was enough to pull out a tiny smile. "Maybe another time. But thanks for the offer."

Ten minutes later she was in her own apartment, prying off a spike-heeled sandal and thinking, irritably, *Now what?*

Get some air in here, that's what. The sandals dangling from one finger, she padded from room to room, opening windows, turning on fans. Not allowing herself to think. Because, really, what was there to think about? She'd said her piece, C.J. had clearly been appalled, and now she'd made more of a mess of things than they already were.

Good going, babe.

Much to her chagrin, there was absolutely nothing even remotely comforting in the fridge. Or in any of the cupboards. She couldn't even make quickie Jell-O because she'd forgotten to refill the ice cube trays. Besides which there was no whipped cream. And, sorry, but as a means of solace, sugar-free fake lemonade wasn't gonna cut it.

The air shuddered around her as she slammed shut the refrigerator door, then stomped to her bedroom, only to discover, after contorting herself into several Kama Sutra–worthy positions, that getting into the dress had been a whole heck of a lot easier than getting out of it. Finally, though, the thing lay on the carpet, like the shucked shell of some large blue insect, as everything that had been confined or hoisted or cinched in spread gratefully back to normal. Really, she thought as she massaged the welts on her ribs, if God had meant her breasts to sit up around her chin, He would have put them there to begin with—

The doorbell rang.

The doorbell rang?

Dana grabbed an old Victoria's Secret kimono out of her closet, still trying to arrange it around her newly freed body when she heard C.J.'s "It's me, open up."

She yanked open the door, the bizarre Hawaiian shirt barely registering before he'd grabbed her by the shoulders so hard she gasped.

"Dammit, Dana! Don't you get it?" Anguish contorted his mouth, choked his words. "I *like* you! I… Oh, *hell!*"

Then he planted one on her she'd remember until her dying day.

He almost groaned in relief when their mouths met, as he poured every ounce of the frustration and need that had built up over the past few weeks into that single, albeit noteworthy kiss. And she kissed him right back, boy, just as hard, just as eager, her fingers curling inside his waistband, tugging him closer…

She teetered for a second when he jerked away, her shoulders soft and slippery beneath his grip. Teetered again when he gently shook her, her hair shuddering around her shoulders.

"How in the hell could you have thought I wasn't attracted to you?"

Slowly, those soft gray-green eyes came into focus, followed by twin creases setting up camp between her brows. "Where would you like me to start?"

With something like a stifled howl, C.J. released her and stumbled over to her sofa in the nearly dark room. He dropped like a stone, his head in his hands, hoping against hope to put his brain back in charge before it shorted out completely.

Talking was all he'd intended to do. Everything he'd wanted to say had been right on the tip of his tongue.

Which had then gone and gotten real cozy with hers. Damn.

He looked up. Oh, God. She was naked under that flimsy little robe, wasn't she? "And if I had come on to you, what would you have thought?"

"Excuse me, but isn't that what you just did?"

"I mean, before."

"Oh, I don't know…." She crossed her arms under her breasts. "That maybe I wasn't chopped liver?"

"Try again," he said wearily, and after a moment he heard a soft "Ohhh," followed by the sofa sinking when she sat beside him.

He heard the release of her breath. "Okay, I guess I would have wondered if you were just, you know. Being kind."

"Or a bastard."

"That, too." Several beats passed. Then, "I take it you weren't being *kind* just then."

He laughed. "No."

"And the other?"

They sat in silence for several seconds, both staring into the darkness, before C.J. finally said, "You want strings, honey. And I don't."

"Oh, for God's sake, C.J.—this isn't about *strings!*"

After a second's recovery from the blast, he said, "Then what *is* this about?"

Dana twisted to face him, folding one leg up underneath her. The robe gapped open, most of one breast softly illuminated in the faint light coming from her bedroom. He didn't even try not to look, and she smiled.

"You really want me?"

"Like you wouldn't believe. But—"

"Geez, I got it, okay?" She hiked her elbow up onto the back of the sofa, her head cradled in her hand. "But you know what? If I can't get Godiva, I'm perfectly happy with Ghirardelli."

"You don't know what you're saying. Hell, *I* don't know what you're saying."

Her gaze was disconcertingly steady for several seconds. Then she brought both hands to her waist, hesitating for barely a moment before deftly undoing the loose knot in her robe sash. A slight shrug and it slithered off her shoulders, a pale blue puddle of silk in the crook of her arms, her lap.

"Is this clearer?"

"Uh…yeah," C.J. said, hoping to hell he didn't look like one of those cartoon characters with his eyeballs out on stalks.

"The point is," she said, leaning forward to cup his jaw in her soft palm, "I know what *you're* saying. So if you're all done being noble, here's where I remind you that I'm a big girl. In more ways than one," she added with a small smile.

"This…is wrong," he said miserably.

"Says who?"

"Me."

"Too bad, you're outvoted," she said, starting to unbutton his shirt.

"And why, exactly, does your vote count more than mine?"

"'Cause I'm the girl," she said, wrinkling her nose at him, and from somewhere deep, deep inside the tangled mess of cells called his brain came the thought, *This could be yours forever,* she *could be yours forever,* and he mentally stuck his fingers in his ears and shouted, *No! Can't hear you, can't hear—*

"Hey," she whispered, apparently misinterpreting his silence as her fingers spread across his chest. "What happens, happens, okay? And with any luck, it'll be lousy and we'll never want to do this again."

"With any luck," he echoed, and gave up the good fight,

easing her back into the cushions, his fingers tangling in her hair as he joined their mouths in a kiss that he'd fully intended to keep tender, gentle. Sweet, almost. Except the cute little she devil in his arms had other ideas, apparently.

Man, could this woman kiss or what?

Man, could he get himself in *deep* or what?

Speaking of getting himself in *deep,* which was looking good for his immediate future... C.J. hauled in a long breath, grateful for her breasts, milk-pale in the scant light, the weightless robe slippery in his fingers as he brushed it away. "You are so damn gorgeous, I can't stand it."

"Okay, C.J.?" she said, nibbling at his neck. "You're already going to get lucky, no need to overdo it."

He lifted himself up, frowning down at her, only to avert his eyes from what sure as hell looked like forgiveness in hers. As if she knew. And understood.

But he didn't want her to be understanding. Or good. Or kind. Or all the things that had brought him to this point to begin with, God help him.

"You think I'm just blowing air up your skirt?" he asked.

"Well, no." She giggled softly. "Since I'm not wearing one."

Actually, the only thing she was wearing at the moment was her perfume, and him, which should have made this one of life's damn-near-perfect moments if it hadn't been for the not-being-able-to-look-in-her-eyes thing. So he moved smartly along to those aspects of the activity that didn't involve locked gazes, thinking, *Okay,* this *I can do.* This *I can give her.* Which, judging from all those sighs and murmurs and clutched fingers in his hair, seemed to be fine with Dana. Except, after some serious breast worship that had her writhing nicely underneath him and had him so hard he thought he'd pass out, he stumbled across a series of angry red marks on her ribcage, visible even in the low light.

"What are these?" he whispered, trying to soothe them with his fingertips, his eyes darting to hers—for only a second—when she winced.

"From that torture device I was wearing tonight."

"Damn. Want me to make it better?"

"Knock yourself out. Um…C.J.?"

"Hmm?"

"There aren't any welts…there…"

"No?" He moved farther down, pressing kiss after soft, lingering kiss in her soft, yielding flesh, as *bastard… bastard…bastard*…played on a continuous loop inside his brain. "My mistake…"

It was hard to tell, what with her crying out and all, when the phone had started to ring. But even after they both froze, listening, hearts pounding, it took another two rings before C.J. finally propelled himself off all that glorious, giving softness and over to the phone, blaring evilly at them from across the room.

He glanced at the lit display, then blew out a breath.

"It's your mother."

Dana instantly sat up, grabbing the phone and trying to shrug back into her robe at the same time. "Mama?…Is Ethan okay?…I know, I'm sorry, I had my cell phone ringer turned off, I forgot to turn it back on. But it's nearly 1:00 a.m., why on earth—?" Right as she'd been about to rake her fingers through her hair, she stilled. "Oh. I see." Her hand dropped. "Uh, yeah, of course. I'll be right over." Then she grimaced, her eyes slanting to his. "Sure. I'll tell him."

She punched the end call button, then sat there, her expression blank, the phone clutched to her chest.

"Dana?" C.J. said softly over the feeling of his chest caving in.

As if coming out of a trance, Dana blinked up at him, then

released a shuddering sigh. "Trish is back," she said, then added, with a rueful grin, "And Mama says to tell you that you may as well come, too."

Chapter Ten

It was like being caught in a hurricane's path, Dana thought as she stood in the doorway to her mother's sewing room, watching her cousin watch Ethan sleep: knowing what was coming didn't make the actual event any less devastating.

"Trish?" she whispered into the half light. The young woman jerked at Dana's voice, her hands tightening around the crib's rails. Anguish radiated from her in palpable waves; in the unforgiving shaft of light seeping into the room from the hallway, Dana could see how thin she'd gotten, the way each vertebrae stood out in relief underneath her cropped top, the jut of a hipbone over the waistband of her low-riding jeans.

"What are you doing here, Dana?"

"Mama called me. She was worried."

"About me?"

"About everything. Come on back to the living room. We need to talk."

Nodding, Trish glanced back at the baby once more, then followed Dana down the narrow, carpeted hallway. Dana's father sat in a wing chair by the picture window in his summer robe and slippers, looking extremely disgruntled; her mother, her hair in curlers and wearing a floral housecoat Dana didn't recognize, stood nearby, arms crossed, frown in place. And in the center of the room, scowling mightily, stood the man she'd been naked with not a half hour before.

Maybe this wasn't the best time to remember that.

"C.J.!" Trish gasped behind her. "Why are *you* here?"

"Because I'm Ethan's father?"

"Trish…" Dana's mother interjected, but C.J. lifted one hand.

"This is between Trish and me, Mrs. Malone," he said softly, the slight curve of his lips doing little to ease the ferocity hard-edging his features. "And Dana."

Clearly befuddled, Trish's distressed eyes darted from Dana to C.J. and back again, before she sank onto the edge of the sofa and began to quietly weep, her face in her hands. If she'd hoped to generate sympathy, it wasn't working, judging from the decided lack of people rushing to her side to offer comfort. Only then she lifted her soggy face and said to C.J., "Except…except he's *not* yours."

Well, that got everyone's attention. Lord, Dana thought her poor father would have another heart attack. If not her mother. As for C.J., he was obviously struggling to check his anger. "Actually, he is."

Trish blanched. "But that's not possible. I mean, I was already…I thought I was…" She swallowed. "Are you sure?"

"Positive. Funny, but when a woman names me as the father of her baby—especially a woman who *abandons* her baby—you better believe I'm going to get proof."

"I didn't abandon him!" Trish's brown eyes took up nearly half her gaunt face. "God, you make it sound like…like I'm some mental case who leaves her baby in the bathroom, or in a trash can somewhere! I made absolutely sure Dana saw him before I drove away!"

"Maybe you didn't endanger him," C.J. said with a lethal softness that made Dana's hair stand up on the back of her neck, "but you still dumped him on Dana and vanished, leaving no way to get in touch with you. And now you say you didn't think I was Ethan's father? Exactly what kind of con were you trying to pull?"

Wedged as far into the sofa cushions as she could possibly go, Trish shook her head, her long, dishwater blond hair gleaming dully. "I wasn't...I didn't mean..." Apology glittered in her eyes when she scanned the room, looking at each of them in turn, before the whole story came tumbling out in semicoherent chunks—that she'd thought she was pregnant by someone else, how she'd been so bummed out that night she ended up with C.J., how she didn't think of putting his name on the birth certificate until after the baby was born and she was already involved with this other dude who really wasn't into kids, you know?

"And then everything completely fell apart. Randall left me, too, and I wasn't making enough to pay for day care, and..." She shrugged with great effort, as though her shoulders were weighted with sandbags. Her eyes at last landed on Dana. "I'm sorry, Dana, I know I took the coward's way out, but I knew how much you'd always wanted kids, and it seemed so ironic that here I was with a kid I couldn't take care of, while you wanted one so badly and couldn't have any. I was worn out and scared and desperate to make sure Ethan would be taken care of better than I could. And I knew you'd never put him in foster care."

"Then why on earth didn't you just *ask* for help?" Dana's mother said.

"Because…because I couldn't stand to see that look in y'all's eyes. Yes, that look right there, Aunt Faye," she said, waggling her finger in a move so much like her aunt's that, under other circumstances, Dana might have laughed.

Instead, she said, keeping her voice as steady as she could manage, "And now you want him back?"

After a long moment, Trish nodded, her eyes glittering. Only everybody jumped when C.J. said, "For how long, Trish? Until you freak out a second time, or a third or fourth?"

"C.J." Dana closed both her hands around his rigid fist, hoping to deflate his anger. But when his gaze jerked to hers, she saw, way past the immediate fury, a raw pain that she realized in an instant had nothing to do with Trish and Ethan.

"No!" Trish said, as Dana caught her mother's all-too-perceptive frown, her glance in Dana's father's direction. "That's not gonna happen! Not this time, I swear! I…I found a pretty good job in Vegas, I've got a nice place and can afford to pay somebody to watch him for me while I work. Look, I'm really sorry for putting everybody through this, but…but I didn't realize how much I'd miss my baby."

"Except you've obviously forgotten something," C.J. said. When she turned perplexed eyes to his, he said, "I *am* his father. And no way in hell am I giving you custody. Not after the stunt you pulled."

Confusion wrinkled her forehead. "But you don't even want kids."

"So why in the name of God did you set me up?"

Leaning forward, her hands tucked around her knees, Trish stared at the coffee table for several seconds before saying, "I was scared. And you were the only decent guy I knew. I guess I figured, if nothing else, you'd provide for Ethan."

Her gaze shifted to Dana. "That was one of the reasons I thought it wouldn't be so bad, if I left him with you, because

I knew you'd contact C.J. Only then I started to feel bad about tricking you," she said to C.J. "Especially now that I want him back." Her hands shoved into her hair, she collapsed back into the cushions. "Oh, man…I've really screwed things up, haven't I?"

"Yes, you have," C.J. said. Then he sighed. "But you haven't screwed things up entirely on your own. And no, that doesn't mean you're off the hook," he said when hope sprang to life in her eyes. "Maybe I *didn't* want kids, but I want this one. And damned if I'd ever do to him what you did. How do you think a judge would feel about that, Trish?"

At that, a determination such as Dana had never seen in her cousin's expression hardened her features. "No matter what, I'm his mama. Yes, I freaked, I'll admit that. And I made mistakes. But nobody can say I neglected him. I love that little boy to death, I swear. How I thought I could just walk away from him—"

"But you did," Dana's mother put in, showing remarkable restraint in having held out this long, Dana thought. And indeed, now she planted herself on the sofa, taking Trish's hand and giving her that now-you-will-listen-to-*me* look that could still make Dana quake in her boots.

"Patricia Elizabeth, all the time you lived here your uncle and I watched you dig yourself into more holes than a prairie dog. But even you have to admit this one's bigger and deeper than all the rest put together. Seems to me it's going to take longer than a couple of weeks and a few promises to dig yourself out."

"I know, but—"

"Honey, I don't doubt you love this baby. Anybody could see you'd taken good care of him. And God knows, I've been waiting for you to turn over a new leaf for a long, long time. But right now, this isn't about you. It's about what's best for your little boy."

"I know that, Aunt Faye," Trish said, defiance edging her words. "Why do you think I came back for him?"

"To appease your own conscience, most likely."

"That's not true!"

"Maybe not. But neither is anything going to be decided tonight. It's late," the older woman said, taking in everyone in the room. "We all need to get to bed. Or back to it, as the case may be. You can stay here, Trish, if you like—"

"If she stays here," C.J. said, "Ethan comes with me.'"

Trish swung around, her face scarlet. "I'm not gonna run off with him, C.J.!"

"No, you're not. Because I'm not giving you the chance."

"You don't trust me?"

"I'm sorry, Trish," he said. "At some point, maybe I'll feel more in a forgiving mood. But not tonight."

Trembling, her eyes sheened with tears, Trish grabbed her purse, muttered something about getting out of everybody's hair, and stormed out of the house.

And nobody—not even Dana's mother, amazingly enough—tried to stop her.

When Dana looked around afterward, however, C.J. had disappeared.

"He went to check on the baby," her mother said, snagging her hand to keep her from going after him. Giving her one of her looks. "You've done it, haven't you? Gone and lost your heart to that man, just like I was afraid you would."

"Actually, last time I checked, my heart was still safely inside my own chest." When the corners of her mother's mouth turned down, she added, "It's okay, Mama. Trust me," then pulled away before the woman could work up a full head of steam.

Of course, she thought as she found C.J. in almost the same position as she had Trish earlier, holding on to the rails of her old crib, staring down at the sleeping baby, that all depended on how one defined *okay*. For sure, things weren't the same between her and C.J. than they had been an orgasm ago. Some lines, you just couldn't cross back over. Nor did she want to. Still and all, they were talking a whole new ballgame, with all new rules.

Only she doubted she and C.J. were playing by the same ones now anymore than they had been.

He glanced up at her entrance, that same tight, weary smile stretched across his mouth, before returning his gaze to the baby. He reached into the crib, carefully rubbing Ethan's back between his tiny shoulder blades.

"It's not that I don't sympathize with how Trish feels…."

"C.J., really, you don't have to explain. Besides, maybe— hopefully—this was a corner-turning moment for her. All her life she's done whatever pops into her head at the moment, screw the consequences. It had to stop sometime."

He nodded, moving his hand up to cup his son's head. "After my mother died, my father…" He took a breath, his voice so low Dana could barely hear him. "My father withdrew into his own world. And didn't bother to take me with him. Nothing mattered but his business. No matter what I did, how hard I tried to please him…" One trembling thumb stroked the baby's temple, over and over. "He gave me everything I wanted—cars, ski trips with classmates, you name it—except the one thing I needed most. Eventually I stopped trying."

Dana leaned against the crib, almost but not quite touching him. "Want me to go beat him up for you?" At his low chuckle, she ventured, "You're not your father, C.J. In case you haven't figured that out."

"No. I can't imagine ever doing to Ethan what my father did to me. But there's still something missing. Although…" He hauled in a huge breath, let it slowly out. "When you heard me on the phone the other night? I was basically reading him the riot act, for all those years he basically ignored me."

"What did he say?" she asked gently.

"Nothing. No apology, no explanation." He shook his head, then pushed away from the crib. "Come on, let's get out of here, let your folks get back to bed."

Except, as they left the room, something nagged at her, that she had a very strong feeling she hadn't heard the whole story. Could C.J.'s inability to forge a lasting relationship really stem simply from his father's neglect, as painful as that must have been? Except what did it matter, in the long run? By now, his resistance was so ingrained, so intractable, the actual cause probably no longer even played into it.

And yet he clearly adored his son.

Hmm. Maybe orchids *could* grow in Antarctica, if given the right conditions.

If they didn't know it was forty below outside the greenhouse.

If someone had the guts to build a greenhouse in Antarctica to begin with.

Not that she could come right out and say any of this to the poor guy's face. That really would send him screaming in the opposite direction. No, this was going to take a little finessing, a bit of good old Southern gal subterfuge. But if *she* didn't believe C.J. capable of change, who would?

Saying she'd meet him at the car, Dana begged off to use the bathroom. Only C.J. had barely gotten to the end of the hall when she heard her father say, "Got a moment, son?"

Man, it had been a long time since he'd been on the receiving end of a father's take-no-prisoners glare. Didn't like it when he'd been seventeen, liked it even less now. Especially since Gene Malone didn't look any more comfortable about the prospective conversation than C.J.

"Let's go on outside," he said. "So the women can't hear us."

"You planning on whupping my butt?"

A brief smile flashed over the man's droopy features, but the look in his eyes said C.J. was treading on very thin ice. "If this had been twenty years ago, I just might." He opened the front door and gestured for C.J. to precede him outside.

The house had no porch to speak of, only a narrow slab of concrete underneath a three-foot overhang. But Gene led C.J. out farther into the small front yard, a circle of grass bordered by crushed rock, sage, a Spanish broom still in flower, its spicy fragrance skating on the cool, feathery breeze. "Lookit that," the older man said. "Even with all the city lights, you can still see the stars. Back home it'd be so hazy with humidity, the sky would be nothing but a big, blank slate." Then he glanced over, his mouth tilted up on one side. "*Whup,* huh?" he said over the incessant chirp of a nearby cricket. "Didn't figure you for a country boy."

"Not exactly. But growing up in the South, you're bound to pick up an expression or two."

A heavy silence preceded, "Seems to me maybe there's one or two other things you should've picked up while you were at it. I don't know what the term is now, but back in my day we called what you're doing tomcatting."

Yeah, he'd known this was coming, ever since he'd caught Dana's parents' exchanged glances when he and Dana had arrived. Together. "Look, I know this looks bad—"

"*Bad* doesn't even begin to cover it. Correct me if I'm wrong, but you spend one night with my niece, get her pregnant, and now you're getting cozy with my daughter? And there's no sense in denying it, it's pretty obvious something's goin' on between you. Now I know you and Dana are both adults, and in theory I've got no right sticking my nose into your business, but…"

His hands rammed into his robe pockets, Dana's father looked across the street. "Dana might be just another woman to you, but she's Faye's and my only child. The one thing they don't tell you, when you become a parent, is that there's no statute of limitation on worrying about your kid."

A concept his own father wouldn't have understood, C.J. thought bitterly, if the words had been branded across his chest. "Your daughter's anything but 'just another woman' to me, Mr. Malone," he said quietly.

Gene looked over. "So you're serious about her?"

"I'm serious about…not wanting to hurt her."

A moment passed. Then, "She tell you about Gil?"

"Gil? No, I don't think so."

"Oh, you'd know if she'd mentioned him. She and Gil had gone together, I don't know, more than two years. She was crazy about him. And we thought he was crazy about her. They were knee-deep in wedding plans when Dana found out she wouldn't be able to have children. And that was that."

"He broke it off?"

"Guess you'd call it that. When he didn't come see Dana in the hospital, or even send her flowers, she got the message." Gene paused. "Had her wedding dress all picked out and everything." The older man's eyes cut to C.J.'s. "Far as her mother and I know, she hasn't dated anybody since—"

"For heaven's sake, Daddy!" Dana said in a hushed voice from the doorway, bustling in their direction. "The Flannigans' bedroom isn't even twenty feet away!"

"They're out of town," her father said, protectiveness once again flashing across his features. Still, how much was too much? God knew C.J. had no intention of tossing his son to the wolves to fend for himself, as his own father had more or less done to him, but neither was it realistic—or even wise— to try protecting a child from ever getting hurt.

Exhaustion suddenly swamped him. As it obviously had Dana, who looked ready to drop, bracing her hand on her father's arm before stretching up on wobbly tiptoe to kiss him on his cheek. "I'll call you guys in the morning," she said, then let C.J. steer her to his car.

Once there, silence jangled between them, until they reached the end of the block and C.J. signaled to turn right. To return to her apartment.

"No," she said softly. "Left."

Not looking at her, he tapped the steering wheel with his thumbs. "You sure?"

"If it's what I want? Yes. Unless *you're* not—"

He changed the turn signal, headed west. A few seconds later, she said, "I'm sure you're right. That no judge in his or her right mind would let Trish take Ethan away from you. Not with her history of instability."

While he appreciated Dana's support, her words didn't comfort him as much as he would have thought. Now the silence was his to break. "So you're really okay with what happened between your cousin and me?" When she didn't answer, he glanced over to see her frowning. He returned his gaze to the nearly empty street as the car glided through pools of viscous, peach-colored light from the overhead halogens. "Or at least dealing with it?"

She laughed faintly. "For the most part. And by the way, whatever we're doing *is* nobody's business but ours."

"Your parents might take exception to that."

After a noisy yawn, she slumped down into her seat, watching him. "My father told you about Gil, didn't he?"

There was no point dissembling. "How'd you know?"

"Intuition?"

It clicked. "You overheard."

"Enough."

"So why didn't *you* tell me about him?"

She shrugged. "Because I didn't want to play the pity card? Because it's past history? Because it has nothing to do with…" She stopped herself.

"Us?"

"Anything."

"He really left you because you couldn't have children?"

"He really did."

"The creep never heard of adoption?"

"And waste all those sperm?" He could feel more than see her smile. "Let me guess. Your fists are itching."

"You have no idea."

"C.J.?" she said after a moment. When he cut his eyes to hers, she said, "I'm not gonna lie, I was devastated when Gil dumped me. He hurt me worse than I've ever been hurt by another human being, and I was very tender for a long, long time. Because I'd trusted him, because he'd made promises to me. Promises that went right out the window when I no longer fit his image of what a perfect wife should be. Here I'd thought for sure I'd finally found someone who'd accept me for who I was…" She faced front again. "He was a liar, basically. You're not."

"Still—"

"Yes, you have issues. But at least you're honest. And since you haven't made any promises, there aren't any to break. I know exactly where I stand. Or more to the point, where you do. No surprises, no curveballs, no—" she yawned "—pain."

"And you don't think you're deluding yourself?"

Her laugh startled him. "No, *deluding* myself would be pretending there's more between us than there is." Her fingertips landed on his wrist. "I may not be the most experienced gal in the land, but I haven't been a starry-eyed virgin for some time. I do know when a man's in it just for the sex. And that's okay, as long as everybody's—" another yawn "—on the same page."

C.J.'s hand tightened around the steering wheel. "I'm not in it 'just for the sex,' Dana. There is more to this than… that."

But when he looked over, she was down for the count, her head tilted to one side against the seat, her breathing slowing, deepening.

God help him, he was drowning here.

It was nuts. On the surface, could this be any more perfect? The company, the companionship, the luscious body of a warm, generous, undemanding woman who expected nothing more than his respect and honesty? By rights, he should feel like the luckiest SOB on the face of the planet.

So the "feeling lucky" thing could kick in anytime now. *Any*time.

His heart punishing his ribs, C.J. drove on, steadily, smoothly, navigating the nearly empty streets a helluva lot easier than he was navigating his own life these days. All those years of striving for an uncomplicated, undemanding existence…

"Oh, shut up," he muttered to that rotten little whoever, or whatever, still laughing his/her/its butt off, even weeks after his discovery that his vasectomy had gone kaflooey.

Minutes later, he pulled into his garage and cut the engine. "Hey," he whispered, stroking Dana's cheek. "We're ho…here."

"Hmm?" She blinked awake, yawning again as she stared blankly out the window. "Oh. Right. Don't even tell me what time it is," she said, pushing open her door. "I don't want to know."

His arm securely around her waist, C.J. guided her inside, amazed to realize how much he'd grown accustomed to Ethan's presence in the house, how off-kilter it already felt not having him there. And he knew, with a sudden clarity that stole his breath, exactly how shattered he'd feel if some judge decided the baby *was* better off with his mother, if Trish took him away.

Who'da thunk it?

"No, this way," he said when Dana leaned toward "her," room, instead steering her toward his.

She came to a dead, if wobbly, halt, looking up at him. "I hog the bed."

"It's a big bed."

"And so it is," she said, even though he wasn't so much of a fool as to think she hadn't at least peeked in here at *some* point during the past two weeks. He caught her head shake at the clothes still piled in the chair before she crashed like a felled tree, fully clothed, on top of the comforter. She curled up on her side, wadding one of the down pillows under her cheek.

"Mmm…" she breathed, and passed out again.

He stood there, watching her sleep, this bundle of contradictions whose very presence made his chest constrict, with joy, longing, regret…this unassuming woman who'd inexplicably goosed his inner white knight into action. And yet, he thought as he eased off her sandals, sending Steve rocketing from the room when he tossed them onto the carpet by the bed, instead of a great, roaring gush of emotion when he looked at her, C.J. still felt only a frustrating trickle, as though his heart was a rusted faucet that turned only so far. Okay, so, yeah, he was crazy about his little boy. He'd admit that. But Ethan was *his*. And a baby. A baby who needed his father to *be* his father. Dana, however…

He fetched a lightweight blanket from the chest at the foot of the bed, carefully draping it over her before curving his body to spoon hers from behind—a slightly unsettling impulse, considering he'd never been much of a cuddler. If only he could strong-arm that faucet open all the way, he thought as his breathing slowed to match hers, then maybe

Dana wouldn't feel compelled to keep hers to a trickle, too, to withhold the one thing he didn't deserve…the one thing, he now realized—selfishly, irrationally—he wanted more than anything in the world. Because what, he wondered, would it be like to bask in the full force of Dana Malone's love?

There was a pointless thought. But if *this* was all there was between them—Dana stirred in her sleep when C.J. kissed her shoulder—then, come morning, he'd just have to make damn sure this was the best *this* she'd ever had.

Chapter Eleven

Dana woke to far, far too much sunlight, the sound of the shower running in the master bath on the other side of the wall, and fish-scented purring in her face. Slowly, she hauled herself upright, raking her fingers through her matted hair as she grimaced at her wrinkled T-shirt and capris.

Only she could wake up in C.J.'s bed with all her clothes still on.

Although "wake up" was probably a stretch, since—she squinted at the clock—she'd only been asleep for five hours. If that. With a sound that was more growl than groan, she crashed back into the C.J.-scented pillows. Who the heck gets up at seven on a Sunday morning? Besides her mother?

Her mother. Who would be here at nine to drop Ethan off before she went on to church. Ethan, yay. Mama…

Dana shut her eyes, as if that would stop…everything. Except Steve was back in her face, rumbling like a '67 Chevy.

An odd, strained *airp* punctuated the purring every now and then, as though he couldn't work up the energy to push out a real meow. A huge yawn—from Dana, not Steve—roused a few more brain cells. And a memory or two of that conversation on the ride home.

She'd felt like one of the characters in her own stories, her words carefully scripted. Except she'd only had one shot at getting it right, no editing allowed. Strangely enough, she'd actually been more sincere about accepting things the way they were between her and C.J. than she might have expected. Hey, getting screwed over by a man you'd completely trusted tends to make a girl *real* cautious. With her heart, at least.

Still, either because she was very brave or very stupid, she still nurtured her precious little hope with all the ferocity and single-mindedness of that crackpot gardener in Antarctica with his orchids. The difference was, she now fully understood the risks involved. She could hope and pray until the cows came home that C.J. would come around, but that didn't mean it would happen—

"Mornin'."

She actually shuddered at the sound of his voice, all low and sexy and silky, only to chuckle when she looked over at him. "Love the hair."

"Yeah?" he said, roughing it up a little more with a small beige towel, the big brother of which was wrapped around his hips. Hmm. Apparently his hair wasn't the only thing at attention.

His gaze followed hers, then slid back up, unmistakable yearning in his eyes, and the room seemed to close around them, an impenetrable fortress shielding them from all that pesky ambivalence.

Well, some of it, anyway.

Eyes crinkling to beat the band, he moved toward the bed. With definite purpose. "Sleep well?" he asked, one knee on the edge of the mattress, his mouth suddenly inches away from hers—

"No!" she shrieked, springing from the bed. "I mean, yes, I slept okay, but um...I need to..." *Floss. Pee. Close the blinds.* "...take care of...things."

"Sure," he said. And ditched the towel. "We'll wait."

Oh, my. Amazing how...*there* things looked in broad daylight. Which meant...oh, dear God. Getting nekkid with the guy in her nearly dark living room was one thing. Doing it here would be like having sex in an operating theater.

"Dana?" he said quietly, jerking her back to attention. A resigned half smile curved his lips. "Look, if you've changed your mind..."

"No, it's not that, it's..." *Weenie, weenie, weenie.* "Hold that thought."

Never had a man looked more relieved. And oddly enough, suddenly the idea of getting it on in the middle of an operating theater sounded...not so bad. Scary as all get-out, yes. But doable.

Five minutes later, brushed and flossed and perfumed and whatnot, and swaddled in the largest towel she could find, she returned to the (still) brightly lit bedroom to find C.J. (still) waiting for her on the bed, his back to the headboard, one pale beige sheet discretely covering his lap. Stretched out beside him, Steve kneaded the air with a goony look on his face (and one eye trained on her) as C.J. idly scratched the thing's belly.

She'd expected...well, she wasn't sure what. An offhand remark, maybe. Instead he rose from the bed, his whole expression softening as he approached her.

And tugged off her towel.

The sunlight slashed across her bare breasts, her belly, her thighs, as the plush cotton sighed to the carpet at her feet...as C.J. gently, softly, sweetly kissed her mouth, tugging her lower lip oh so tenderly between his teeth before gathering her in his arms, hot skin to hot skin, to tongue the hollow of her throat, and it didn't take long for the filmy haze of sun and sex to soft-edge any lingering reservations about things sagging and swaying and jiggling.

He lowered himself to his knees in front of her to suckle her breasts, and she smiled, bending forward to shield him with her long hair, the room's deep silence swallowing her sighs, the sounds of a lover's worship, her own soft cries of sharp, achy pleasure when he pulled her deeper, deeper into his mouth, as though he couldn't get enough of her, give enough to her…

She braced her hands on shoulders like rock, eyes closed, savoring, reveling…trusting, that he wouldn't hurt her, wouldn't take her anyplace she didn't want to go, wouldn't let her fall…as his hot, moist breath heralded a hundred lazy, lingering kisses across her breasts, her ribs, her belly, lower…

Dana whimpered, her fingers tangled in C.J.'s hair, as he spread her, loved her, brought her to climax, once…twice…

"Oh! *Oh!*"

She cried out, in amazement, in gratitude, as the pulsing peaked a third time, as she felt more glad to be a woman than she ever, ever had in her life.

"Your skin…" Sounding slightly amazed himself, C.J.'s voice cut through her après-climax haze. "It's the color of the light."

"W-what?"

"Your skin. Look."

He got to his feet, pulling her over to face the huge mirror over his dresser, and the "No!" of surprise, of embarrassment, escaped before she could catch it. Acute self-awareness surged through her, a furious blush following in its wake. Not a second before, she'd felt beautiful, almost ethereal, and now he'd ruined the moment, *destroyed* it, by making her see herself as she really was.

"Damn you!" she cried, struggling to get free, but C.J. only chuckled, wrapping one strong, darker arm, around her waist, pulling her back against him. When she dropped her eyes, he tightened his hold, making her gasp again.

"Look at yourself, dammit!" he hissed, his breath hot in her ear. "See what I see. Yes, like that," he said when she forced herself to look at her reflection, watching his splayed hand track across her stomach, cup her full breasts, his thumb rhythmically circling her rosy nipples.

"Don't you see?" he said, pressing his temple against hers, and she met his gaze in the mirror, saw something in it she'd never seen in another man's eyes. "You're *real*, Dana," he said, touching her, stroking her wherever he pleased without an ounce of compunction, one finger tracing the faint, silvery pink scar from her operation. "You're so…damn…real, you make my mouth go dry."

Her skin flushed anew, this time with arousal, as the sharp, delicious sting of anticipation bloomed once more between her legs. "How on earth could you not know how beautiful you are?" he said, and tears threatened.

"Because I never saw myself through your eyes," she whispered.

"Oh, Dana…" he said on a rush of air, ribbons of fire streaking her hair when he sifted it through his fingers, then let those fingers skim her neck, shoulders, down her goose-bumped arms to claim her hands, pull her toward the bed. And he started all over, his exploration thorough, unhurried, making her blush again and again when he'd pause for a moment in the proceedings to extol, in explicit detail, her many—as he put it—charms.

"C.J.…." she said, laughing, when things had gone on in

this manner for far longer than most men would even consider, especially since it was patently clear that he wasn't doing all this to buy time for himself "…you must be about to explode!"

"Now that you mention it…" Wicked amusement danced in his eyes. "Yeah. I am. But, oh, what a mind-blowing explosion it's going to be."

"Wow. You sound pretty sure of yourself."

"Call it—" he said, kneeing apart her legs, his eyes darkening "—an educated guess."

"Prove it," she said, sighing in pure *okay-I-can-die-now* happiness as one very ready Tab A plunged effortlessly into one even more ready Slot B, as he tormented her with tantalizingly, agonizingly slow thrusts, each one deeper than the last, filling her more…and more…and more, until their bodies finally said to their brains, *Move over, our turn,* and then there was nothing but heat and friction and lots of heavy breathing and the mad, frantic pumping that if you thought about too hard, you'd laugh, and then there were moans and cries and just before that final, glorious burst of stars and white lights (because, yes, sometimes it really is like that), Dana opened her eyes to see the barely concealed terror in C.J.'s.

Then it was over, their hearts the only things left pumping, their cries already faded into the silence. Only before she could catch C.J.'s eyes a second time he wrapped her so tightly in his arms she could hardly breathe.

And she thought, *Damn you, C.J., what am I going to do with you?*

"I still haven't decided whether I should thank you or smack you."

At Dana's teasing words, C.J. looked up from his three-cheese omelet. As he watched Dana spoon applesauce into Ethan's baby-bird-wide mouth, it struck him that he couldn't even remember the afterglow hanging around for more than ten minutes, let alone two hours. But not even the baby's return—accompanied by the noxious cloud of disapproval radiating from Dana's mother—or the mundane tasks of feeding him his lunch and preparing their own breakfast, could fully eradicate the lingering vestiges of a hunger not nearly as sated as one might have expected.

The edge to Dana's voice brought him back to earth with a resounding *thud.*

"For what?"

With a rubber-tipped spoon, she scraped leaked sauce off Ethan's chin and shoved it back into his mouth. "For raising the bar. Because, really…" She glanced over, her ponytail—still damp from their second shower, finished mere minutes before Faye's arrival—falling over one tank-topped breast. "I'm not sure how the next guy is ever going to be able to top your…talent."

His fingers tightened around his fork. "The next guy?"

"Sure," Dana said lightly, softly dinging the spoon against the bottom of the jar. "Since this is only for the moment and all. I was just thinking ahead, you know. Oh, for heaven's sake—why the long face?" She stood, screwing the top back on the jar. "I would think your ego would be puffed up like the Pillsbury Doughboy after that compliment," she said, grabbing the container of wipes off the counter to clean Ethan's hands, earning her a squeal of protest. "And I was taught—oh, now, quit squirming, sugarpie, I'll be all done in a sec—to always give credit where it's due."

"I wasn't alone in the bed, Dana," C.J. grumbled. But she'd turned the water on at the sink and hadn't heard him. And what was with his nose getting out of joint, anyway? It wasn't as if he had any claim on her future affections, after all. Still, at least she could have had the good grace not to bring up the subject now.

Since *now* was all they had.

"Hey," he said, "why don't we take Ethan to the zoo today? My client cancelled his open house, so—"

"Oh…I'm sorry, C.J., I can't." Wiping her hands on a dish-towel, Dana faced him. "The workers are coming tomorrow to start on the new place, so Cass and Merce and I already made plans to meet there this afternoon to prepare. But there's no reason why *you* couldn't take him to the zoo. By yourself."

"Well…no, I suppose not. Except…I just thought it would be fun. All of us going together."

"Yes, it would," she said softly. "But…"

"What?"

"With Trish back in the equation, maybe we shouldn't get too carried away with acting like a family. For Ethan's sake, if nothing else. It would only confuse him."

C.J. frowned. "She's not getting custody, Dana."

"You don't know that. And even if you two get joint custody, that kinda removes me from the equation, doesn't it?"

His chest felt as though it would cave in. "It doesn't have to."

"Of course it does," she said gently, patiently, waiting for him to connect the dots. Which he finally did.

"You're going to leave already?"

"Not until things are settled about Ethan, obviously. But since it appears that's going to happen sooner than later… Oh, come on, C.J.—you know as well as I do that if it weren't for Ethan, I wouldn't even be here. Let alone that we'd've gotten naked. Our lives just happened to bump up against each other, and we both took…advantage of the opportunity."

She came up behind him to slip her arms around his neck, laying her cheek against his temple. "You're an incredible lover," she said, giving him a squeeze. "You're incredible, period. But even you have to admit that the longer I hang around, the harder it's going to be to keep things casual. And

I know that's the last thing you want. So I'm just saying…
maybe Trish's return is a blessing in disguise. Oh, shoot," she
said, her gaze glancing off the microwave clock, "it's later
than I thought, I need to get my butt in gear—"

"Dana?" he said, catching her before she got all the way
out of the kitchen.

"For the life of me, I can't figure you out. And it's beginning to seriously piss me off."

She lifted her hands in a *that's-the-way-it-goes* gesture,
then walked away.

"Okay." Mercy swept her hair back with her wrist,
adorning her forehead with blobs of cobalt-blue paint.
"Explain to me again why we didn't hire painters?"

"Because we're cheap," Cass yelled from the other side of
the room over the constant hum of floor fans, the pounding
of hammers, the continuous stream of Spanish—off-color
jokes (according to Mercy) from the other side of the house.

Mercy slammed her roller against the wall. "No, I think it's
because we're stupid."

"And who said the more sweat equity we put into the place,
the bigger stake we have in its success?"

"Yeah, well, *there* was a delusional moment."

Curled up apart from the fray in a window seat with her
laptop, Dana allowed herself a wry smile as she put the finishing touches on the print ad to run in the paper the following Sunday, Monday being the grand opening for the new
location. Insanity, is what this was, allowing only a week to
get everything up and running. She'd hardly seen either Ethan
or C.J. the past several days, one of those good news/bad
news kind of things.

But she couldn't dump everything in her partners' laps,
and closing the store for longer would wreak havoc with

their cash flow, already stretched to the max as it was. Even with Mercy's father's construction company doing the lion's share of the work, it was still costing a fortune to retrofit the old house. God alone knew how they were going to afford an elevator, an absolute must if they wanted parents with strollers to even consider going up to the second floor.

At least—she hit the Send button to e-mail the ad to the paper—the craziness here distracted her (somewhat) from the craziness that was the rest of her life. Who would've guessed she'd have the guts to toss that little gauntlet down between her and C.J. the other morning, putting him on notice that she was already thinking about the future? The one in which sex wasn't on the menu?

Not that she'd expected C.J. to pick it up. Not then, anyway. Even if he had looked slightly ill. But nothing strained the old ego more than an ignored gauntlet, lying there collecting dust as everybody stepped over it, day after day.

Dana slipped the laptop back into its case, resisting the temptation to sneak a peek at the last few pages of her book, finally written in the wee hours the night before. At least she had that. Now all she had to do was work up the gumption to actually ask editors and agents if they wanted to read it.

Thinking about it made her heart beat so hard, it actually hurt.

"Hey!" Mercy barked. "You over there in a fog. Got a roller here with your name on it. And did you call the sign people?"

"I did," Dana said, unfolding herself from the seat and wending her way through ladders and paint buckets and drop-clothed display cases, her hands sunk into the pockets of a pair of ancient denim overalls she'd unearthed from the bowels of her old closet. "They'll be here tomorrow. Hey, you missed a spot—"

"Dana?"

She spun around to see Trish silhouetted in the open doorway, a vision in a belly-baring tank top and short-shorts, the ends of her twisted-up hair fanned around the top of her head like a worn-out paintbrush. By some unspoken mutual agreement, they hadn't seen or spoken with each other since that night at her parents' house. Despite Trish's having left Ethan with Dana, whatever happened about the baby now was between Trish and C.J., a realization which produced a little burst of anger in Dana's chest.

"Trish! What are you—?"

"Aunt Faye told me y'all were over here," she said, sidestepping a stack of lumber, her eyes darting between Cass and Mercy, who were assiduously pretending not to listen, before meeting Dana's again. "I need to talk to you."

"Why?" The word came out hard enough to make her cousin flinch.

"Dana, please don't be like this. I know I put you in an awkward situation and all but—"

"Not me, Trish. Ethan. And C.J. I'm just…" She waved her hands. "A bystander."

"Is…is there someplace we can talk?" Trish whispered. "In private?"

"I've got a million things to do—"

"This won't take long, I promise."

"Outside, then. And make it snappy."

And indeed, they'd barely gotten out onto the porch before Trish said, "I've changed my mind. About wanting custody of Ethan."

"Oh, for the love of God, Trish! *Again?*"

Her cousin's eyebrows slammed together over her nose. "Don't you dare go gettin' mad at me when you know good and well this is what you wanted all along!"

"And I repeat, this isn't about *me*. It's about you not being able to stick with a decision for longer than five minutes! So how long is this one going to last? Until you get back to Vegas and miss Ethan again?"

A couple of seconds passed before Trish pushed out a sigh, then clomped over to the steps in her platform shoes, plunking her butt down on the top one. "I'm not goin' back to Vegas. I'm stayin' here."

"What do you mean, staying here? What about your job? Your apartment?"

Trish seemed to take a sudden interest in the mail carrier across the street. "The job was only temporary, some under-the-table thing in one of the casinos. And I was living with an old friend from school who'd moved out there."

"So you lied."

"Yeah. Well, sorta. Becky does have a pretty nice place."

Dana exhaled. "Why?"

"I don't know, I just… All I wanted was to see Ethan again, make sure he was okay and stuff. Not that I thought he wouldn't be. Except then I saw him and…I kinda went a little crazy. And then C.J. was there, and I guess I freaked, and then I heard myself telling C.J. that Ethan that wasn't his."

"Wait a minute. So the story you told C.J., about thinking you were already pregnant…?"

Bony, bare shoulders shrugged.

"Oh, Trish." This was the problem with Trish—how could you stay mad at somebody that screwed up? Shaking her head, Dana joined her cousin on the steps. "Honey, don't take this the wrong way, but you really, really need help."

"Yeah," the girl said on a sigh. "I know. But…"

"You know we'd all help with the expense, if that's what's holding you back. As long as you're willing to try to make it work this time."

After a moment, her cousin nodded, not looking at her.

"God, Dana," she said in a small voice, "you have no idea how much I hate my life. Sometimes I even hate myself, for making such a mess of things." She twisted around, tears glittering in her eyes. "But I do love Ethan, you've gotta believe that. I always have. And if things'd been different, I wouldn't've left him with you to begin with. But now that I've been back for a while and had a chance to think things through, I know I really can't take care of a baby right now. And probably not for a very long time. So whatever you and C.J. want to do about custody's fine with me. Although I'd still like to be part of my baby's life. I mean, if that's okay?"

After a moment, Dana took her cousin's hand in hers. "I'm sure we can work something out."

"Really? Because I'd like him to know who his mama is, that she loves him. That way, maybe he won't hate me so much for giving him up."

"He won't," Dana said over the lump in her throat. "I won't let him."

"Swear?"

"Swear."

"What about C.J.?"

Ah, yes, C.J. C.J. with the parent-abandonment issues. Still… "I can't see C.J. letting that happen, either. Although you need to talk to him yourself."

"Already did, earlier today. But I needed to tell you in person. It's part of my new resolve, facing things head-on instead of runnin' from 'em, or hidin' behind a lie. Or six," she added with a small smile. Trish glanced back at the house, then faced Dana again, rubbing her palm over her bare knee. "You suppose maybe y'all might need some extra help, once you open again?"

Dana started. "You mean here? At the store?"

"I can run a register like nobody's business. And I've always liked kids, you know that." The girl's face fell at

Dana's apparently poleaxed expression. "But if you don't think it's a good idea, I totally understand."

"No, it's not that." Dana pushed out a breath. "I'll have to discuss it with Mercy and Cass. And if—*if*—we do hire you, you cannot flake out on us. Is that understood? Because I've worked too hard for this business to put it in jeopardy."

Trish grinned, then saluted. "Got it. And I *swear* you won't be sorry—" Dana held up a hand to cut her off; Trish giggled, then angled her head. "And...d'you think I could stay with Aunt Faye and Uncle Gene until I save up enough to get my own place?"

Honestly. If the girl ever got the common sense to go with the cojones, there'd be no stopping her. "Knowing Mama?" Dana said. "What do you think?" Then she pushed herself to her feet. "And now I've really got to get back in there, or Mercy's gonna have my hide."

"You do believe there wasn't ever anything between C.J. and me, don't you?" Trish said, standing, as well. "Well, apart from the one night, I mean."

Dana thought of her previous jealousy—because that's what it was, no sense pretending otherwise—about that "one night." Not an issue any longer, she thought with a flush. "Yes, actually. Although...did you want there to be more?"

"Oh, heck, no. He's not my type at all. Not for the long haul. I mean, it was fun and all—"

"Trish? TMI, okay? And anyway, I'm not sure what that has to do with anything."

At that, her cousin reared back to look at her, incredulity swimming in her eyes. "You're not serious? Anybody with two eyes in their head can see how crazy you are about the guy. The way you looked at him that night at Aunt Faye's?" She shook her head. "Shoot, I'll bet nobody's ever loved him like you do."

An embarrassed, nervous laugh popped out of Dana's mouth. "How on earth would you know that? You worked for him for, what? Six months?"

"Hey. Maybe I've got problems, but I can read people a lot better than you might think. And besides, that office manager of his is a gold mine of information," Trish added with a grin. Then she sobered. "And from what Val told me, I'm gathering not many women liked C.J. for just himself, if you get my drift. Either they were after his money, or because he was arm candy, or both. You're not like that, Dana."

"Maybe not, but—"

"Oh, for pity's sake, do I have to spell it out for you? One of the reasons I don't feel as bad as I might about giving Ethan up is because I can see he's got a shot of havin' two parents. Obviously I didn't even consider that when I left him with you, because I honestly didn't think C.J. would step up to bat the way he did. And of course I had no idea you and C.J. would hook up, so that part's a total fluke, but now...well, it couldn't be more perfect, could it—? Ohmi*god!*"

"What?"

"You're playin' hard to get, aren't you? Instead of puttin' yourself on the line and goin' after the man, you're gonna let him get away." Trish laughed, shaking her head. "And you think *I'm* the dumb one?"

Her cousin was halfway back to the front door by the time Dana found her voice again. "What are you doing?"

"I think it's called *going for it*," her cousin said from the open doorway. "A concept apparently some of us on this porch are currently havin' a little trouble with?" When Dana rolled her eyes, Trish giggled and said, "Heck, I need a job. And if slapping paint on the walls is what it takes to get in y'all's good graces, then that's what I'll do."

After Trish disappeared inside, Dana collapsed onto the top

step, a million thoughts pinging around inside her head like drunken moths. Well. Trish's change of heart about Ethan pretty much annihilated her "out" with C.J., didn't it? Stay or not, whatever decision she made, using Ethan and/or Trish as a reason was no longer an option. Ball was in her court and all that.

But what really chapped her hide was the mortifying realization that her spacey cousin had read her a heckuva lot better than she'd read herself. Because what kind of risk *was* she taking, really? As long as she kept her heart locked up in its safe little cage, how on earth could she expect C.J. to trust her enough to reciprocate? Or even try? At the very least— she sucked in a steadying breath—he deserved to know how she really felt. That she did love him.

What he did with that information was completely up to him.

Chapter Twelve

Stretched out on a chaise by the pool, C.J. jerked out of his doze when he heard the patio door open behind him. He twisted his head as Dana sank into a nearby chair, her breath leaving her lungs in a long, obviously exhausted whoosh. Odd how, these days, he could never fully relax until she was once again where he could see her, hear her. Touch her. Reassure himself that she was safe.

Stupid.

"What time is it?" he asked, sitting up.

"After nine. Ethan go down okay?"

"Not really, no." He paused. "I think he misses you."

"I doubt it." She plucked something off her knee. "Trish came by."

"Yeah, she said she was going to. So you know."

"Yes. Congratulations, by the way," she said, leaning her head back against the cushion, ruffling Steve's fur when he jumped up onto her lap and began to knead that awful, baggy, paint-spattered thing she was wearing. "That must be a huge load off your mind. Or will be, once it's all on paper."

"Frankly, I think it's a huge load off Trish's, too," C.J. said cautiously, trying to gauge Dana's obviously strange mood. Fraught with danger though that might be. "Knowing she never has to worry about Ethan being taken care of. I suppose you and I need to work out something official now. I'll make an appointment with my lawyer sometime next week."

In the darkness, he sensed the slight smile she offered in lieu of a response. Then she got to her feet, jettisoning the cat. "Is there anything to eat? I'm starved."

C.J. stood, as well, opening the patio door for her. "Guadalupe brought homemade tamales, will that do?"

"God bless Guadalupe," she said, moving past him to the kitchen. Keeping her gaze trained straight ahead.

"You look beat."

"Twelve hours straight of manual labor will do that to you."

"Sit," he said, pointing to the table in the breakfast alcove. "Nuking, I can do. How many do you want? Two or three?"

"How about a dozen?" she said, dropping like a stone into one of the chairs. "Although I'll settle for three." She'd pulled her hair back into a ponytail, but great hunks of it hung around her face as though they were too pooped to stay up in the clip. But it was the look in her eyes that sent shockwaves coursing through his veins. Shuttered, cautious. Guilty, although what Dana would have to feel guilty about, he had no idea.

He put three tamales on a plate and shoved them in the microwave.

"Tea?"

"Please."

He poured her a large glass, handed it to her, then said, "Talk, Dana."

She took a long sip of her tea, carefully setting the glass back on the table. Then she wiggled her mouth from side to side before saying, "Well, it's like this, see…" Her eyes met his. "I'm in love with you."

C.J.'s ears rang for several seconds. Then, on a groan, he leaned heavily against the edge of the island, eyes squeezed shut, shaking his head. "Oh, Dana…" He looked over at her. "Honey…no."

She shrugged. "Sorry. Can't be helped. Oh, yay," she said when the microwave beeped. "Food."

In a daze, C.J. removed the tamales and put them in front of her, followed by a container of sour cream. She pried off the top, slathered both tamales with the cream. "But you said—"

"That I knew where I stood with you, that I didn't expect anything more. And I still don't. I just left out a salient fact or two."

"Why?"

She smiled the smile of someone who knows things can't get any worse. "Why do I love you, or why didn't I tell you?"

"Why didn't you tell me? Everything we said, about being honest with each other—"

"You don't want honesty, C.J.," she said, chewing. "Not really. You want…I don't know." She swallowed. "Absolution?"

"Absolution? For what?"

"For whatever it was I saw in your eyes when we made love. For that tiny, but oh so crucial part of yourself you just can't let go of."

He felt every muscle in his body stiffen. "Dana, I told you—"

"You know," she said softly, pressing the side of her fork into the next tamale, "if you didn't want me to fall in love with you, maybe you should have rethought that whole knight in shining armor routine." She tilted her head. "Nobody's ever made me believe in myself the way you have. Or pushed me to trust my instincts. Pretty powerful stuff for a gal who's always been surrounded by people hell-bent on protecting her."

Whether she would have brought the subject up on her own without his prodding, he had no idea. What difference did it make? It didn't make the pain any less excruciating, knowing whatever he said was only going to hurt her. Knowing he already had.

"I was just being a friend."

A tiny smile touched her lips. "I don't believe that. Hey," she added when he flinched. "You said you wanted honesty."

"I know, but…" He frowned. "What do you mean, you don't believe me?"

"I didn't say I didn't believe *you*. There's a difference. C.J.… Over the past several weeks, I watched a man so rattled by the idea of being a father he initially didn't even want to hold his own baby, turn into this big old softie who can't hold his baby enough. So it's not your *capacity* to love that's in question."

"It's different with Ethan."

"Because he's yours? Because you had no choice?"

"Well…yes."

Dana got up from the table, carrying her now empty plate to the dishwasher. "You didn't have to take him into your home," she said, putting her dish inside. "You didn't have to fight his own mother for him. You didn't have to fall in love with him." She turned. "But you did. Every step of the way, you made choices. Just like you've been making choices all your life, about where you'd live, your career…your relationships."

He smirked. "If you could call them that."

"My point exactly. Still, having me live here was your idea. And heaven knows, nothing compelled you to sleep with me. You could have turned me down," she said when he opened his mouth to protest. Then her hand was on his cheek, warm and slightly trembly, and his heart nearly cracked in two. "You knew full well what you were getting into," she whispered. Her hand dropped. "And so did I."

"Oh, God, Dana…" C.J. said on an exhaled breath, then gathered her in his arms, tucking her head under his chin, stroking her hair. "Okay, so you're more than a friend," he said, and she chuckled into his shirt. "But if you're implying that I'm somehow making a choice about loving you or not…I'm sorry. Your intuition's let you down with that one." He held her slightly apart, his hands framing her face. "Because believe me, I'd kill to be able to feel what you're feeling."

She looked at him steadily for a long moment, then said, "Actually, I think you'd kill not to be feeling what you are right now."

He flinched. "What?"

"You remember how I said I knew the difference between when a guy's in it just for the sex, and when he isn't? Well, you're not. Oh, you can deny it up one side and down the other, but you're dangling off the precipice, aren't you? And you're absolutely petrified. If you're looking for honesty, C.J.," she said gently, "you have to start with yourself. And until then…" With a shrug, she pulled out of his arms. "Things are going to be crazy for the next week or so, but I'll be completely out of here right after that, if it's okay with you."

"You don't have to—"

"Yes. I do." Steve rubbed up against her shins; she bent over to pick him up. "Look, this is probably a stretch—and God knows none of my business, really—but have you ever tried to fix things with your father?"

"What's my father got to do with anything?"

"Don't be disingenuous, C.J.," she said with a slight smile. "It doesn't suit you. And frankly, I think your father has everything to do with this. And you know something else? If I ever meet the guy, I just might deck him, for doing whatever he did to you to make you so afraid to accept somebody's love."

"Dammit, Dana, do you honestly believe I *like* being like this?"

"Honestly?" she said. "Yes. I do. In some ways, anyway. Oh, come on, C.J., keeping things simple is what you do. And that's not a criticism—exactly—simply an observation. Except, I'm wondering where you get off telling *me* to take risks, to put myself on the line, when you don't take your own advice?"

She released the cat. "Now if you'll excuse me, I'm half-asleep on my feet. And joy of joys, I get to do it all over again tomorrow—"

"What about Ethan?"

When she met his gaze, he saw tears flooding her eyes. "You're his father, C.J.," she said, her softly spoken words pummeling him like hailstones. "Whatever you decide about how we should divide our time with the baby is fine with me."

He watched her leave the room, knowing better than to ask where she'd be sleeping tonight.

Steve meowed at the patio door, asking to go outside again. C.J. opened the door, followed him out into the cool, still night. The water's surface grabbed the moonlight, shredding it into thousands of shimmering strands. Once Ethan became mobile, he realized, he'd have to keep the pool covered when they weren't actually using it. A high fence around it probably wouldn't hurt, either. With a good lock.

With a jolt, he realized he was thinking, for the first time in his life, about a house, *this* house, in terms of permanent. The house where his son would grow up, learn to walk, learn to swim, bring buddies over after school, return to during college breaks.

The house where he'd finally, fully understood what "making love" really meant.

C.J. dropped into one of the chairs, staring bleakly at the glittering water. When was the last time a woman's exit from his life had provoked much feeling one way or the other, with the occasional exception of relief? This time, however…

He let his head fall back, his gaze sweeping the vast, star-studded sky. This time, he felt hollow. No, worse—gouged out, a fragile shell of BS that protected the horrible, aching emptiness.

Except Dana hadn't caused the void. She'd only exposed it.

Because she was right, about his making choices. Careful choices, choices guaranteed—or so he'd hoped—not to bite him in the butt. Until a baby entered his life, not by choice, but by…what? Happenstance? Stupidity? And suddenly, he found himself faced with a whole new set of the suckers.

Not to mention a woman with the courage to call him on his sorry-assed excuse for a life.

Regret spasmed through him, as palpable as any physical pain. But with the regret—for things he couldn't change, perhaps—came, at last, a resolve. To face the past he'd spent twenty or more years avoiding, with those "choices."

To face himself. Or at least, the himself he'd never let anyone see.

A long shot, at best. But he owed it to his son.

And to the woman who'd honored him with her love.

Even if he couldn't return it.

Her cursor hovered over the Print icon, Dana listened to the *whoompa, whoompa, whoompa* of her heartbeat in her ears. One little click, and her baby would soon be ready to send out into the world.

To be judged. And most likely rejected. She knew the odds,

and they didn't exactly make a girl's heart sing. Of course, there was always option number two, which was to cop out altogether.

"Cowabunga," she whispered. And clicked.

The laser printer in C.J.'s home office whirred awake. From the playpen, Ethan looked up at the sound, a bland curiosity filling his big, blue eyes. Steve, however, who'd been curled up in a splotch of sunlight on the desk, leaped onto the printer, all the better to attack the pages as the printer spit them out. Yeah, toothmarks would add a nice touch, huh?

"Hey!" Dana squawked, swatting the cat on the rump. He went flying, his indignant expression when he landed butt-first on the carpet making her laugh in spite of the heaviness inside her chest.

Oh, the grand opening two days ago had gone over like gangbusters. And a two-bedroom had opened up in her complex, one with better views and more light than her old apartment. Not to mention brand new carpeting and a new fridge. C.J. had insisted on making up the difference between her old and new rent, and she'd decided it was stupid to argue, especially since it wasn't as if he couldn't afford it. Downright gallant of him, in fact. So now she'd have a lovely extra bedroom for Ethan, when it was "her turn." But—

As if reading her mind, the baby screeched to get her attention, grinning hugely when she picked him up. On a sigh, she sank back into the leather desk chair, imagining it smelled like the man whose bed she'd hadn't even seen in more than a week, let alone shared.

And she'd thought giving up Doritos had been hard.

Her car was already packed; as soon as this was printed and C.J. got home, she'd be outta here. Odd to think that by this time tomorrow living here would be only a memory. No more chats by the pool, no more sharing a bowl of Jell-O in the middle of the night, no more—she hugged the baby closer—grocery trips together, or watching a movie together, or doing anything else together. That particular gamble, she'd lost. And annoyingly, it stung a lot more than it should have, considering she'd been well aware of the odds against that, too.

Still, even though hope whimpered in its sleep inside her, she had no real regrets. Not about sleeping with C.J., or telling him how she really felt. Had she let the opportunity slip by she would have regretted it for the rest of her life.

You could guard your heart, or you could give it, but you couldn't do both. *Safe risk* was an oxymoron.

Which is why she now watched the printer spew out page after page of the novel she could have started sending out feelers for months ago, if she hadn't been such a scaredy-cat. If she'd had the guts to trust her instincts instead of listening to the nasty little voice demanding to know who the hell she thought she was, to think someone might actually want to even read what she'd written, let alone buy it. At this point, it wasn't about whether it sold or not, it was about having the guts to take chances.

"I take it that's your book?" C.J. said from the doorway.

Dana turned awkwardly with the baby in her lap, ignoring her overeager-beagle heart leaping in her chest. Funny how that same little—actually, brass-band-huge—voice had also asked her who the hell she thought she was, expecting to attract someone like C.J. There was one worry, at least, that could be put to rest. So she could take some comfort in knowing—really knowing, not just telling herself—that this wasn't about her. And that if she hadn't taken a chance, she *wouldn't* know that.

"It sure is," she said with a smile. "I already printed out the query letters, and I'm sending them out tomorrow."

"You promise?"

"Cross my heart."

"Excellent." His smile was tender. Damn him. He hadn't

changed out of his work clothes yet, although he'd ditched his suit coat, loosened his tie. The babbling-idiot effect of his handsomeness on her brain had more or less worn off by now, although she still suffered the odd weak knee now and then. "I'm proud of you, Dana. This is a huge step."

And if it hadn't been for his cheerleading, his pushing her past her fear, she wouldn't be taking this step. For that, if nothing else, she'd always be grateful.

"We should celebrate," he said.

"We definitely should," she said, although she knew they wouldn't. Not now. "Thanks for letting me use your printer, by the way. I'll be more than happy to contribute toward the cartridge replacement—"

"It's a laser," C.J. said patiently. "Your manuscript will barely make a dent. Forget it."

"Well. Thanks. Because my printer sucks."

"So you said."

Jerks, she was used to. Jerks, she could deal with. Jerks, she could get over. But this…

This would all be so much easier if they hated each other.

Go away, she thought when he simply stood there, as though *basking* in the awkward silence. Just a few more minutes, though, and it would all be over—

"I have something to tell you," he said, the edge to his voice making her head snap up.

"What?"

He took the baby from her, smiling when Ethan squealed and batted at his face. Then he looked at her again, a mixture of apprehension and resolve in his eyes.

"I've decided to take Ethan back to Charleston to meet his grandfather."

Her breath caught. "Oh, C.J.…are you sure you want to do this?"

"I'm sure I *have* to do this." His gaze rested on the top of Ethan's head for a moment, then swung back to her. "I find I don't much like being a hypocrite."

She got up to straighten out the already printed pages before the printer choked. "Imagine that," she said, as lightly as she could considering how loudly her brain was screaming. Which in turn woke hope up all over again. And here the poor thing had been having *such* a nice snooze. "When do you leave?"

"Late tomorrow morning."

"Wow. Nothing like striking while the iron is hot."

A smile touched his lips. "I think this falls into the 'before I chicken out' category. But I'll be back in a couple of days. Sooner, if things don't go well. But at least this will give you some time to get settled into your new apartment without worrying about taking care of the baby, right?"

And hope said, *You woke me up for that?*, yanked the covers back up over its head and went back to sleep. Grumbling.

C.J.'s cell rang at the same time the printer spit out the last page and whined to a stop. He fished the phone out of his pocket, laughing when Ethan tried to grab it away from him. But instead of handing the baby back to her, he moseyed on out of the office, contentedly—at least, so it seemed—balancing phone and baby. Her stomach churning, Dana quickly smacked the sides of the manuscript pages against the desk to even them out, then stuffed them into a Tyvek envelope.

Then, a minute later, she quietly left the house she'd grown a lot more fond of than she should have, knowing full well that C.J. would be ticked at her for not saying goodbye.

C.J. idly wondered, as he maneuvered a child, a stroller, a car seat, a diaper bag the size of Texas and his own carry-on through the Charleston airport, how someone a tenth of his size could generate five times more *stuff*. He also wondered, not so idly, whether he'd ever be able to show his face again on a Delta flight. Oh, Ethan had outdone himself in the cute department, charming the flight attendants and making everyone in first class swoon. Until they were airborne. Apparently his son was not a natural-born flyer.

"Oh, poor thing," the flight attendant—a motherly type somewhere in her fifties—said. At first. "Try giving him a bottle, the sucking will make his ears pop."

"Hmm," the same attendant said ten minutes later over the screaming. "As soon as the Fasten Seat Belt sign goes off, why don't you walk him? I'm sure that'll do the trick."

Forty-five minutes later—and right about the time C.J. was getting some strong *"Who wants to shove them both out the emergency exit?"* vibes from the other passengers—Ethan passed out in midshriek.

Only to do a number in his diaper C.J. was sure could be detected back on the ground. Or at least in the seat across the aisle, if the prune-faced expression of the woman sitting there was any indication. Well, let's see…change the diaper of a baby who'd been screaming his head off the past hour, thereby risking waking him, or pass out clothespins? Fortunately, they only had another half hour before the plane landed in Dallas.

Unfortunately, their layover was only twenty minutes.

And their first plane was five minutes late.

To say that C.J. wasn't exactly in the best of moods by the time they touched down in Charlestown was a vast understatement. Exhaustion and ringing ears will do that to a person. Ethan, however—changed, fed and back on terra firma—was happy as a little towheaded clam, grinning at everybody they passed in the airport, and generally getting a head start on his 2044 Presidential bid. Then C.J. went to put his son in the car seat in the back of the rented Lexus, and the baby gave him a huge *"Hey, how's it goin'?"* grin, and his heart felt close to bursting, and he thought, *How could a father not want to have anything to do with his own son?*

Well, that's what he was going to find out. Come hell, high water or stinky diapers.

By the time they left the airport, it was already close enough to rush hour for traffic into town to be a pain. But eventually C.J. pulled up in front of the three-story, wrought-iron-trimmed redbrick that had been in the family for three generations. As someone who appreciated fine architecture, C.J. should have loved the stately house, infused with both charm and provenance as it was. Instead, memories flooded his thoughts like raw sewage, years of hurt suffocating him more than the oppressive humidity, obliterating whatever affection he might have, should have, felt for his childhood home.

He parked in the driveway alongside the shallow front yard, underneath a massive live oak twice as large as he remembered. Dense foliage—ten-foot-tall hydrangeas, azaleas, rhododendron—hugged the side of the house, nearly concealing from view what had once been the carriage house in the back, where a lonely little boy had spent far too much time playing make-believe.

Pretending he was "away on business," like his father so often was. Only when *he* returned home, it would be to a large, loving family who'd missed him terribly and were thrilled to have him back.

"Hey, guy," C.J. whispered to the baby, who'd conked out again. He stroked one down-soft cheek with his fingertip until Ethan squirmed, his golden eyelashes fluttering. With a start, C.J. noticed for the first time the slightest hint of Dana in the boy's coloring, the same dimples when he smiled, even the directness of his gaze. Then again, he could be full of it, seeing a resemblance that only existed in his head. "Time to meet your grandfather. Just remember," he said, hauling the solid little body out of the car seat, "I've got your back."

As expected, the maid, or housekeeper, or whoever the woman was who opened the pristinely white, multipaneled door at the top of the steps, was deferential and black, and—except for the brief conversation he'd exchanged with the woman a few days before, to make sure his father would be around—completely unfamiliar. C.J. idly wondered how many there had been between her and Jessie, the last one he remembered.

A broad, but somewhat cautious, smile rounded cheeks nearly the same warm, rich color of the polished banister sweeping behind her to the second floor. "Oh, you just *have* to be Mr. Cameron," she said, bright green eyes sparkling underneath a meringue of white hair. "I recognize you from your graduation photo, the one Mr. James keeps on the living room mantle. I'm Carmela, I don't usually stay this late, but no way was I gonna miss meeting *you*." Trim gray eyebrows rose behind oversized, eighties-vintage eyeglass frames. "And would you *look* at this handsome boy? And don't you know it?" she said, laughing softly when the baby opened his eyes and flashed his two teeth at her. "What's his name?"

C.J. grabbed the baby's hand before his chubby little fingers latched on to all that irresistible fluffy hair. "Ethan."

"Ethan Turner," she said, tumbling the sounds around in her mouth as though tasting wine. Then she nodded. "I like it. A good, solid name. I put one of those little mesh folding cribs in the closet in your old room for the baby. My daughter just moved her youngest into a bed so she wasn't usin' it."

"Thank you, you're a lifesaver."

"Yes, I am," she said with a low laugh, "and don't you forget it. Well, I best be gettin' on home, before my husband calls out the dogs."

"Before you go, may I ask you something?"

"Yes?"

"How long have you been working for my father?"

"Long enough to know it's been at least six years since you came to see him."

Letting the gentle chiding pass, C.J. said, "That's three times longer than any of your predecessors was able to hold out."

She chuckled. "Oh, yes, I know all about the revolving door in this place. Knew it before I was hired, since word does gets out. Your daddy still can't keep a cook to save him. Either finds some half-baked reason to let 'em go, or else drives 'em so crazy they leave of their own accord."

"Then how have you managed to stay on so long?"

"Lord only knows," she said with a smile. "Wasn't anything I did or didn't do, I don't think. Except maybe… seems to me like he just got *tired* of all the changes. Gettin' old'll do that to a person. You'll be here in the morning, I take it?"

C.J. breathed out, "That's the plan."

"Well…" Carmela gathered her things from the hall table. "Whatever your reasons for showin' up now," she said softly, laying her hand on his arm, "just remember, he's probably more scared of you than you are of him."

The front door had barely clicked shut behind her when C.J. heard behind him, "Cameron?"

C.J. turned, meeting the clearly stunned, ice-chip-blue gaze with a steady one of his own. The old man commanded his space as completely as he ever did, no pot belly straining the waistband of his Dockers or marring the smooth fit of his light blue knit shirt. In fact, if it weren't for the white hair, the less sharply defined jaw, this could have easily been twenty years ago.

Except twenty years ago, C.J.'s father had the power to hurt him, to intimidate him, a mental stranglehold broken only by C.J.'s leaving. And by never looking back. Now, however, they stood as equals. Not in terms of wealth or social status, but simply as grown men.

Neither of whom was about to take any crap from the other.

C.J. shifted Ethan in his arms, protectively cuddling his son against his chest.

"Hello, Dad," he said quietly, gathering strength from his baby's smile before again facing his father's incredulous expression. "Meet your grandson."

Chapter Thirteen

"This might come as a surprise," Dana's mother said, wrapping Dana's largest casserole dish in a towel, "but I'm not the enemy."

A pile of books in her arms, Dana glanced up from the cardboard box at her knees. From her bedroom came much grunting and cussing as her father tried to take apart her bed frame. The books clunked into the box, raising an embarrassing cloud of dust. "Why would I think that, Mama?" she said mildly.

"Oh, I don't know. Maybe because you rarely tell me what's going on in your life anymore."

Dana struggled to her feet, swiping a lose strand of hair out of her eyes, catching sight of the time as she did. A little after two-thirty. Two hours later in South Carolina. C.J.'s plane would have landed a half hour ago; he might even be at his father's by now.

"I am over thirty, Mama," she said, yanking her thoughts

back to the here-and-now. "I kinda caught on to the concept of taking care of my own problems a while back."

"And what problems might those be?"

She smiled. "Nice try."

"I'm just saying—" Faye reached up on her tiptoes to snag a serving platter from the cupboard, letting out a huff when she had the thing firmly in her grip "—there's nothing says you outgrow needing your mother."

"Never said there was. Would you toss me the packing tape doohickey, I left it by the sink."

Instead of tossing it, however, her mother brought it to her and slapped it into her hand. "So are you ever going to tell me what really happened between you and C.J., or do I have to keep guessing for rest of my life?"

"I pick option *B,*" Dana said, *wrrrratching* the tape across the box.

Faye let out a sigh. "It was your father's talking to him, wasn't it? He scared him off."

Said father chose that moment to wander back into the living room, wiping his forehead with his handkerchief. "I did not scare him off, Faye. I *warned* him. And anyway, it was your idea to talk to him, so don't you lay all this on me."

"Hey, guys?" Dana said, hands up. "There is no 'all this' to lay on anybody. Okay," she said on a rush of air when they both frowned at her. "Maybe I was sort of hoping things would get off the ground. They didn't, case closed, let's move on. Some men simply aren't the marrying type." A gross oversimplification of the situation, true, but hey, life was short.

Her mother snorted. "That's what your father said. I changed his mind."

"You did not," Gene said. "I was just…puttin' up barriers until I was sure you were 'the one.'"

"And if that isn't the most ridiculous thing I've ever heard—"

"No, Mama, he's right. Some men say they're not the marrying kind when what they really mean is they're waiting for the right woman. Others really don't want to get married." *Or face their fears.*

"I take it back," Faye said after a moment. "*That's* the most ridiculous thing I've ever heard."

On a shrug, Dana went back to her book packing—a far more productive endeavor than arguing with her mother—while her father, grumbling about crazy women, went back to wrestling with Dana's bed. She flinched, though, when she felt a soft hand land on her shoulder, a move that—dammit!—threatened to jar loose the tears Dana had been holding in for the past week.

"When I first saw C.J. with Ethan," her mother said, revealing a sadistic side to her character Dana had never quite noticed before, "I had serious doubts. But eventually…well. I think he's going to make a fine daddy, don't you?"

"Absolutely."

"I think being around this family helped him, don't you?"

Dana swallowed her laugh. "I'm sure it did."

Faye patted her back and moved away. Thank God. Then Dana heard, "What's this?"

Her hands full of old paperbacks, Dana turned to see her mother flipping through the pages of her manuscript. Which she'd deliberately left out.

"My book," she said quietly. "I finally finished it. In fact—" she took a deep breath "—I've already starting sending out query letters to agents."

Her mother's eyes shot to hers. "Oh, honey, do you really think you want to set yourself up for more disappointment? Especially so soon after…you know."

Irritation—no, outrage—flashed inside her. The books

clattered onto the carpet as she dropped them, then stomped over and around boxes and piles of crap to snatch the manuscript off the dining table, clutching it to her. "*This* is why I don't share things with you anymore, Mama," she said, her voice shaking. "Because instead of encouraging me, supporting me, all you ever see are the pitfalls."

"But the odds of actually getting published—"

"Are a thousand to one. *Ten* thousand to one. I know, Mama. Dammit, I *know.* But if I don't ever try, the odds are zip."

"I just don't want to see you get hurt."

"So what are you saying? You'd rather I never put myself out there, never see what I'm capable of? Yeah, rejection hurts," she said, her eyes watering. "Like a b-bitch. But…" She stopped, willing herself not to lose control. It didn't entirely work. "But it's not fatal," she finished in a small voice.

"Oh, honey." Her mother lifted one hand, wiping a stray tear from her cheek. "You really love him, don't you?"

One tear, then another, trickled down her cheek. "You have no idea."

"His loss," her father said from the doorway. Dana looked up, offering him a shaky smile.

"Yeah, that's what I'm thinking."

The birds' twittering filled the silence for several seconds, a silence broken when her mother cleared her throat, then asked, "Do you…think I could read it? Your book?"

The pages actually seemed to squeak when Dana increased her stranglehold on them. "I don't know." She leaned closer, whispering, "It's got s-e-x in it."

"I should hope so," her mother said, and they both laughed. Then the older woman frowned.

"If you don't like it, that's okay," Dana said. "I can take it."

"Yes," Faye said, understanding dawning in her eyes. "I suppose you can."

* * *

Judging from the maître d's somewhat disdainful expression, the restaurant—a favorite of Charleston's old guard—wasn't exactly family friendly. However, the staff graciously rose to the occasion, even rustling up a high chair for Ethan. Who seemed to be settling quite nicely into his new role as a grandchild of the Southern aristocracy, calmly taking in his surroundings while gumming an oyster cracker. And occasionally flirting with the carefully coiffed matron at the next table.

Ostensibly perusing the menu, C.J. stole a glance at his father from across the linen-shrouded table. Ethan, apparently bored with both the cracker and the matron, began batting the high chair table and gurgling. After thirty seconds or so, the old man's gaze at last veered toward his grandson, eyes glowering underneath dark, formidable eyebrows. He'd already expressed his bewilderment at C.J.'s not having an au pair or nanny to "keep the kid out of his hair," as he put it.

"This is why babies don't belong in restaurants," he grumbled.

Ethan went completely still, eyes huge. Then he laughed, a great big belly laugh that made heads turn and lips curve upward within a ten-foot radius. His father grunted, returning his attention to his menu. Ethan looked over at C.J., who palmed the baby's head in reassurance.

"You keep coddlin' the boy like that," his father said, not looking up, "you'll turn him into a sissy for sure."

The waiter appeared to take their order, giving C.J. a chance to tamp down the flash of anger. Once the man was gone, however, C.J. selected a warm roll from the basket in the center of the table, buttering half of it before he said, "And there we have it, friends…" He leaned back in his chair, giving Ethan a tiny piece of the roll, which the child crammed into his mouth. "The core philosophy behind my father's child-rearing method."

They'd said very little to each other up to this point, other than C.J.'s bare bones explanation of the hows and whys of his having a son. But C.J. had no doubt that his father knew as well as he did that this was showdown time. And if only one of them was left standing when it was over, C.J. had no intention of it not being him.

After a moment, his father also chose a roll, separating it with excruciatingly deliberate slowness. "In more than forty years," he said quietly, not looking at C.J., "I never made a single bad investment. Goes to a man's head, thinking he's infallible. That he's somehow incapable of making a mistake." He lifted his gaze to C.J.'s. "But I sure as hell screwed it up with you, didn't I?"

Well, hell. Instead of a shootout, his father had laid his gun down in the dirt, backing away with his hands raised. If the old man thought, however, that was his ticket to freedom, he was sorely mistaken.

"Yes, Dad. You did."

The waiter brought their salads, offered the peppermill, which both men passed up, disappeared. His father stabbed his fork into the sea of romaine, then lanced C.J. with his gaze. "So, why are you here? The real reason."

It shouldn't have been a surprise, his father's scramble to regain the upper hand. But C.J. doubted the sudden acid taste in his mouth had anything to do with the tart vinaigrette dressing on his salad. "Ethan's not enough?"

"My guess is he's an excuse. Not the reason. Not after the way you reamed me out over the phone."

"Fine." C.J. set down his fork, lifted his wineglass. "Now I want to know *why* you couldn't stand the sight of me."

His father waited out a burst of laughter from the next table, then said, "If I died tomorrow, you wouldn't feel much one way or the other, would you?"

C.J. refused to let the out-of-the-blue question knock him off balance. Neither was he about to buy into whatever guilt trip the old man was trying to lay on him. "Can't say that I would."

His father seemed neither taken aback nor disappointed by his answer. Instead, he nodded, almost in approval, before spearing a cherry tomato with his fork. "Ever been in love?"

C.J.'s stomach twisted. "No."

Liar, something whispered inside him.

"So you've never had your heart broken?"

He rammed his fork into a chunk of lettuce. "No."

Liar. Liar, liar, liar.

"Then I guess my plan worked, after all," his father said.

"Your...plan?"

The waiter returned to clear their salads, replacing them with their entrees—halibut for C.J., filet mignon for his father. The older man picked up his utensils, seeming to weigh them in his hands before cutting into his steak.

"Your mother didn't die in a car crash," he said softly, not looking at C.J. "She killed herself."

C.J.'s fingers vised the stem of his water goblet. "What did you say?"

Almost irritably, his father hacked off another slice of steak. "Took her own life. Pills. I found her. I..." The knife and fork clattered to his plate as he reached for his own water glass with a shaking hand.

"Why on earth didn't you tell me?"

His father's eyes snapped to his. "To *protect* you, why the hell do you think?"

"From *what,* for God's sake? Especially after I was grown?"

"And what difference would it have made?"

"I don't know! But I would have at least appreciated the gesture."

Once again, his father picked up his utensils, although

with little enthusiasm. "Sheila was my life," he said, his words barely audible. "I'd never met anyone like her. The way she could see straight through me…" C.J. was startled to see tears in his father's eyes when he looked up. "The pain afterward…it was unimaginable."

"I'm sure," C.J. said, trying to reconcile the obviously crushed man in front of him with the cold, imperious figure from his youth. Another bite of steak disappeared into his father's mouth, but he chewed it with great difficulty, as though the tender meat had somehow turned to rubber.

"So tell me, Cameron," he said after he'd finally swallowed. "What kind of father would I have been if I'd left *you* that vulnerable?"

"Vulnerable? To what?"

"To having your heart ripped out of your chest." His father leaned forward, his dinner forgotten. As was C.J.'s. "I didn't keep my distance because I couldn't stand the sight of you, I did it because I wanted to spare you that kind of pain. No attachment, no risk of getting hurt."

And at last, understanding shuddered through him.

"Spare me, hell," C.J. said in a low voice. "You *robbed* me."

"For your own good, dammit!"

"Bull." His even voice belied the inferno raging in his gut. "You cut yourself off from me—your only child—so *you* wouldn't get too attached, so *you* couldn't be hurt again. And how twisted is that? Especially considering that under your *plan*—" he spat out the word "—instead of occasionally suffering the normal, human pain of loss, I ached with it constantly. *Constantly,* Dad. Every…single…damn day of my childhood. I could never figure out what I'd done to make you hate me so much."

"I never hated you, Cameron."

"Yeah, well, you had a pretty bizarre way of showing it."

Obviously picking up on the tension, Ethan started to whimper. C.J. grabbed his napkin off his knee, throwing it down on the table before rescuing the baby from his high chair. He sat back down with the child on his lap, giving him a very messy sip of water, tiny teeth clinking on the glass. "You at least knew what it felt like to be loved. Where did you get off denying me that right?"

"It's not all it's cracked up to be," his father said wearily.

"That wasn't your decision to make for me, dammit. What you did was wrong, Dad. Not misguided, *wrong.* But you want to hear something really ironic? I thought I'd *escaped* your poison, by leaving. By not coming back. Now I'm sitting here, realizing every choice I've made over the past twenty years has only increased its potency. No, wait, that's not entirely true." C.J. set down his glass, then pointlessly tried to smooth down Ethan's flyaway hair. "Because, your fine example notwithstanding, I *choose* to be everything for this little boy you never were for me. If I screw up, I screw up, but at least I'll have *tried*—"

C.J. sagged back in his chair. "Oh, God," he whispered. "That's it, that's…" After a second, his eyes found his father's confused ones again. "You're wrong, Dad. Getting attached, making that connection, *love*…it *is* all it's cracked up to be. Hey, you want to live in your cold, empty little world, you go right ahead. But despite your best efforts…" He leaned forward, the white-hot light of epiphany melting his anger. "In the end, your plan didn't work."

His father's eyebrows took a dive. "Thought you said you'd never been in love."

"Apparently I was wrong," C.J. said in wonder, then let out a startled, high laugh as that old, rusty faucet finally, and completely, gave way. "Hell, I was still trying to deal with what it felt like to just be on the receiving end. And to think I very nearly…"

"Where the hell are you going?" he said when C.J. popped up out of his chair.

"I'm not sure. To make a phone call, I think—"

"Sit down, Cameron," his father said under his breath. "People are beginning to stare."

"So let them stare! I'm in love! *I'm in love!*" he announced to the room at large, earning him a smattering of applause, a titter of laughter.

"For crying out loud," James said, "sit *down!*"

C.J. sat, and Ethan gave one of his belly laughs, and C.J. released a huge breath, and with it more than three decades of misery and mistakes and misapprehensions. And man, that felt good. Then, holding Ethan sideways (a position perfect for batting his eyes at the lady at the next table), C.J. said, "And you know the craziest part of all this?"

"What?"

"That maybe I could have helped get you through your pain. Only you never gave me the chance."

They stared each other down for a long moment, until his father finally pushed out a sigh. "You're a lot like her, you know."

"Like my mother?"

He nodded. "Bright. Passionate." His father's throat worked for several seconds before he whispered, "*Kind.* God, she was a far better person than I'll ever be. And, oh, my, how she loved *you.* I see…I see the same thing in your eyes, when you look at Ethan. I just didn't…I had no idea she was so sick."

"It wasn't your fault," C.J. said over the knot in his chest. "Not that, anyway."

His father actually chuckled, then signaled the waiter for the check. "What do you say," he said, tugging his credit card out of his wallet, "we blow this joint. Then you can tell me about this obviously extraordinary woman who somehow managed to undo all my damage." He glanced up. "Or is it too late?"

"Well, I need to get Ethan to bed pretty soon—"

"I don't mean that," his father said, with something very much like hope in his eyes. And regret.

C.J.'s mouth pulled into a half smile. "Why don't we just take it one step at a time?"

"Fair enough," his father said.

Dana pulled into her parking space, only to shut her eyes, letting out a long, *well*-you're-*an-idiot* sigh. Because this wasn't her parking space. Not anymore. *Her* parking space—the tires squealed when she backed out, clearly startling the old guy from R building walking his stiff-legged poodle—was over…*here*.

She got out, slammed shut her door and stomped up the steps to her apartment. Her larger, lighter, closer-to-the-laundry room/playground/pool apartment that she absolutely, positively despised with every fiber of her being.

Huh. Guess she'd moved into the angry phase of her grief.

Because, she'd realized this morning—right about the time she moved from *numb* to *sad*—grieving was exactly what she was doing. No, she and C.J. hadn't exactly broken up—it being kinda hard to break up when you were never really a couple to begin with—but apparently her heart hadn't gotten that particular memo.

Because *okay* was the one thing she did not feel right now. What she felt right now, she thought as she kicked—yes, kicked!—her door open was—

"Ohmigod!"

Clearly, a band of marauding six-year-olds had broken in and thrown the mother of all birthday parties. It was every-where, in pinks and purples and oranges and a hideous Day-Glo green, hanging from the ceiling fan and draped over her furniture and all the unpacked boxes, even dangling from the bottom of the birdcage, a veritable spider web of—

"Strings," C.J. said, sending her back into her door with a shriek.

"Wh-what?"

His teeth flashed in the semidarkness of the hallway. In his arms, wearing a blue-and-red T-shirt, green shorts and an orange hat, Ethan bobbed and babbled, reaching out for her.

"You want strings," C.J. said, moving out of the shadows. The mini fashion disaster lurched for Dana; she caught him before he landed on his nose, as C.J. calmly surveyed his handiwork. His gaze—hopeful, pleading and almost frighteningly sure all at once—returned to hers. "So strings, you shall have."

Their gazes tangoed for another couple of seconds until her brain caught up. Then she sucked in a breath. Hard.

"No…" she said, coughing, waving her hands, the movement sending the nearest veil of Silly String into a gentle hula.

"It's not enough? Because I've still got a can or two left, I can certainly do more." While she stood there, rabbit-eyed, he wrapped his hand around the back of her neck, touching his forehead to hers. "In case you missed it," he whispered, "I love you, too."

Her heart went *ka-thud.* Birds twittered and baby babbled while she took a few more seconds to bask in his smile. Then she burst into tears. Great, honking, *somebody-pinch-me* sobs, sobs that a second later were buried in C.J.'s soft knit shirt as he wrapped both of them up in those long, solid arms. Sobs that, a second after that, turned to a yelp when Ethan grabbed a handful of her hair and called it lunch.

They group-hug-shuffled over to her sofa, where she sort of melted into C.J.'s side, thinking, *Ohmigod, ohmigod, ohmigod,* while Ethan, sitting in her lap in his little baby world, happily chattered away to the birds.

"You're sure about this?" she finally whispered, leaning

against C.J. "This isn't just jet lag talking? Or—" she waved one hand, making a face "—Silly String fumes?"

"Yeah," he said, his chuckle vibrating in her ear. "I'm sure. You and Ethan…you're the most important things in the world to me. And if I can't spend the rest of my life with you, then what's the point?"

"None that I can see," Dana said, smiling like a goof. Then she frowned. "But how did you get in?"

"Your mother," C.J. murmured into what was left of her hair. "She gave me her key. Apparently she likes me."

"Because clearly you didn't let her in on the Silly String scheme." Not moving—which she didn't intend to do until she had to eat, pee or change a diaper—she surveyed her living room. "How many cans are we talking, anyway?"

"Have no idea. I just told the kid at Party Barn to give me all he had."

A fresh round of tears threatened. She swallowed, twice, then said to the baby, "Daddy made a big mess."

"I know," C.J. said softly, his breath warm on her temple. "So I figured I'd better do something to fix it."

"You didn't—"

"I did. So shut up and let me grovel."

Dana twisted around, frowning up into his eyes. "Wow. That must've been *some* trip."

C.J. kissed the top of her head, then stood, pulling the baby up with him and carrying him to stand in a shaft of sunlight in the dining area, his gaze fixed outside. "Turns out my mother wasn't killed in a car crash. She committed suicide."

"Oh, C.J…how awful. But why didn't your father tell you?"

"I suppose because he saw it as a personal failure when she took her own life." He jiggled the baby, making him laugh. "He was obviously crazy about her. I wouldn't have believed it possible, until I saw the look in his eyes when he finally told me the truth. I honestly believe he was devastated. Frankly, I think he still is."

As much as she already loved this man, hearing the obvious forgiveness—or at least, the *desire* to forgive—in his voice melted her heart even more. She got up from the sofa and walked over to thread her hands through C.J.'s arm, laying her head against it. "And that's why he shut you out?"

"If only it had been that simple," he said on a sigh. "In some sort of bizarre, misguided attempt to spare me that kind of pain, he decided to never let me become attached to anything. Pets, nannies, house servants…the minute I'd start to get close, he'd get rid of them. Needless to say, by the time I reached adolescence, I'd learned to never let down my guard, never trust anyone to stick around."

She squeezed his arm, in part to quell the outrage threatening to choke her. "But what about friends?"

"Oh, I had them. After a fashion. But I'd learned my lesson well," he said softly, sadly, brushing his lips over the baby's head. "So when I started to date, it was the same thing. Pick someone you know from the outset won't last, and you're safe." He angled his head to look into her eyes. "Then you and Ethan happened into my life. And suddenly I was being pulled in two, between all those years of habit and self-protection and everything I was convinced I could never have. Could never be. And yet…deep down, wanted so damn much. You had no idea, how right you were. About the precipice thing. I *was* scared. Hell, I was terrified."

"Then what changed your mind?"

He smiled. "Other than the obvious remorse in my father's eyes? Finally realizing that the only power he'd ever really had over me is what I'd given him." He tilted her face up to kiss her softly on the lips. "That the choice is, always has been, mine. Even if I didn't know it. I can either stay in my safe, but empty, excuse for a life. Or I can have a *real* life. With you. And my son." His expression gentled. "And maybe someday we'll find Ethan a little brother. Or sister. Or both," he finished on a laugh.

Dana's breath caught. "Ohmigosh, C.J.—are you sure?"

A funny smile on his face, he reached into his shirt pocket and pulled out a small, silver ring. "It's the best I could do on short notice. But it seemed appropriate."

With trembling hands, Dana took the delicately crafted Celtic knot ring from his fingers and slipped it on. "It's perfect," she said, tears making her voice wobble.

"Let's go home, honey," C.J. whispered, and all she could think was...

Wow.

Epilogue

Being put to bed when it's still light out gives a guy a lot of time to think. To reflect on his purpose in life. Oh, please— you don't really think all we do is babble at those stupid mobiles dangling over our cribs, do you? Trust me, that gets old real fast. And this one has these creepy clowns, for Pete's sake—I'll be lucky if I'm not scarred for life.

So now you know. When we give you those funny looks? It's not gas. We really do know a heckuva lot more about things than we let on. Or can verbalize. But the thing is, from everything I've heard, by the time our facility for coherent speech catches up with our brains, a lot of the inside info we were born with has pretty much faded. By my second birthday I won't remember any of this. So take notes.

Common wisdom says I shouldn't even have happened. Slim odds and all that. Well, here's a newsflash—you can hereby forget everything you've ever believed about things happening for no good reason. Trust me, there's a plan. Trish, my birth mother, didn't just *happen* to cozy up to my dad. I mean, yeah, I was skeptical, too, when they told me who my father was going to be. "Him?" I said. "The guy who doesn't want kids? What kind of sick joke is that?"

"Trust me," the Big Guy said.

Not that I had any choice. We just go where we're assigned, it's not like we have any input or anything. "They need you," He said. Implying lives were at stake, the fate of civilization was in my itty-bitty hands, the whole enchilada. Man, that's an awful lot to put on a little dude's shoulders. But hey, when the Big Guy gives an order, you do what you can.

Although, if Trish sounded a little Looney Tunes about the whole should-she-keep-me-or-not thing, or even whether my dad was my dad, that's understandable, when you think about it. You know, that whole "mysterious ways" thing and all. Hard for some people to swallow. Please don't feel bad for her, though, because I've got some pretty heavy-duty inside info that she's going to come out of this on top. That having me actually *was* the wake-up call she needed to get her act together. Don't quote me on this, but I think I heard something about a hottie cop and more babies down the road? And a career? I might be fuzzy on the details—like I said, it's all fading pretty fast now—but I do know it's good.

Uh-oh, I hear Dana and my dad coming down the hall to check on me. If I'm not asleep there will be *H-E*-double hockey sticks to pay. Where's that rag I sleep with? Got it. Thumb in place, check. Eyes shut, check. Butt up in air (that gets 'em every time), check.

I crack open one eye to notice Dad's got his arm around Dana's waist. Again. Sheesh, those two cannot keep their hands off each other, it's disgusting. Not that I mind all the hugs and kisses *I* get from them, but please, people—a little decorum, okay?

"You think he has any idea how much he's changed our lives?" my dad says, and Dana laughs. It's a nice laugh. Good thing, considering how often she does it.

"Of course not, he's just a baby. All he knows is that he's loved."

Well, not exactly. But, yeah, I know I'm loved. Every single second of my life. It's a nice feeling, what can I say?

"'Night, sweetie," she whispers, even though she's already told me that once tonight. Not that I mind hearing it again. Then my father's hand lands on my back, and I feel...safe. Wanted. And very, very glad to be here.

"'Night, Scooter," he says softly, and I give him one of those precious fluttery smiles. In my sleep, of course.

They both tiptoe out, but I keep smiling.

Mission accomplished.

* * * * *

*Experience entertaining women's fiction for
every woman who has wondered
"what's next?" in their lives.
Turn the page for a sneak preview
of a new book from Harlequin NEXT,
WHY IS MURDER ON THE MENU, ANYWAY?
by Stevi Mittman*

On sale December 26, wherever books are sold.

Ambience is everything. Imagine eating a foie gras at a luncheonette counter or a side of coleslaw at Le Cirque. It's not a matter of food but one of atmosphere. Remember that when planning your dining room design.
—Tips from *Teddi.com*

"Now that's the kind of man you should be looking for," my mother, the self-appointed keeper of my shelf-life stamp, says. She points with her fork at a man in the corner of the Steak-Out Restaurant, a dive I've just been hired to redecorate. Making this restaurant look four-star will be hard, but not half as hard as getting through lunch without strangling the woman across the table from me. "*He* would make a good husband."

"Oh, you can tell that from across the room?" I ask, wondering how it is she can forget that when we had trouble getting rid of my last husband, she shot him. "Besides being ten minutes away from death if he actually eats all that steak, he's twenty years too old for me and—shallow woman that I am—twenty pounds too heavy. Besides, I am *so* not looking for another husband here. I'm looking to design a new image for this place, looking for some sense of ambience, some feeling, something I can build a proposal on for them."

My mother studies the man in the corner, tilting her head, the better to gauge his age, I suppose. I think she's grimacing, but with all the Botox and Restylane injected into that face, it's hard to tell. She takes another bite of her steak salad, chews slowly so that I don't miss the fact that the steak is a poor cut and tougher than it should be. "You're concentrating on the wrong kind of proposal," she says finally. "Just look at this place, Teddi. It's a dive. There are hardly any other diners. What does *that* tell you about the food?"

"That they cater to a dinner crowd and it's lunchtime," I tell her.

I don't know what I was thinking bringing her here with me. I suppose I thought it would be better than eating alone. There really are days when my common sense goes on vacation. Clearly, this is one of them. I mean, really, did I not resolve less than three weeks ago that I would not let my mother get to me anymore?

What good are New Year's resolutions, anyway?

Mario approaches the man's table and my mother studies him while they converse. Eventually Mario leaves the table with a huff, after which the diner glances up and meets my mother's gaze. I think she's smiling at him. That or she's got indigestion. They size each other up.

I concentrate on making sketches in my notebook and try to ignore the fact that my mother is flirting. At nearly seventy, she's developed an unhealthy interest in members of the opposite sex to whom she isn't married.

According to my father, who has broken the TMI rule and given me Too Much Information, she has no interest in sex with him. Better, I suppose, to be clued in on what they aren't doing in the bedroom than have to hear what they might be doing.

"He's not so old," my mother says, noticing that I have barely touched the Chinese chicken salad she warned me not to get. "He's got about as many years on you as you have on your little cop friend."

She does this to make me crazy. I know it, but it works all the same. "Drew Scoones is not my little 'friend.' He's a detective with whom I—"

"Screwed around," my mother says. I must look shocked, because my mother laughs at me and asks if I think she doesn't know the "lingo."

What I thought she didn't know was that Drew and I actually tangled in the sheets. And, since it's possible she's just fishing, I sidestep the issue and tell her that Drew is just a couple of years younger than me and that I don't need reminding. I dig into my salad with renewed vigor, determined to show my mother that Chinese chicken salad in a steak place was not the stupid choice it's proving to be.

After a few more minutes of my picking at the wilted leaves on my plate, the man my mother has me nearly engaged to pays his bill and heads past us toward the back of the restaurant. I watch my mother take in his shoes, his suit and the diamond pinkie ring that seems to be cutting off the circulation in his little finger.

"Such nice hands," she says after the man is out of sight. "Manicured." She and I both stare at my hands. I have two popped acrylics that are being held on at weird angles by bandages. My cuticles are ragged and there's marker decorating my right hand from measuring carelessly when I did a drawing for a customer.

Twenty minutes later she's disappointed that he managed to leave the restaurant without our noticing. He will join the list of the ones I let get away. I will hear about him twenty years from now when—according to my mother—my children will be grown and I will still be single, living pathetically alone with several dogs and cats.

After my ex, that sounds good to me.

The waitress tells us that our meal has been taken care of by the management and, after thanking Mario, the owner, complimenting him on the wonderful meal and assuring him that once I have redecorated his place people will be flocking here in droves (I actually use those words and ignore my mother when she rolls her eyes), my mother and I head for the restroom.

My father—unfortunately not with us today—has the patience of a saint. He got it over the years of living with my mother. She, perhaps as a result, figures he has the patience for both of them, and feels justified having none. For her, no rules apply, and a little thing like a picture of a man on the door to a public restroom is certainly no barrier to using the john. In all fairness, it does seem silly to stand and wait for the ladies' room if no one is using the men's room.

Still, it's the idea that rules don't apply to her, signs don't apply to her, conventions don't apply to her. She knocks on the door to the men's room. When no one answers she gestures to me to go in ahead. I tell her that I can certainly wait for the ladies' room to be free and she shrugs and goes in herself.

Not a minute later there is a bloodcurdling scream from behind the men's room door.

"Mom!" I yell. "Are you all right?"

Mario comes running over, the waitress on his heels. Two customers head our way while my mother continues to scream.

I try the door, but it is locked. I yell for her to open it and she fumbles with the knob. When she finally manages to unlock and open it, she is white behind her two streaks of blush, but she is on her feet and appears shaken but not stirred.

"What happened?" I ask her. So do Mario and the waitress and the few customers who have migrated to the back of the place.

She points toward the bathroom and I go in, thinking it serves her right for using the men's room. But I see nothing amiss.

She gestures toward the stall, and, like any self-respecting and suspicious woman, I poke the door open with one finger, expecting the worst.

What I find is worse than the worst.

The husband my mother picked out for me is sitting on the toilet. His pants are puddled around his ankles, his hands are hanging at his sides. Pinned to his chest is some sort of Health Department certificate.

Oh, and there is a large, round, bloodless bullet hole between his eyes.

Four Nassau County police officers are securing the area, waiting for the detectives and crime scene personnel to show up. They are trying, though not very hard, to comfort my mother, who in another era would be considered to be suffering from the vapors. Less tactful in the twenty-first century, I'd say she was losing it. That is, if I didn't know her better, know she was milking it for everything it was worth.

My mother loves attention. As it begins to flag, she swoons and claims to feel faint. Despite four No Smoking signs, my mother insists it's all right for her to light up because, after all, she's in shock. Not to mention that signs, as we know, don't apply to her.

When asked not to smoke, she collapses mournfully in a chair and lets her head loll to the side, all without mussing her hair.

Eventually, the detectives show up to find the four patrolmen all circled around her, debating whether to administer CPR, smelling salts or simply call the paramedics. I, however, know just what will snap her to attention.

"Detective Scoones," I say loudly. My mother parts the sea of cops.

"We have to stop meeting like this," he says lightly to me, but I can feel him checking me over with his eyes, making sure I'm all right while pretending not to care.

"What have you got in those pants?" my mother asks him, coming to her feet and staring at his crotch accusingly. *Baydar?* Everywhere we Bayers are, you turn up. You don't expect me to buy that this is a coincidence, I hope."

Drew tells my mother that it's nice to see her, too, and asks if it's his fault that her daughter seems to attract disasters.

Charming to be made to feel like the bearer of a plague.

He asks how I am.

"Just peachy," I tell him. "I seem to be making a habit of finding dead bodies, my mother is driving me crazy and the catering hall I booked two freakin' years ago for Dana's bat mitzvah has just been shut down by the Board of Health!"

"Glad to see your luck's finally changing," he says, giving me a quick squeeze around the shoulders before turning his attention to the patrolmen, asking what they've got, whether they've taken any statements, moved anything, all the sort of stuff you see on TV, without any of the drama. That is, if you don't count my mother's threats to faint every few minutes when she senses no one's paying attention to her.

Mario tells his waitstaff to bring everyone espresso, which I decline because I'm wired enough. Drew pulls him aside and a minute later I'm handed a cup of coffee that smells divinely of Kahlúa.

The man knows me well. Too well.

His partner, whom I've met once or twice, says he'll interview the kitchen staff. Drew asks Mario if he minds if he takes statements from the patrons first and gets to him and the wait-staff afterward.

"No, no," Mario tells him. "Do the patrons first." Drew raises his eyebrow at me like he wants to know if I get the double entendre. I try to look bored.

"What is it with you and murder victims?" he asks me when we sit down at a table in the corner.

I search them out so that I can see you again, I almost say, but I'm afraid it will sound desperate instead of sarcastic.

My mother, lighting up and daring him with a look to tell her not to, reminds him that *she* was the one to find the body.

Drew asks what happened *this time*. My mother tells him how the man in the john was "taken" with me, couldn't take his eyes off me and blatantly flirted with both of us. To his credit, Drew doesn't laugh, but his smirk is undeniable to the trained eye. And I've had my eye trained on him for nearly a year now.

"While he was noticing you," he asks me, "did *you* notice anything about him? Was he waiting for anyone? Watching for anything?"

I tell him that he didn't appear to be waiting or watching. That he made no phone calls, was fairly intent on eating and did, indeed, flirt with my mother. This last bit Drew takes with a grain of salt, which was the way it was intended.

"And he had a short conversation with Mario," I tell him. "I think he might have been unhappy with the food, though he didn't send it back."

Drew asks what makes me think he was dissatisfied, and I tell him that the discussion seemed acrimonious and that Mario looked distressed when he left the table. Drew makes a note and says he'll look into it and asks about anyone else in the restaurant. Did I see anyone who didn't seem to belong, anyone who was watching the victim, anyone looking suspicious?

"Besides my mother?" I ask him, and Mom huffs and blows her cigarette smoke in my direction.

I tell him that there were several deliveries, the kitchen staff going in and out the back door to grab a smoke. He stops me and asks what I was doing checking out the back door of the restaurant.

Proudly—because, while he was off forgetting me, dropping by only once in a while to say hi to Jesse, my son, or drop something by for one of my daughters that he thought they might like, I was getting on with my life—I tell him that I'm decorating the place.

He looks genuinely impressed. "Commercial customers? That's great," he says. Okay, that's what he *ought* to say. What he actually says is "Whatever pays the bills."

"Howard Rosen, the famous restaurant critic, got her the job," my mother says. "You met him—the good-looking, distinguished gentleman with the *real* job, something to be proud of. I guess you've never read his reviews in *Newsday*."

Drew, without missing a beat, tells her that Howard's reviews are on the top of his list, as soon as he learns how to read.

"I only meant—" my mother starts, but both of us assure her that we know just what she meant.

"So," Drew says. "Deliveries?"

I tell him that Mario would know better than I, but that I saw vegetables come in, maybe fish and linens.

"This is the second restaurant job Howard's got her," my mother tells Drew.

"At least she's getting *something* out of the relationship," he says.

"If he were here," my mother says, ignoring the insinuation, "he'd be comforting her instead of interrogating her. He'd be making sure we're both all right after such an ordeal."

"I'm sure he would," Drew agrees, then looks me in the

eyes as if he's measuring my tolerance for shock. Quietly he adds, "But then maybe he doesn't know just what strong stuff your daughter's made of."

It's the closest thing to a tender moment I can expect from Drew Scoones. My mother breaks the spell. "She gets that from me," she says.

Both Drew and I take a minute, probably to pray that's all I inherited from her.

"I'm just trying to save you some time and effort," my mother tells him. "My money's on Howard."

Drew withers her with a look and mutters something that sounds suspiciously like "fool's gold." Then he excuses himself to go back to work.

I catch his sleeve and ask if it's all right for us to leave. He says sure, he knows where we live. I say goodbye to Mario. I assure him that I will have some sketches for him in a few days, all the while hoping that this murder doesn't cancel his redecorating plans. I need the money desperately, the alternative being borrowing from my parents and being strangled by the strings.

My mother is strangely quiet all the way to her house. She doesn't tell me what a loser Drew Scoones is—despite his good looks—and how I was obviously drooling over him. She doesn't ask me where Howard is taking me tonight or warn me not to tell my father about what happened because he will worry about us both and no doubt insist we see our respective psychiatrists.

She fidgets nervously, opening and closing her purse over and over again.

"You okay?" I ask her. After all, she's just found a dead man on the toilet and tough as she is that's got to be upsetting.

When she doesn't answer me I pull over to the side of the road.

"Mom?" She refuses to meet my eyes. "You want me to take you to see Dr. Cohen?"

She looks out the window as if she's just realized we're on Broadway in Woodmere. "Aren't we near Marvin's Jewelers?" she asks, pulling something out of her purse.

"What have you got, Mother?" I ask, prying open her fingers to find the murdered man's ring.

"It was on the sink," she says in answer to my dropped jaw. "I was going to get his name and address and have you return it to him so that he could ask you out. I thought it was a sign that the two of you were meant to be together."

"He's dead, Mom. You understand that, right?" I ask. You never can tell when my mother is fine and when she's in la-la land.

"Well, I didn't know that," she shouts at me. "Not at the time."

I ask why she didn't give it to Drew, realize that she wouldn't give Drew the time in a clock shop and add, "...or one of the other policemen?"

"For heaven's sake," she tells me. "The man is dead, Teddi, and I took his ring. How would that look?"

Before I can tell her it looks just the way it is, she pulls out a cigarette and threatens to light it.

"I mean, really," she says, shaking her head like it's my brains that are loose. "What does he need with it now?"

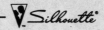

SPECIAL EDITION™

Logan's Legacy Revisited

**THE LOGAN FAMILY IS BACK
WITH SIX NEW STORIES.**

Beginning in January 2007 with

THE COUPLE MOST LIKELY TO

by

LILIAN DARCY

Tragedy drove them apart. Reunited eighteen
years later, their attraction was once again
undeniable. But had time away changed
Jake Logan enough to let him face his fears
and commit to the woman he once loved?

nocturne™

**WAS HE HER SAVIOR
OR HER NIGHTMARE?**

HAUNTED
LISA CHILDS

Years ago, Ariel and her sisters were separated for
their own protection. Now the man who vowed
revenge on her family has resumed the hunt, and
Ariel must warn her sisters before it's too late.
The closer she comes to finding them, the more
secretive her fiancé becomes. Can she trust the man
she plans to spend eternity with? Or has he been
waiting for the perfect moment to destroy her?

On sale December 2006.

In February, expect MORE
from

HARLEQUIN® *Romance*®

as it increases to six titles per month.

What's to come...

Rancher and Protector

Part of the
Western Weddings
miniseries

BY JUDY CHRISTENBERRY

The Boss's
Pregnancy Proposal

BY RAYE MORGAN

Don't miss February's
incredible line up of authors!

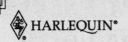

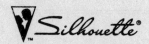

COMING NEXT MONTH